STRUTTING
AND
FRETTING

Kevin McKeon

For all who passed through.

Oh, it offends me to the soul to hear a robustious periwig-pated fellow tear a passion to tatters, to very rags. Pray you, avoid it.

– Shakespeare, from HAMLET

STRUTTING
AND
FRETTING

MAY

1

Mostly we talked about who the best songwriter was, because months had passed since John Lennon's *Playboy* interview came out, in which he revealed who actually wrote different parts of different songs, and we had a lot to discuss. I said it had been obvious all along who wrote the songs by who would (as a rule) take the lead vocal on any particular track. You could tell "Eleanor Rigby" was written by Paul, right? "Ob-La-Dee Ob-La-Da." Bouncy, unmistakably Paul. And then Ripley, a huge Lennon-is-better-than-McCartney guy, said the main issue he had with Paul is that his songs were too lightweight, unsubstantial. McCartney always writes about other people, Ripley said. Lennon's songs are all personal. Even dating back to "This Boy." Listen to the pathos. McCartney wrote pop, Lennon wrote songs that revealed how human he was.

Maybe, I said, but who can deny the grooves, the creativity McCartney displayed in his work? Can you possibly disregard the infectiousness of "Penny Lane"? And so we went around on this for a hundred miles, and I have to admit, it burned up a lot of the boring stuff between Sacramento and Fresno.

Because the bus is, let's face it, a horrible sweat-soaked naugahyde nightmare of coughing fits, airborne filth, crazy people talking too loud, gum wads and questionable stains. If I'd had to make the trip alone, I would have left a few days earlier and hitchhiked. But Ripley's companionship made the bus ride tolerable. Even though Ripley could be a clueless ass about most of life, he was an opinionated and intelligent conversationalist.

Ripley and I had caught the bus outside the Sac State commons on a Saturday evening a day or so after classes had ended and our final show had closed. We had both been in graduate acting school there, along with Sue Henley, some skinny fornicator named Mark Sanders, six or seven other people, and Gina. More about her later. Ripley liked to say that after three years of dressing in sweat pants and lying on the floor and *finding our cores,* they gave us our MFA degrees. I figured I would have been far worse off for it, after spending three years of my mid-twenties finding my core but being no further along on a career path, if I hadn't landed this summer job with a major repertory theatre. Ripley had scored the job too, and that's why we were headed down to Santa Maria, to be in the acting company there for the summer. We considered ourselves extremely fortunate to have the work, *any* work, in our line of study. My contract paid me $1000 for the summer, and I would have been riding an extreme high and lording my fortunes above all else if it hadn't been for the Gina stuff.

Gina and I had met in college back in that decade of wonderment known as the seventies. But now it was all over, college, grad school, the seventies *and* the marriage. We had some good years, Gina and I. I could tell myself I didn't miss her or anything, but I guess I'd be lying. I suppose I was pretty hurt. Everything hurt that last year. I think I hurt because Gina had been so miserable those last few months.

2

Ripley looked over at me with his eyes lowered. "How you doing?" he asked.

"You've asked me nineteen times," I said.

"You getting nostalgic or anything? Need to talk?"

"Nah."

"Like about why she got the car and you didn't?"

"Because it was hers to begin with."

"Yeah, but… now you don't have a car."

What could I say?

"If you had the car we wouldn't be taking the bus," he said.

"Change the subject," I said. "I don't want to talk about Gina."

Ripley had the seat at the window and he turned his head toward it.

"Do you think she had an affair with Mark Sanders?" I asked.

Ripley looked like he got hit in the head with a football. I swear, his hair stood on end and swayed to the right.

"I don't know. What do you think?"

"I think she did," I said.

Ripley turned to the window again. "There was a rumor I guess."

I leaned back, depleted. "People were talking about it?"

"Well, just a few people. You knew, didn't you? Everybody knew. You didn't know?"

Maybe I had known. I thought of Gina gyrating beneath Mark Sanders' white, skinny body. I had run the scene over in my head a million times and it brought a familiar lump to my throat.

"Sorry, man. I didn't think this was new information," Ripley said.

"No. It's not. Not new."

"I don't know why you want to dredge this up. You're here. She's in Minnesota. Your marriage is over. Why don't you just take that wedding ring off. Let's put it on a train track or something."

"Yeah."

"Huh?"

"You're right," I said.

It was a long time before either of us spoke after that, and I knew that thought priorities had shifted, and Ripley was undoubtedly running over the lines of his audition pieces in his head. The auditions the next morning were important. They were for the benefit of the individual directors so they could cast the seven shows that PCPA mounted in repertory over the summer. We had endured two rounds of auditions already just to get into the company. But we had never set foot in Santa Maria, as the audition wagon came to our campus for preliminaries, and the callbacks had been in San Francisco.

PCPA was short for *Pacific Conservatory of the Performing Arts,* an uncomfortable mouthful of a name worthy of reducing to initial caps for convenience:

Pacific was in the title because that's where it was: near, at least, to the Pacific Ocean.

Conservatory was the catchall term for the masses of people PCPA recruited over the summer to stoke the fires of their impressive machine. PCPA was headquartered at Allan Hancock College, a community college that allowed its theatre department to balloon into a producing juggernaut that employed about 150 people during the summer. If you were among the chosen, like Ripley and I were, being a part of the acting company, you had it made, because that's all you did – you acted. But PCPA also needed lots and lots of less fortunate souls to build sets, make costumes, hang lights and do all the behind-the-scenes work so we actors could get all the credit. There was a built-in romance to being a part, any part, of a theatre company. Tech kids clamored for the jobs. PCPA could offer someone a contract of $600 for the summer and call it a scholarship, and that kid would be happy to throw down a sleeping bag in somebody's garage, live on Top Ramen and weld sets together at 3:00 in the morning. Funny thing is, the same kid would be back the next year, working for $650.

Performing Arts was another phrase for "crowd-pleasing shows amenable to a wide demographic with the occasional risky artistic gamble." The menu every year would include two or three venerable workhorse musicals like *The King and I* or *South Pacific,* interspersed with a couple offerings from the eponymous Shakespeare canon, and one or two others which might or might not be contemporary, like *Picnic* or *A View*

From the Bridge, or a Shaw, or maybe an Ibsen, and whose inclusion in the lineup would lend a sense of daring and credibility to it all. The musicals were sold out months in advance, and even though the acting company included a plethora of singing talent, the raspy-throated Ripley and I had definitely not been hired to fill hearts with the sound of music. PCPA cast its *lead* roles from a very well-known company in San Francisco called the American Conservatory Theatre (ACT), whose actors, at least some of them, summer-vacationed at the farm team in Santa Maria. PCPA offered a way for those actors to stay employed year-round. So all the big roles, the Willy Lomans and the Hedda Gablers and the Stanley Kowalskis, were pre-cast from the ACT company. Ripley and I knew we were hired as ballast, to fill in the chorus, to carry the spear, to fill out the stage picture, maybe to score one or two decent scenes as a featured supporting player if we truly impressed one of the directors. But it didn't matter. For the next four months, we were high up in the food chain. We were working and living among our peers and we were being paid for acting. And that was a great thing.

Santa Maria, it turned out, was a flat, nondescript clearing in a corn patch off the freeway. Squat houses and buildings could gradually be discerned from the greasy bus windows as we headed into the center of town. From what I could see, the place was not radiating as the cultural hub of the Central Coast.

Tire stores, five-and-dimes, places where you could get your tv fixed, Denny's, Sprouse-Reitz...

"Maybe this is just the slummy part of town," Ripley said, hopefully.

But as we collected our backpacks and started hoofing it south to the college, it became evident that each unremarkable single-story block was indistinguishable from the next.

The sun was slanting and casting an oblique orange glow on the olive trees, the ranch-style houses, the oleander bushes; the light getting weaker each block we walked. After twenty minutes we found the college. It was practically deserted. It was summer on the academic calendar, so normal classes had let out, leaving the campus vulnerable to takeover by the actors and technicians, who, apparently, had checked in

5

and dispersed hours before. The theatre building squatted before us, beige and cylindrical, resembling a flying saucer that had landed and burrowed partway into the ground. It was dark and underwhelming. Ripley lit a cigarette. A light wind blew from the west, cool from the ocean and unimpeded by geography or buildings of any considerable size. To the north, sprinklers chirped and whirred and sprayed birdlike plumes of water over quads of green grass. To the south, the manicured lawn gave way abruptly to much higher brown grass, acres of it, that stretched as far as we could see. To the east, we could hear the freeway roar past an embankment. Somewhere on the lawn in front of us, a skinny guy in a camouflage coat and long hair whirled around, karate-chopping an imaginary enemy while screaming: Kick! Mother! Your! Ass!

"You suppose he's the check-in guy?" Ripley asked.

I smiled and looked at Ripley full on, like you look at somebody before you jump out of an airplane. He didn't look back. The smell of onions, still in the ground, wafted in on the breeze. It was the moment of change, the tipping point. I knew, and Ripley knew that I knew, that this was the moment we left our little cocoon of family behind. We had held on to the camaraderie we had felt at State all the time we had been on the bus. But it was over now. Grad school was over, my fucked-up marriage with Gina and the little life we had tried to build in our funky apartment with the lime green bathroom and the walnut-stained cupboards was over. The coffee shop was gone, the classes were gone, even the seventies, those terrible years of enlightenment that had brought us screaming into adulthood, were gone. All the bitching we had done that bonded us close against the outside world had no relevance here, in this corn patch at the end of the continent.

Ripley stepped on his cigarette, as if in acknowledgement of the era's finality. We both hefted our backpacks and walked silently toward our new lives.

The admin office was not in one of the institutional beige buildings of the Allan Hancock ilk but rather was situated in a whitewashed quonset hut stuck like an afterthought behind the security and maintenance facilities. Some stragglers were still getting checked in. There were other actors I could have met, socialized with, and maybe dispelled some tension about the morning auditions, but I didn't feel like doing anything but finding my living quarters and getting some sleep. Ripley and I emerged from check-in about the same time, papers and maps in hand. We were heading in different directions.

"Make me a tape of that Cars album," I said.

"Okay," he said.

"And that Tom Petty one too." *Damn the Torpedoes*. The new one.

"Okay," he said, cocked his chin, and headed off.

It was, according to the route the woman had drawn in blue on the xeroxed street map, a sixteen block walk to the garage apartment I was to share with a married couple. Apparently, as I understood it, the apartment was actually built on *top* of the garage, which surely would have distinguished the structure as being one of the only two-story buildings in town. Santa Maria was subdued in an after-dinner stupor. The sun had set in a cold, white blanket of fog, which was beginning to waft inland. I stopped after eight blocks or so, got my sweatshirt out of my pack and put it on. Every house was a mid-century stucco rambler with a fake brick or slumpstone skirt, blocks and blocks of them, their pastel colors nothing but grey and shadow in the darkening remains of the day. Through just about every picture window I could see the blurry blue rectangle of a tv set through the curtains, or see the cathode ray light bouncing off the dining room walls, or even hear the familiar intonations of Walter Cronkite. I turned down the correct alley and found the correct stairway above the correct two-car garage. Midway up the stairs, a blonde woman was sitting on the landing.

"Yikes," she said. "Hello."

Apparently I startled her. "Hello," I said. "Sorry."

"Why are you sorry?" she said.

"Sorry to scare you like that."

"Never be sorry. Sorry is a terrible thing to be. You only scared me because I thought you might have been the landlady and I was about to roll this joint. She's a little uptight, I think. Have you met her?"

"No. I just got here."

"Right. We got here last Thursday, so we've had a chance to look around a bit. You must be Bob."

"Yes," I said. "I am. Bob."

"Would you like to smoke some pot?"

"Oh, well, actually, right now…"

"Ah, of course," she said. "You just got here. Where are my manners?"

She hopped up from the landing and faced me. She wore a loose-knit sweater over a sleeveless blouse and jeans. Her straight hair hung below her shoulders. She was reasonably tall but I was sure my pack weighed more than she did. "I'm Angie," she said, holding out her hand.

I shook it. "Bob," I said. "But you knew that."

"Yes I did. Come on in."

And she led me up the stairs. She opened the screen door and I stepped in. The tiny living room had a burnt orange carpet with thin brown trim, furnished with castoffs from the landlord's 60's remodel. It looked comfortable enough.

"Have you eaten today?" she asked.

It was past eight o'clock. "Kind of," I said.

"I can't remember if I've eaten. Oh yeah. I had a bagel. This is your room."

She opened a door in the tiny hall and switched on the overhead light: single bed, dresser. "We took the bigger room with the double. Is that all your stuff?" she asked as I dropped my pack on the bed.

"The rest of it's being shipped to the admin office," I said. "Should be here this week sometime I guess. Couple boxes."

"My husband's name is Willie. He's not here right now because he's working. He builds sets at the theatre and so his contract started a week ago."

"He's a tech guy, huh?"

"He starts early and works late, if you must know the truth. We come from Iowa State. I'm in the acting company so I've been doing nothing all week but hanging out. There's not much mystery to Santa Maria, if you know what I mean."

"I know what you mean."

"And an apple. I had an apple. Are you hungry?" She stuffed her joint into a little box of matches and closed it in her palm.

"Yes."

"Maybe I can get Willie to take me out for pizza when he gets home."

"Will he be home soon? Because it seems like this town rolls up the streets after dinner. And it's Sunday."

"Ah," she said. "Good point. Maybe I'll have him stop by the market on the way home. Pick up a couple of those pizza crust in a tube things with the sauce in a red can. He calls, you know. He always calls to check in before he leaves work."

"Yeah?"

"We'll have a nice late dinner. You can join us. Welcome our new roommate."

"I should contribute something," I said.

"Oh, don't worry. We'll work all that out. Your half of the refrigerator and all that. Tonight, you're our guest."

"Thanks Angie."

"Hopefully he'll be leaving before it gets too late. You want a beer?"

The phone rang. Angie braced herself in the doorjamb and looked at me like she was about to dive naked into a snowbank. "There he is. That's our meal ticket. Good old reliable Willie, calling to check in on Old Wifey-Poo." She headed for the wall phone.

Okay. She's fun, I thought to myself. I opened the top drawer of the dresser and started to unpack.

I heard her answer the phone. "Hi babe," she said.

Then there was a pause.

"Oh hi," she said. "My name is Angie."

My heart sank.

"No, he's here. We were just talking about pizza."

How did she get the phone number? She got the number already? I had no idea what my phone number was.

"Yes. Well, you know, I'm hungry because all I had was an onion bagel and an apple all day long."

I jerked into action. My blood was pounding.

"We were just talking about having dinner. Do you want to talk to him?"

I was in the living room.

"Nice talking to you," Angie said. "Here he is."

I practically snatched the phone from Angie's hand.

"It's –"

"I know," I said, my hand over the mouthpiece. I waited for her to back away.

Angie looked at me, her lips forming a grimace, and she fluttered her hands above her head and ducked out the front door.

"Hello Gina," I said.

I didn't sleep too well that night. Willie eventually came home, but I didn't meet him. Angie wound up shopping while I was on the phone, and by the time she came back I had my door closed and the night was over. She never knocked, out of respect, I'm sure. I heard them bang about in the kitchen, heard them take turns in the bathroom, heard the springs groan as they got into bed, heard their muffled conversation die out. It was a long time before morning.

The thing about Gina is she doesn't see stuff from anybody else's perspective. It's all me me me. I this. I that. Anyway she got upset over one thing or another and it wasn't a great phone call. She basically wanted to talk about divorce stuff and I wasn't in the mood. Then I asked her about Mark Sanders. I had that familiar lump in my throat the rest of the night.

It would have been simple if we could have just stuck to the script. There should be scripts for successful marriages, just like good plays. You should be able just to pick a script off a shelf and run with it. Everything written out, everything prescribed. This is where this happens. This is the way the story goes. Gina plays her part, I play mine. Thing is, the story isn't written yet, so you have to write your own. After all, good stories are just elaborate lies. I'd written a million plays in my head by the time I was twenty. I was a good liar. Surely I could script out a good marriage. So I decided to take a whack at it.

I started lying first. Innocent lies designed to spare feelings. They were successful lies and I played them well, convincing enough to build a whole first act.

"What's wrong?" she'd ask.

"Nothing," I'd say.

"Is everything okay?"

"Fine."

"Do you love me?"

"Yes."

Then I thought: This is not comfortable. The script is not *right* yet. There's room for improvement. What if we move this part around, add this in here?

Like the part where I feel empty.

So I began to let little truths sneak in:

"Do you like the way I look?" she'd ask.

"Well, I guess I've been meaning to tell you something."

"What?"

"Maybe you've gained a little weight."

Of course, one line of improvisation opens the door to a profusion of adlibs.

"How can you say that?" Etcetera, etcetera. Understandable outrage and defiance from the lead actress.

So I discovered that improvisation was dangerous. Then the backpedaling lies began:

"I didn't mean it. I really love the way you look."

What I didn't and couldn't say is that no matter how beautiful and personable Gina was, she could never meet the ideal of the woman who should have had the part – the woman I had in my head. Because I held Gina to a standard that was unattainable for her, I was unable to see her clearly and appreciate her for who she was. But you have to make all this shit up as you go along, all this improvisational shit, and so the script lacks clarity. It lacks refinement. Besides, too much truth at this stage of the marriage would be devastating. It would have made the scene read like this:

"What's wrong?" she'd ask.

And if I'd said: "I realize that I sought you out because I needed to feel better about myself and I mistakenly thought that marrying you would solve my problems. I mistook feelings of love for dependency, and now I'm angry because I'm expecting you to be everything I need, and you can't possibly be that for me. So where I should be seeing you for who you really are, I'm seeing only your weaknesses, and I hate myself for it."

...It would have made for a very short story.

Instead, you have to work in the truths sporadically and try to preserve the structure of the piece without permanently pissing off your scene partner. So the second act becomes interspersed with bits of truth.

Gina could write some decent dialogue of her own:

"I'm going out," she'd say.

"Where are you going?"

"I'm going out with a friend."

"Which friend are you going out with?"

"Just a friend."

"Is this friend a girl or a guy?"

"You're always grilling me. You don't trust me. You think I'm a whore."

"I don't think you're a whore. Why can't you tell me who you're going out with?"

"If you loved me you'd trust me to have an evening out by myself without always having to go through your interrogation."

Partial truths. Not full truths. Full truths would have taken all the intrigue away. Full truths would have made the script read like this:

"I'm going out to sleep with Mark Sanders. Because of my reliance on you to fill the void of the father I never really knew, I'm cheating on you to get even with Daddy. Because you love me, you have become my enemy, because anybody who loves me doesn't see me as I really am: a horrible person. Therefore I want to hurt and destroy you."

Exposition over, the third act would have written itself.

No, it was easier to coast along in the preordained manner. Just say the words.

Except *that* didn't work out either.

On the phone, regarding Mark Sanders, she said to me:

"Things were really screwed up at that time, Bobby. I swear, I didn't know what I was doing."

I got maybe two hours' sleep.

2

I must have drifted off sometime toward morning. Willie had already left the house by the time my alarm rang. I had set it for 8:30, but I waited until I heard Angie in the shower before I got up, and got out of there before she finished. I didn't want to split my focus by making polite conversation on the big audition morning, or, God forbid, *apologize* for any social faux pas I might have made. I needed to stay concentrated, keep my edge.

Our audition times had been posted on sheets in the hallway between the auditorium and the green room in the cylindrical theatre building. Actors were thronging the hall, craning their necks to see over heads and shoulders. I was craning my neck with everybody else. I was hoping for a later-in-the-day audition time to allow myself some recovery from my emotional disorientation and fatigue, but there I was, scheduled for 10:10, practically right out of the chute. My heart started pounding immediately and I felt the rush of blood to my chest. I verified it five times visually before I left the callboard: my name, my time, my name, my time, then I turned away and involuntarily started bouncing on my toes, trying to exhale away the serpentine beast that had wound itself around my breathing apparatus. Instead of whiling away hours around the picnic tables like the lucky ones with afternoon call times, I needed to get serious immediately and start doing warmups.

I saw Ripley bobbing amid the hordes. "What's your time?" he yelled.

"In about fifteen minutes," I yelled back.

"You're lucky." He elbowed his way toward me and patted me on the back. His later-in-the-afternoon slot meant he'd be a basket case most of the day. "Give it hell," he said, his voice creaking uncontrollably.

Maybe Ripley was right. I just had to get through the next twenty minutes and I could relax. But the pressure was on. I strode to the green room, going over every little movement, every line reading of my audition, carefully choreographed for maximum effect; not too subdued, not too over-the-top. The pieces, one classical, one contemporary and one song, time and peer group-tested for over a year and a half, picked apart and reconstructed by grad school pundits, teachers and entrusted fellow actors, had been trotted out for Noah Manning, the big honcho at PCPA, not once, on his way through the boonies with his traveling audition wagon, but twice; again at the callbacks on Geary Street. How could there be any surprises? But this time it was for the directors, I told myself. Stay the course. Don't worry about surprising Manning, he's immured to surprise anyway, as he sees thousands of auditions every spring and fall. Just do your job, I thought, stick to the plan, stay on the script, and relax.

"Bob? You're next."

The serpentine beast tightened its grip around my heart and lungs, forcing me to take quick, shallow breaths. An usher led me from the green room through the heavy stage door, which shut silently behind me, and I stepped from the melee of the crowded hall into an imposing quiet and an enveloping darkness. I was in the backstage area, surrounded by black curtains. I felt the usher's hand on my chest, a welcome touchstone as I waited for my eyes to become accustomed to the blackness. I realized there was a person standing in front of me, female, I could tell by the scent of hand cream, and my widening pupils could faintly discern her bare shoulders in the dark. I heard her clear her throat, gently. *Don't damage the instrument. Got to have clear pipes.* There was the sound of applause from the auditorium. The person onstage had finished. I could feel the adrenaline of the woman in front of me shoot up another notch. She blew some quick breaths, cleared her throat again, louder this time, shook her hands, jogged in place and bounced three times. Then the usher parted the curtains and the woman squared her shoulders and walked into the stage light, stately and statuesque, projecting as much confidence as she possibly could. She looked like every other female there that day, in some variation of the prerequisite audition costume: Danskin leggings, black dance skirt and neutral blouse. The curtains fell back into place in front of me, and I heard her say "Hello" into the dark auditorium, deeply and slowly, her voice no doubt warmed up for hours. She was a singer, I could tell already, which probably meant she wouldn't make a big impression with the dramatic stuff, but she was going to wow them with the resonant high E. "My name is…" Blah de blah whoever. There was silence, and I could imagine the directors in the audience circling her name and shuffling her picture and resume to the front of the pile. There were other actors in the audience as well, those with time slots comfortably in the afternoon, sitting in to watch, no doubt gauging this woman's training quotient, assessing how thoroughly prepped she was, everybody of like gender silently hoping she would fail and take herself out of the unspoken competition for the available roles that season. "Today I'll be doing Portia from *The Merchant of Venice,* and…"

How many times had they seen actresses do Portia from *The Merchant of Venice,* I thought. How many times had they seen some ham like me do my cutting from *Macbeth?* How original was that? The dagger speech, big deal. Of the seventy some actors there, how many guys were doing *Macbeth?* Three? Five? Maybe more. Hell, Shakespeare didn't write that many plays, there weren't that many to choose from. And how about my contemporary piece? What surprises could I bring to Neil Simon's *Prisoner of Second Avenue*? Why did I pick such pedestrian twaddle? Simon was wrong for me and Macbeth was out of my league, I thought. And what about my singing voice? Crap, at best. It would have made me hurl, I thought, seeing hams like me and Ripley and Gina and that skinny fornicator Mark Sanders do their off-the-shelf George and Marthas, their *Equuses* and their *Streetcars* and their *Man in the Moon Marigolds,* their just-the-way-Ian McKellen-did-it Richard III's and worst of all, their fruity, limp throated *Pippins* and *Fantastiks* and *Little Night Musics*. I fought the urge to bolt from the auditorium. I felt sick to my stomach. The woman ahead of me had finished her contemporary piece. There was no response from the assembled, which was customary protocol for these kinds of things. Their job was not to be effusive one way or the other. They were simply there to assess. She would end with the song, for her, in chosen order, the pièce de résistance. She had kept her monologues short, as I suspected, to avoid belying too much of her lack of acting talent, but would fill out her time with the song. I had maybe two minutes before my name was called and I would have to step into the light. I shook out my hands, jumped up and down, trying to dissipate the Golem-like layer of stone that had encased my body. I briefly entered a nightmare state, where I envisioned myself unable to form words, my lips frozen and forced to utter only monosyllables by the tons of rock that had poured down upon my head. Who was I to think I could do this? My marriage was failing, my tenure in the Ivory Tower of Education was over and I had already realized that my MFA degree was actually a great credential for a career in fast food. What did it matter to the deep fryer guy that I had done the definitive Macbeth at age 24? All that mattered were the next fleeting moments in the cavernous flying saucer in the grass.

The woman onstage finished on the predictable high note, flawlessly executed. "Thank you," she said, and strode confidently off the other side of the stage. There was customary polite applause from the auditorium.

The usher parted the curtains. "Okay," the usher said. I walked. It looked like it would take only a few strides to reach center stage, but as I traversed the distance, it seemed to take me forever to get there. And my legs felt like they didn't belong to me at all. I gave my sheet music to the piano guy, took my place under the lights, and stood perhaps just a little too straight in my standard auditioning clothes (sensible pants, light shirt,

shirt always lighter than the pants, no tie). There was silence in the auditorium. I could imagine them circling my name, thumbing my picture, trying to assess how many years it would take for me to go completely bald. "Hello," I said. The sound felt like it traveled five inches in front of my face and then fell to the stage, dead. I opened my mouth again and for a split second, I actually forgot my first and last name. It came to me before the time lapse would have been perceptible and I managed to croak it out. But that was a bad sign. It meant I was not connected, not concentrating, not centered. I needed to galvanize myself.

I had to do something desperate.

We used to play this blindfold game in acting school. It was a test to see how thoroughly you could trust your fellow actors, who are gathered in a circle around you, with you in the middle, blindfolded, your arms clasped at your sides, and you see nothing, have no way of protecting yourself as you fall backward into the circle and are passed around from person to person, bobbing and tilting on the axis of your feet. All you are required to do is remain stiff and silent, like a board. And if you do this and you trust that your partners will not let you fall, the experience is heavenly, much like what a baby must feel when it is being rocked and cradled in its mother's arms. But all your partners must be attentive, and treat you carefully, because only if you trust them can you fall without worrying. If you panic and try to reach out, or adjust yourself to regain your footing, you wreck the game and could actually get hurt or hurt someone else. So the reward for being calm, for trusting, is to be coddled and passed around the group and laid gently, blissfully to the ground.

I felt like I had learned a lot from this exercise, and I dubbed the lesson I had learned the Freefall Theory. I employed the theory a lot as an actor, because as an actor, I had to trust that when I said my line, it would be there. Just like the people in the circle were there. You see? Because, as the exercise had shown us, acting was all about trust. Now if for whatever reason the line I was about to say was not in my head when I needed to say it, it meant I was too tense and that I should relax, and in that split second of relaxation, the line would most likely appear. Say you're playing a word game like Concentration or something where you try to think of as many state capitals as you can in 30 seconds. The pressure's on, all the people are watching and nothing's coming except maybe Olympia and Sacramento. But when all the sand has run out of the hourglass and you let out that big breath, you get this flood of information: Salem, Boise, Bismarck, Juneau, Des Moines. They were there, you were just trying too hard. Moreover, once it wasn't *important* that you remembered them, you could remember them with ease. I was convinced that this was not only the key to great acting, it was the key to life. If something was too important, make it less important.

So to encourage spontaneity in my acting, I would play this game with myself. I would learn my lines as fast as I could and then forget them, pretend I never learned them, and then recall them the moment I opened my mouth. They came out differently each time. Same words, but different. It was very risky to do it this way. I imagined it was like falling into space when you're not sure there's anything to catch you. To fall freely, your trust, your level of confidence, has to be really high. Being worried about remembering your lines meant you didn't really know them. Worrying was not an option. Your head had to be clear.

Audition pieces went against the entire Freefall Theory, because they were so pat, so minted, so polished and refined and sanitized. Where was there room for any spontaneity?

So there I was, under the glare of the lights, my years of training boiling away to the next two and a half minutes. "Today I'll be doing..." I introduced my classical monologue as my customary classical monologue, and my song as my song, feeling I couldn't radically depart from performing them. But when I announced my contemporary piece I plucked a title and the name of some bogus playwright out of the air. Just made it up on the spot. Who would know? Somebody they never heard of, something new, to my benefit, I thought. I had no idea what I was going to say, but it was going to be a new experience, good or bad, for them and for me.

I began to intone the all-too-familiar *Macbeth* stuff: "Is this a dagger I see before me" and blah de blah. Same words, but something was different. Because I had set a challenge for myself, I had let go of all my reserve, all my self-consciousness. I had nothing to lose. I felt remarkably relaxed. I wasn't examining every syllable, I didn't care what they thought. I was centered, my head was clear, and I felt like I commanded attention. Because I had told myself there was no pressure. I made the pressure go away. Whatever was happening was happening right there, in the moment, without any worries clogging up my brain. I even fared okay with my song. At the very least I figured my musical choice of "What's New Pussycat" ought to win me points for originality. And then I opened my mouth to begin my contemporary monologue, and I fell back into the circle of hands.

Spontaneity is a real high. I maintain that I've had moments on stage that are better than any orgasm, even the ones with Jessica Murphy, the Very Oral First Girlfriend. But this was most excellent. Here was Noah Manning, mover and shaker of one of California's largest theaters, sitting in the audience, and all these revered directors and fellow actors with time on their hands, listening to me go on about throwing up on Diane Kern on the ferris wheel at the county fair. I figured, the most exciting moments I've seen on stage are when actors forgot their lines. All of a sudden they have to really communicate! Here I was totally flying by the seat of my pants, relating this completely unrehearsed and rather intimate story about me and Diane Kern, and I was communicating with Noah Manning and he was perhaps even laughing. And people did laugh, several times, which I felt was definitely to my credit. And I let it feed me and kept going, talking to my imaginary confidant somewhere mid-level in the auditorium, telling this person how even though I had tried to aim the puke stream out through the metal window, the cage of the ferris wheel actually caught the puke and dumped it back over both of us. When I was sixteen, the experience nearly killed me, and I could never look Diane Kern in the eye again. But I had ventured a bet that I wasn't the only one who had suffered humiliation in high school, and I felt the story resonating with the developmentally-arrested braces-and-glasses-wearing teenager in all of them.

I don't remember thanking the auditioners, but I hope I did. I went through the crowded hall and out the stage door and kept walking.

Blocks later I bought an enchilada at a food cart parked near an auto re-pair place, and sat on the guardrail at a cul-de-sac near the high school to eat. I watched some guys collapse some bleachers on the field.

From my new vantage point, Santa Maria didn't look so bad.

JUNE

3

They called the town Solvang, which, I figured, had something to do with *Sun*. At least the *Sol* part. *Vang* must have meant Burn. Or Stroke. Solvang was a 35 minute road trip south and inland from Santa Maria, and its geographic location to the east meant it was exponentially hotter than the temperate coastal towns. For some reason Solvang was built to resemble some Bavarian village conceived in an opium dream by a Hollywood set designer. It had all been calculated to bring in tourists, probably after the success of the kitschy Andersen's Split Pea Soup place out on the freeway. So Solvang was all about stucco facades resembling post and beam Tudor, colored flags atop pointy turrets, cobblestones inlaid in asphalt. Everything newly built had to resemble something old and Northern European. Thing was, Northern Europe was not known for its blistering heat.

I was the only person sitting in the audience of Solvang's outdoor ampitheater, which was broiling in the late afternoon sun. I was sitting there because I was the only actor in the place whose presence onstage was not imminently required. This didn't mean I had an insignificant part. Okay, maybe I had a *small* part, but at least it was a speaking role, big enough to escape the anonymity and repetition of the spear carrier ranks. Okay, maybe I didn't get to do any fancy swordplay like the spear carriers did, but I had plenty of downtime.

Despite my enviable job, I was not altogether willing, at that moment, to drop to my knees and sing the praises of my good fortune. I had lots of crap on my mind. I was dealing fairly well with the Gina stuff, but I really needed some perspective. And I needed perspective from somebody who knew me, so I was waiting for rehearsal to end at 5:00 so I could talk to Ripley over dinner.

It hadn't felt right talking to Kathy Bishop about all my junk. She was the one I was watching on stage at that moment, as she stood there in short, frayed cutoffs and a green bikini top. She was the only thing worth watching, frankly, as the guy onstage with her was about as exciting as watching milk sour. Kathy was playing Catherine in that famous French scene in *Henry V.* I had helped her learn the scene while we sat on the grass near the scene shop a week before, and it would have been a great time to unburden all my junk on her, because I sensed that if I had played it right, I might have been able to haul her off to the sack, even though we barely knew each other. But for some reason, I balked. She had been wearing a blue halter top then, which I tried not to stare at while she kept asking me why Gina, who she didn't know and had no business asking about, and I weren't together anymore. Instead of being vulnerable and offering her the "oh, poor me" type of bullshit, I was evasive and kept steering our conversation back to benign topics. We mostly talked about what a ham the guy playing Henry V was and how she hated doing her scenes with him. His name was Verden Price. He was the only actor I had ever seen who actually got worse during rehearsal. He auditioned like a pro. Best audition I had ever seen; commanding, exciting, fluid. But each day he rehearsed he cramped up and got stiffer and stiffer until, with opening night looming, he was practically catatonic. Really, it was like he was trying to speak underwater. Shakespeare was boring to begin with and if you had a catatonic ham playing your Henry, you had sheer tedium.

We were in the third week of our residency at PCPA, and things had sorted themselves out after the auditions. I was opening the first show in order of the three I was cast in, that being *Henry V,* and we were opening the show in Solvang because, believe it or not, PCPA ran two, count 'em, two stages in these two towns, and rotated most of their seven plays in repertory between them. Solvang had figured out years before that it needed to provide some sort of quaint nighttime entertainment for its tourists, so the City Council invited PCPA to road its shows down there. Solvang had built an outdoor thrust stage identical in every way to the indoor stage at Allan Hancock College, so PCPA's sets could be broken down and set up on both stages. But Solvang wanted an open-air experience for their theatergoers, so the auditorium was built without a roof. Same blueprint exactly for the stage, but the seats were all out in the open. After dark the theatre was the only game in town, so Solvang's vast tourist population flocked there. If we thought about it, which few of us did, being self-centered actors and all, we would have realized it was an amazing feat of civic engineering.

The assembled *Hank V* company was in Solvang preparing for the evening's technical rehearsal. "Tech" happened right before a show opened. It was the time where all the elements came together – sets, lights, costumes, props, and us actors who had rehearsed for weeks in street clothes and tennis shoes on a blank stage with tape outlines on the floor that indicated the platforms and wall units being built. Believe me, Verden Price's monologues had even less of an impact when you had to watch them over and over again on a gym floor under fluorescent lighting, so we were all at least somewhat grateful we had made it to tech. We actors were off the hook. We knew all our lines and were essentially clay pigeons for the tech folks to punt around. There was a lot of "Hold please!" called by Stage Manager Lou Bowman, a short, red-haired, bespectacled woman who wielded the power of someone five times her size, and commanded everyone's respect in a forceful Texan accent. During tech you would stand on stage for an hour while they adjusted the lights or whatever and you could crack jokes. Nobody cared as long as you didn't get too loud. When they'd built the cue to the director's liking, you'd hear Lou say "Okay, we're going back to [some point in the play]." And you'd go offstage and start where they told you. Trying to act during all this was futile so nobody tried. A five minute scene could take an hour if it had a lot of complicated cues in it.

So that's why I was sitting in the audience trying to discern the impressions of Kathy Bishop's nipples through her green bikini top. We were close to dinnertime, and a shadow, cast from the fake turrets which loomed above the stage, had crept up the amphitheater and had finally reached my row. I was sitting in shade when I put my shirt back on and went backstage to find Ripley.

"Hey Ripley. I'll buy you a bratwurst. Let's go to dinner before the crush."

He looked at me like I had barfed in his lunch bag. "I can't go now. What if Lou skips ahead to the battle scene?"

I had anticipated Ripley's reaction. His list of phobias was as long as your arm. He was standing in the wings, listening intently for his cue to enter, with Hanover, a mean third baseman in inter-company hardball, who had a mischievous sense of humor. Both of them wore plastic helmets and clutched prop spears.

"It's six minutes to dinner and they're at a dead stop," I said. "She's not going to get to anything else before the break."

"I'll cover for you," Hanover said to Ripley.

Ripley glanced around. "I don't want to get in trouble."

"What can she do in six minutes? But – suit yourself." And I was prepared to wait it out.

"I'll cover for you," Hanover said again. "Leave your stuff. I'll take it to the prop table."

Reluctantly, Ripley put down his spear and followed me out the stage door. "If I get in trouble because of you guys…"

What did I know? We were halfway down the block when Hanover stuck his head out the door and shouted "Ripley!"

"Dammit, Bob! I told you!" Ripley cursed, panicking, a break in his voice. He ran back. I trotted behind him in sympathy.

Hanover held open the stage door. "I thought they were speeding up, but now they've stopped again," he said, winking at me while Ripley frantically re-attached his helmet strap.

"Dinner break," Lou said over the loudspeaker. "Back at 6:30. We'll start at the top of the show with lights and costumes."

"Do you think he was messing with me?" Ripley asked as we walked along Glockenspiel Avenue outside the theater.

"Nah," I said. "Just being thorough."

We grabbed a seat at Das Doggenhaus. A cute waitress in Heidi braids and lederhosen took our order. They had good bratwurst.

"What did you want to talk about?" Ripley asked.

"Me," I said.

"Holy Jesus, Bob. Don't you think other people have lives too?"

"Maybe. But theirs are not as important as mine." I was half serious. "On the bus you asked me a million times if I was okay. So – have my problems paled in importance since then?"

"Frankly, yes."

"Come on. Just give me five minutes. Then we can talk about *you* if you want."

I knew Ripley was mostly giving me shit. I knew he loved me, and would tolerate my indulgent introspection, because he was as self-absorbed as I was. Maybe more so.

"Five minutes," he said. "Go."

"You've known me awhile. Do I seem different to you?"

"Since when?"

"You know, since the breakup. Since she went to Minnesota."

"I don't know. Not really."

Not the answer I wanted. I tried again. "If you were to assess me as a person right now, today, and describe me to somebody else, how would you describe me?"

Ripley looked at me with squinty eyes.

"I'd say you were a decent guy with an annoyingly positive outlook on life."

Goddammit. "What about the mystery?" I said. "Do you see a dark side to me anywhere? Because I feel – I don't know – dark! I mean, what about my vast well of hurt that gives me the fuel to do my art?"

"What about it?"

Ripley was an unobservant fool. Surely anybody off the street could see I was one of the walking wounded. A dangerous character with a razor tongue. The raccoon with the leg in the trap. This was the dark and quiet kid who stayed in his room drawing pictures while all the other kids were out playing football. The only child. The observer. The wounds inflicted from childhood had been subsequently uncovered and rubbed raw by a stunning betrayal in love.

"I don't feel the same," I said.

"Of course you don't."

"I mean I feel like I'm not a good person anymore."

"Define 'good.'"

"Here I am 25 years old and I'm practically divorced once already. I'm damaged."

"You've always been damaged." He looked at me blankly. "Ever since I've known you. You got married way too early. You were a kid. Live with it and move on. You're still wearing that wedding ring. Take it off. Open your eyes. Do you know how many available women there are in this company? Have you even noticed?"

I had noticed. But something about wearing the ring: it kept the women away when you needed to heal. Hands off the damaged goods. Having been cheated on and lied to, I didn't want to have anything to do with another woman. Not right then. Not ever. I was a card-carrying misogynist. All women were the same.

"I'm emotionally unavailable," I said.

I fiddled with the ring on my finger beneath the table. I needed to wear it. I needed to be sick at heart. I wanted to be down in the muck. When the marriage started to unravel I found myself ceasing to care, and

I liked the strange power it gave me. I stopped caring, and everything became so much easier. I didn't have to adhere to my own tight standards anymore. The ring was a reminder that I was a failure, and I liked that because being optimistic and positive took a lot of energy. When you're a failure you can sit in the shadows, head bowed, with mean slits for eyes, and lob caustic snipes at people who hurt you. Sweet. Easy. And the best part of it? You don't have to give away any part of yourself.

I felt cheated by my upbringing. I had been burdened from birth. This was the thing: I was an only child and pretty much a shut-in growing up. I didn't have great socialization skills. I would have loved to have had a sister so I could have grown up knowing *something* about girls and what makes them tick. I hadn't a clue. I thought the way you got a girl in the sack was to impress them and make them notice you, so you could convince them that you were a nice enough person to fall in love with and then, once they did, you could have sex with them whenever you wanted. How was I to know *I* was supposed to chase *them?* How was I supposed to know girls were built to be the object of pursuit? Here I was, working on being Mr. Nice Guy so girls would flock around and – what? What did I think they were going to do? Plus, I had no idea that girls didn't *want* nice guys. They wanted Jim Morrison. They wanted the beefy red pickup with DANGER written all over it. I had led myself down the wrong path. I hadn't made the male-female correlation properly. The answer was in nature. See that flower? V-A-G-I-N-A. See that bee? That's the guy in a tux. This garden is the high school prom. I think this basic mistake in sexual orientation led me to become an actor. I was still trying to show off, win approval. Then I would use the adulation I received to my advantage and make women do whatever I wanted.

Sap.

I met Gina in my first play in college. We became good friends and because of this screwed up idea of male-female bonding, I thought our friendship was a terrific foundation for a long and loving marriage. I was, I suppose, wrong.

"Bad self image," Ripley said. "That's why most of us become actors. We don't like who we are."

Ripley was raised Catholic. He knew all about self loathing.

For the rest of the evening our tech rehearsal ran its due course. I was wrapped in my misery and kept to myself. We did have costumes, but my cloak was still being worked on so I had to wear my sweatshirt over my black tights and ill-fitting pantaloons. I looked like a moron, and felt even worse. Backstage poker games hadn't begun yet because the maddening stop/start pace kept everybody anxiously listening for cues, so all us supporting players and spear carriers could do was hang out and wait. Finally the rehearsal lurched to the point of my big entrance, but Stage Manager Lou barely let me croak out three words of my first line before she said over the loudspeaker "Thank you, Bob," and skipped to my exit cue.

I came offstage and decided that women were horrible things and I hated them all. Lou was okay – she was just doing her job. But she was the only one. All other women were simply, irredeemably horrible. But, paradoxically, at that moment, I needed to get laid.

Prospects for spontaneous sex did not look promising, however. Because *Hank V* was one of Shakespeare's histories, there were only three women in the cast, which did not allow for a lot of backstage intrigue. Kathy Bishop was hot for me. I knew it. She knew it. I had made points with her on the grass that day, but perhaps because of my seemingly low level of interest in romance she had moved her attentions toward Peter Ross. Now, they found shadows together and spoke in low tones, punctuated with coy smiles. Another woman in the cast was older and married and had NOT INTERESTED painted all over her. And Henry V's main squeeze, played by a woman named Wanda Dare, was from another planet that I had never been to. She was an established actress at ACT in San Francisco. Wanda Dare was quite attractive but in that weird silicone doll way which left you wondering if Barbie had actually sprung to life without you knowing it and slipped into an Elizabethan costume. I can say truthfully that Wanda Dare looked great in her costume. She had some acting talent but there was apparently room for nothing else in her head, as her conversational skills seemed to stop after "How do I look?" Perhaps because I had only a minor speaking part and was, in fact, one step above the spear carrier ranks, Wanda Dare had decided I was not to be fraternized with. I noticed, however, that she was chummy with Verden Price, the facile Henry V himself, due completely to the fact, I'm sure, that he had the biggest part in the play. Never mind that he was a catatonic ham, he was the lead.

There were in fact, some very good actors in the company, but none of them seemed to find their way into *Henry V*. This was probably the fault of the director, the Darkly Effeminate Mario, who apparently decided that his high-minded directorial concept would fill the void left by the dearth of acting talent.

I had to forget about the getting laid thing for awhile, at least until after the bus ride home.

I found Angie sitting outside on the front steps as usual, wearing jeans and a white, sleeveless blouse, her feet bare, legs apart and sprawled out in front of her. A large hunk of hair dangled in front of her face at eye level. As roommates go, I could have done a lot worse. I found Angie really attractive, and even though I was currently *emotionally unavailable*, I was convinced that the connection we shared could, in some alternate reality, allow me to whisk her away from that loser Willie, who after all wasn't even an actor and surely could not provide Angie the aesthetic stimulation she needed to remain committed. Angie and I hadn't been cast in any shows together. Her good looks and singing voice had landed her squarely in both musicals, and they had given her a small role in *The Country Wife*.

"Wanna smoke some pot?" she said.

"Okay," I said. "Let me put my crap away first." I checked their bedroom. No Willie.

"Where's Willie?" The screen door banged loudly behind me as I sat down beside her.

Angie blew a strand of hair out of her eyes. "Bob," she said, "You obviously didn't hear the news that my old man has been promoted to scene shop foreman. Not out of, you know, commendation or good deeds or skill or whatever but because he was the only guy that would take the job after Fred Norton split town."

"Fred Norton split town?"

"You are so behind the times, mister."

This was real news. Nobody *ever* left mid-season. "When did this happen?"

"This morning. Ol' Fred didn't show up for work this morning and everyone thought he must be dead or drunk or something. So Willie goes over to his place and it's cleaned out from top to bottom. Just... whoosh. Gone."

"Does this mean Willie makes more money now?"

"Duh! Yes! More responsibility means Willie stays up all night but makes more money for meeee. I'll be lonely but we'll be rich."

"So what happened to Norton?"

"Don't know. Willie's in Noah's office after lunch? And these two FBI guys come in looking for him."

"Looking for Willie?"

"No! Looking for Fred Norton. It turns out he's this criminal or something. There's a warrant out for his arrest."

"You're kidding me."

"In more than one state. He was hiding out."

"What did he do?" I asked.

"I just told you. He left town."

"No. I mean what did he do to get in trouble?"

"Nobody knows. Do you want me to make something up?" Angie said, taking a hit of her joint. "Don't you want any of this?" She said without exhaling.

"No thanks," I said. I didn't know how to tell Angie I never really liked getting stoned.

"Anything you want to talk about?"

How did she know there was? "Not really," I said.

"Is it the Gina thing?"

"What Gina thing?"

"Don't be a jerk, Bob. You guys going to get back together? Are you working on it? Why does she call you?"

"I don't know. Beats me."

Angie exhaled exasperatedly. "Look Bob. I hate this. If this subject is off limits or something just let me know and I won't waste my time trying to get anything out of you. I won't ask you about her. Or is it that you feel you don't know me well enough?"

By broaching the Gina subject, the conversation had turned from the mildly informative to the highly pertinent. This was just what I needed to talk about. A spouse's blatant infidelity was great for gathering sympathy points. With The Wronged Husband label attached to me, Angie would see me as at once vulnerable, sensitive, and in need of love. So, as I pulled out my ace, I looked her square in the eye and got ready to collect my bonus points.

"I found out she was sleeping with someone behind my back," I said.

She blinked. "Did you cheat on her?"

"Did I what?"

"It's a two-way street, you know."

"Yeah, I know."

"There's two sides to every story. I'm sure she believes she had her reasons for cheating on you. So what were they? Do you know?"

"Not..."

"I mean, maybe she was really pissed at you. Did you guys talk about your problems? Most people just don't sleep with other people for no reason. And there's different kinds of betrayal. She may have felt let down by you. Did you abuse her? Abuse can take many forms. It doesn't have to be physical abuse. You may have been manipulating her without even knowing it."

Hey. This was not the way this was supposed to work. Where were my conciliatory "ohhh"s and "I'm sorry"s, the reaching out, the touching of my hand?

"I mean, I know you well enough to realize that communication is not your strong suit," she said.

"You don't know me well enough to say that."

"Really? Because you haven't been, you know, incredibly verbose."

Maybe it was the way I looked at her, but she finally cocked her head reflexively and said:

"Sorry. I do that. I Just go off. And then I realize I'm way too direct with people I hardly know. Did I hurt your feelings?"

Yes. "No."

"I need to edit myself. I mostly just say what I feel. Bad habit. Most of the time I'm right, though."

"You shouldn't have to edit what you say," I said.

"But you really should think about opening up a little, Bob. It would do you good." She got up and brushed ashes off her blouse. "You know? Because maybe you and me could be friends. But you have to share something. Information, the way you feel about things, something." She turned and walked up the steps. "Think about it."

And she went inside.

4

The next morning I showed up in the dance studio early. In the mornings we rehearsed *Once in a Lifetime,* an old Kaufman and Hart chestnut about Hollywood shenanigans dating back to 1930 or so. All of the jokes were dated but our director, Mr. Lark, loved all of them because they were at least as old as he was. Mr. Lark reminded me of my grandfather. And he had no first name. At least we never knew it. His age and stature simply demanded that everyone refer to him as Mr. Lark.

We still had a week before tech, so the cast was off-book. *Once in a Lifetime* was one show with some good people in it. Like Richard Siebert. I had first seen Richard in *Moon for the Misbegotten* at ACT. He was not striking in appearance – just a very normal-looking guy – but I couldn't keep my eyes off him. Not because he was showy or grandiose or hammy or anything, but because he was the antithesis of hamdom. He was simple and real. He made difficult roles seem effortless and found ways to perform them without artifice. In *Once in a Lifetime*, he was getting a chance to show his comedy chops. Richard played one of a trio of vaudevillians who head west for fame and glory in Celluloid City. Ripley and I found ourselves in the large ensemble, doubling up on characters and running around chewing cigars and opening and shutting doors and wearing different straw hats and what-not. The play didn't amount to much in terms of it being a literary benchmark or anything, but it was a lot of fun to work on. I didn't have a lot to do, though I had more stage time than I did in *Henry V*. And it was a pleasure just being in the room with actors I respected. The other two leads were being played by Curt Harnick, a beak-nosed virtuoso with a commanding presence, and the oh-so-hot and talented Barbara Ledbetter.

Bronson, another actor in the cast, came up to me during a break. He motioned to Barbara Ledbetter. "She's really a man," he said.

"He wears it well," I said.

Bronson was a big actor from Texas. Mr. Lark was off working with Richard and Curt and Barbara Ledbetter and we ensemble guys were standing by onstage.

"I'm actually a woman," Bronson said.

"Funny," I said. "I would've pegged you for a Republican."

Bronson would have been a scary guy in the real world, because of his size and weird sense of humor. But this was the theatre, and guys like Bronson, even if they were from Texas, were only there because their hearts were made of decent stuff.

"Did'ja hear about that guy that skipped town?"

"Fred Norton," I said. "My roommate is taking his place."

"What do you think he did?"

"Pillow tag removal?"

Bronson glanced over his shoulder, checking things out. "Real estate fraud. He sold a house that wasn't his."

I looked over at Bronson's roommate Lloyd, who was listening in. Lloyd was a shorter guy who in casting vernacular would have been pegged a *character type*. Lloyd silently nodded his head.

"Did he make any money?" I asked.

"Five thousand dollars earnest money." Bronson said.

"And they haven't caught him?"

"He's done it at least twice before," Lloyd said.

On our break the three of us went outside so Lloyd could smoke.

"Goddammit," Bronson said. "You have to smoke out here?"

"Go back inside if you don't like it," Lloyd said.

"I hate it when you fuckin' smoke."

"Go back inside then," Lloyd said, standing his ground.

"Too bad it was illegal what Norton did," said Bronson. "Otherwise it's a good idea."

"Real estate is the way to go, especially for an actor," Lloyd said. "You can make a lot of money in your spare time."

"The Army is selling all this land down near Nipomo for a thousand dollars an acre," Bronson said. "It was used for artillery practice but they don't need it anymore."

"That could be a goldmine," Lloyd said.

"Somebody could put in a road, bring in the electrical, tie in the sewer..."

"You could sell those lots for $20,000 an acre," Lloyd said.

"It's three miles from the beach."

"Would anybody want to live down there?" I asked.

"Look at how this place is expanding," Bronson said.

"Jeez," Lloyd said. "If we could just buy ten of those lots we could be rich. Where could we get $10,000?"

"That's easy. We could sell shares," Bronson said. "Anybody who can come up with a thousand dollars. Then we pool the money, turn the deal and pay everybody a high percentage. We still come out rich."

"But everybody in the company is broke," I said.

"Hell. We don't go after people in the company," Bronson said. "We just put a want ad in the paper. These people in Santa Maria are loaded."

"We should drive down there on our first day off," Lloyd said.

"All we need is a car," Bronson said. He looked at me. "How about you, Bob?"

"What?"

"You got a thousand dollars?"

"Or a car?" Lloyd said.

"I have seven dollars until payday," I said.

"You interested? We could split the profits three ways and we wouldn't have to work for five years," Bronson said.

"Who told you about those lots?" I asked Bronson.

"Fred Norton," he said.

I looked at Bronson. I looked at Lloyd.

"The criminal? The guy on the run for real estate fraud?"

I waited for an answer, but they both looked at me blankly.

"You guys are nuts," I said. "Maybe you should partner with him."

Something? Anything? They both looked at me blankly.

"Say what you will about Fred," Bronson said. "But that guy knows real estate."

"He knows how to make a fast buck," I said. "And he's going to be doing time for it."

"He's got to be a good salesman," Lloyd said.

"Next thing you're going to be telling me he's hiding in your attic or something," I said.

"Not our attic," Lloyd said.

"No attic in our house, right Lloyd?" Bronson said.

"Right."

Bronson kicked the curb. "I never had any trouble with him," he said. "I always thought he was a nice guy."

In the afternoons I rehearsed *Death of a Salesman*, directed by none other than the guy who ran the whole theatre company, Noah Manning himself. Getting cast as Biff was a real achievement for me, a first-timer in the company, having somehow been cast over a lot of the A.C.T. guys who had better training. As I was rehearsing Biff I was trying to employ my Freefall Theory and be spontaneous and dangerous with the lines and all, but it was difficult because the lines hadn't been in my head long enough to be confident with them. My hero, Richard Siebert, was playing my father, Willie Loman, and I was slightly intimidated because he had his role *down* already. I would have been much more freaked if Richard hadn't been such a nice guy. He treated both the guy playing Hap and I like peers, which we were, I suppose, but Richard never lorded his status as an actor above us. So each day, for me, was about relaxing with my lines. The angry stuff was easy for me. You know, where Biff shouts at his father because he's angry about being lied to. I could at least come close to matching Richard in voracity. Those scenes were connecting. But the flashbacks to Biff and Happy's boyhood were giving me trouble. I figured, just perhaps, I was intimidated. Because, there I was, a 25 year old, and in those flashback scenes, I'm supposed to be playing a fourteen year old.

Okay I'll just say it: my hair was thinning. It wasn't chronic or anything, but I wouldn't necessarily say I was hirsute. My hair was blond, which had helped me avoid the cue ball with a beard look that some guys develop, but you could definitely see some skin on the back of my head. I wasn't convinced I could pull off playing someone half my age. Mr. Manning had cast me anyway, never mentioning it, of course, though he did say my hair looked good since I had it buzzed real short, because after all they were growing up in the forties and all, but I wasn't sure I believed him. The day the costumer sat in on rehearsals I couldn't help but keep one eye on her the whole time. I could just imagine her sitting there thinking: "Holy cow. This guy is bald. How is he going to pull off playing a fourteen year old?" It was her problem to make us all look right.

So I wasn't surprised when I saw on the board a "special costume fitting" slotted in for me that afternoon. I knew that she wasn't worried about the slacks and shirts I was going to be wearing. This fitting was all about something I swore I would never resort to. It was about the dreaded H word.

Hairpiece.

"Hi Bob," she said. She was a fairly attractive lady but her hips were a little big and she wore long, nondescript dresses to cover it up. "I've brought you in here today to talk about whether you would be comfortable wearing a hairpiece."

"What does Mr. Manning think about this?" I had my reply all thought out.

"He thinks you look fine. But I told him I would like to see how you look."

"I just want to be believable in the part." What I really wanted to say was *You think I'm bald, you meddlesome cow?* But I figured it would have hurt her feelings.

"Mr. Manning said he would pop in to take a look at it later."

She took it out of the box. It looked like a thing of evil. I had worn a stick-on mustache in a play once. As if in my worst nightmare, half of it worked free during the second act and drooped down the right side of my face. I swore never again.

"Is it like a mustache?" I said. "Because I've had bad experiences with those things."

"I think you'll find this very easy to work with," she said, referring to the toupé like it was a committee member or a square dance partner.

I held it as far away from me as I could, as if it smelled.

"This is a very realistic and very expensive piece. And it's a good match for your coloring."

I thought, Why don't you just send me out there with a red nose and a Bozo wig?

She fussed and mucked about with it, combing it and patting it like some animal. I must have sunk way down in my chair because she kept lifting me up by my chin like a barber does. Her fingers were cold and clammy. The top of my head felt like it was being pinched.

"What do you think?" she asked.

I had to admit I was surprised. I stared at myself in the mirror. I looked pretty normal. The piece was short, very much like my own hair, but fuller.

Before I could answer, Noah Manning opened the door.

"Ah," he said. "What do we think?"

"I think it looks extremely natural," said the costume lady. "I'm not sure what Bob thinks about it."

It was like getting used to a new baby brother. I needed time. "I don't much like the idea of wearing it," I said. "But I guess it doesn't look too bad."

"Wear it in rehearsal if you like," said the costume lady.

"It's up to you," Mr. Manning said. "We don't want you to be un-comfortable. The acting comes first."

I thought, Why has fate determined that I must go through the em-barrassment of this afternoon? Why have my grandfather's genes snuck up and given me the old fish slap in the back of the head? I don't deserve this. Just when you start getting used to THE WAY THINGS ARE NOW, something like this comes along and leeches all your self confidence. And worse yet, Noah Manning himself says "It's up to me" whether I wear it or not. Meaning what? Meaning if I choose not to wear it I risk humiliation in the eyes of a disbelieving public?

If the costume lady thought I looked bald, other people would too. It was all her fault for setting the wheels in motion in the first place.

I wanted to ask Angie what she thought and was pissed off that I had to wait until after the Marathon of Monotony the cast of *Henry V* had to suffer that evening in Solvang. They made us board the bus at 5:00, and we arrived too early for any relief from the heat. I had my shoes off like a lot of people and we hot-footed it to the shade of the dressing rooms. Af-ter dinner (a bunch of us ate at Haggenfeffer!) the fireworks started.

Wanda Dare was livid.

"How am I supposed to move in this thing?"

And I thought I was testy about the hairpiece.

"This dress makes me look like a fucking turtle!"

There were three costume people standing at a safe distance from Wanda Dare, tape measures dangling, their arms crossed, protecting themselves. Mario, our director, was trying to soothe Wanda Dare, who was whirling about the stage, skirts flying, in some exaggerated display of angst. Ripley and I and most of the spear carriers had gathered in the vomitoriums, observing the fray from the safety of darkness.

"I just want to know how this fucking thing could have gone so terri-bly wrong!"

"Wanda Darling, we'll fix it," Mario was cooing. "Just wear it for tonight and we'll have them work on it or get you a new dress by tomorrow."

I could see the costume people shift and slump in disgust. They had bags under their eyes the size of tennis balls.

"You can't trust these idiots to get anything right," Wanda sobbed. "My fucking cat could have done a better job sewing this fucking thing."

Stage Manager Lou's voice boomed across the speaker: "Mario? We've got to get started now. It's 8:05."

Mario wheeled in the direction of the loudspeaker. "We've got a bit of a crisis here, for Christ's sake!" The spear carriers and I had caught a glimpse of this before, the ferocious child that clawed and scratched to break free through that little doorway in Mario's otherwise austere facade. It was not pretty. "Let's just take five minutes, all right? We can keep them here five minutes longer if we need to for fuck's sake."

You knew things were dire when people invented creative uses for the word "fuck."

We began rehearsal at 8:32, and Wanda Dare appeared that evening in her rehearsal skirt. Two gals were backstage in the dressing room, quietly ripping seams from the dress in question. I wish I had gotten to know them better, these girls, whose names I hadn't even bothered to learn. I offered them a pleasant smile (or so it felt like) but they only gave me blank stares in return. I felt like a white slaveowner surveying the plantation.

"Poker?" Hanover asked.

I thought we might be testing the waters a bit early in the proceedings to try poker when we hadn't actually settled into a rhythm of running the show yet. It was hard to gauge entrances with all the distractions of the technical stuff.

Indeed the evening had grown long. Lou had to stop and start quite a bit for problems with costume changes and light cues, and it seemed old Verden Price was intoning his long-winded speeches with less variety than usual. It was precisely 11:23. I was three dollars up and holding a pretty good hand when Wanda Dare's piercing squeal ripped through the intercom:

"Where is the FUCKING MESSAGE?"

"Jesus!" said Ripley. He bolted up, white as a sheet, and blundered up the vom, adjusting his helmet and grabbing his message scroll.

Lou said "Ripley? Please deliver your message," over the loudspeaker. The spear carriers and I were shocked into immobility, wanting to laugh but fearing for our mortal souls. Wanda Dare had completely stopped the rehearsal and stood waiting, hands on hips, for Ripley to appear.

Director Mario had rushed up on stage to attend his starlet. "Thank you, Mr. Ripley. Glad to see you could make it."

Under his helmet, I'm sure Ripley's hair was doing that standing on end thing.

"Ripley, try to pay attention, all right?" Lou said over the loudspeaker. "Can we pick up from here and go on?"

Normally we would have done exactly that. But Mario had to put on a show for Wanda Dare.

"Just a minute, Lou," he said. "I think we need to all be aware that our fellow actors are up here trying to concentrate, and it's episodes like this that make it extremely difficult on all of us. It's because of the thoughtlessness of a few individuals that we all are here well past the time we should be. Blah blah blah." Now let's get to work and blah blah blah. Ripley had turned from white to red and moved very slowly back down the vom. Mario had taken Wanda Dare aside, urging her, I'm sure, to muster up the courage to finish the rehearsal. Even Kathy Bishop and Peter Ross had gathered to observe. Kathy had her hand on Peter's butt. Verden Price looked like someone had driven a semi over his fondue lunch.

I wasn't able to get much out of Ripley on the way home. We boarded the bus well after midnight and most everybody had their eyes closed. But Ripley's eyes were glowing red.

"Why does she hate me?" Ripley said. "What did I ever do to her?"

"Forget about it. Don't take it personally."

"You should have seen the way she looked at me."

"Yeah?"

"Yeah."

"Like how did she look at you?"

"Like all funny and shit."

"Yeah?"

"Yeah."

"Like how, funny?"

"Just funny."

"Like 'I'll kill you' funny?"

"No, no... there's more there. Kind of like 'you don't understand me.'"

"Yeah?"

"I think she was just as humiliated as I was. I think she wants me." And he didn't say anything else.

Wanda Dare had given Verden Price a ride back to town in her Mustang. They had seemed quite jolly, to me.

I walked back to the apartment with high hopes of talking with Angie. I was surprised to find myself thinking about her so much. I was expecting to find her sitting on the stoop and rolling a joint, as was customary. Willie would still be at work. We'd smoke a little weed and this time we'd have a very meaningful conversation about whether or not she thought I would look good in a toupé. I'd tell her "I've been thinking a lot about what you said, Angie, and you're right. I really do need and want to open up to people" and she'd say "Yeah?" and I'd say "Yeah." And she'd say "I knew it was just because you're shy" and I'd say "That's right" and we'd begin sharing and talking and communicating intimately, like lovers do. But this would be a real love, a pure love that would transcend sex and gender and carnal appetites. We would share a bond that was unique.

The living room was well lit so it looked promising when I walked in. The stereo was on but the record had finished playing (Lou Reed's *Rock 'n' Roll Animal*, mine, by the way). Angie and Willie's bedroom door was closed. That was a bad sign. Angie barely closed the door halfway if she was dressing or showering. I felt like she wanted me to look at her, catch glimpses of her nakedness, shoot me a little smile and go on combing her hair. I imagined opening the door wider, watching her eyes watch me in the mirror. I'd place my hands gently on her shoulders and I'd feel her relax, close her eyes and roll her neck languidly beneath my touch.

Willie's jacket was on the couch and half a joint was in the ashtray. There would be no meaningful talks tonight. I opened my half of the cupboard and surveyed the food situation. There were Cheerios, and lo and behold Willie or Angie had bought a quart of milk (organic). As I wrote them a note ("IOU 1 cup of milk approx") and taped it to the carton, I heard soft laughter from their bedroom.

The kinky thing is I moved closer to the wall. I chewed my cereal as quietly as I could, straining to hear more muffled sounds. I heard the low rumble of Willie's voice, then the softer, mellower tones of Angie's. There were long intervals of silence, and it was during these that my imagination went into overtime. I washed out my bowl in the sink and turned out the lights but instead of getting into bed I found myself lingering outside their door. This close, I could hear that the silences were being filled with occasional smacking noises, little moans and sighs, cooing sounds. I had developed a boner that wouldn't quit. I went into my bedroom but I have to admit I crept back into the hall like a complete perv a couple times to get a better listen. I could tell when they started to actually do it, because I heard headboard bumps and Angie began emitting sharp rhythmic grunts. That was enough for me. I jumped into bed, jacked off like there was no tomorrow and came in about half a minute, right when Angie was having what sounded like a huge orgasm.

I can't say I laid awake for very long that night. I would have, except having sex with myself usually calms me right down, and because it was very late, thanks to Wanda Dare and Ripley and the Darkly Effeminate Mario, it wasn't very long before I was out. In those last waking moments, though, I felt that familiar lump rise in my throat, and I thought of Gina and me painting the kitchen cabinets in our first apartment. She had wanted a peach color, and I remember being against it at first, but thought it looked good when we had it done. We turned out all the lights except for this funky blue night light thing she had kept from her dorm room days and she fell asleep as the FM station was premiering Heart's second album, the one with "Barracuda" on it. She bought it for my birthday about six months later. I thought of our cat who ate her food on the counter. I thought of the smell of Gina's closet. I thought of the way the afternoon sun streaked our back porch. I thought of our dining table, a wedding gift from woodworker Don. I thought of walking home from Ethics class in the rain together, and opening a can of chicken gumbo soup. I thought of the sound her paisley dress made when she walked in it.

Angie and Willie's door was still closed when I went past it the next morning.

5

Mr. Lark was a guy who expended a lot of energy when he directed. Even though he was old, ancient probably, somewhere over 40, grey, bi-focaled, no doubt reliant on Geritol and prunes and colostomy bags and God knows what else, typical for people over 40, he had more stamina than I did. He would bound onstage in *Once in a Lifetime* rehearsal to give directions and then bound off to take a seat. Up again. Change rows. Onstage to adjust Ripley's slumping shoulders. Back in the audience. Cross his legs. "Wait, wait." Leap onstage to talk to Barbara Ledbetter. Slap her on the back. "Pace, now! Pick it up everybody!" Hunker down in first row. Laugh. "Wait, wait." And back up again, all day long. I came up with some stage business of pulling out a razor and having a shave on a street corner during a scene, which Mr. Lark liked, because he laughed heartily when I first did it, but then insisted on fussing with the bit until it wasn't fun anymore. "Shave this way," he said. "With precision – on Jer-ry's line – there!" I thought: What the hell do you want to screw with it for? It's funny enough. But I could tell, begrudgingly, from people's laughter in the room, the bit was better after he choreographed it.

"Ripley?" Mr. Lark said, clapping his hands, "Shoulders!"

Ripley was getting a lot of attention from the Wanda Dare incident. At break, Richard Siebert wanted to hear the whole story, and was grinning and chuckling as Ripley went on about how Mario and Wanda Dare had singled him out for ridicule and what a ham Verden Price was. Soon six guys had gathered around him, even Bronson and Lloyd, who had to wait until lunchtime to try to tempt me with titillating business ventures.

"So here's the story on those government lots," Bronson said. "Polluted groundwater. Won't be buildable for awhile, at least not until after our season's over."

"Maybe not even for ten years," Lloyd said.

"Good thing the Army fessed up," I said.

"Oh they didn't," Bronson said. "Hell, they would have sold us those lots in a heartbeat and stuck us with unbuildable wasteland."

"They wouldn't have cared," Lloyd said.

"How'd you find out about it?" I asked.

"Friend of ours did some research down at the county courthouse."

"You have a friend down at the courthouse?"

"Well, he doesn't work down there," Bronson said. "It's a matter of open record. Anyone can walk in there and look."

"He was just a guy off the street," Lloyd said. "You or I could have done it."

"But this friend of yours did it for you," I said.

"That's right," Bronson said. "Because he has lots of time on his hands during the day." Bronson and Lloyd looked at each other. "Anyways, we got a better idea for an entrepreneurial venture."

"Brace yourself," Lloyd said.

"Are you ready?" Bronson asked. And then he made a wide, expansive gesture. "Bumper stickers."

"Bumper stickers?" I said.

"And buttons," Lloyd added.

"Bumper stickers and buttons," Bronson concluded. "We settled on this endeavor because we're low on start-up capital and we figured this was an easy entré into the world of Novelty Printing and Merchandising. All we have to do is set aside twenty dollars a week between the two of us, and with the help of another partner, by the middle of August we'll have enough for an initial print run," Bronson said. "In the meantime we can do some pre-sales, you know, start establishing a network of accounts."

"Mañuel at Timbales Music already said he'd take a few," Lloyd said.

"You mentioned you had another partner?" I said.

"Now, if you want, we talked about it and we decided we'd let you in as another partner if you wanted to make some serious money," Bronson said.

"The offer is only open to you because of your impressive drawing talent," Lloyd said.

When you're a kid and you stay in your room and draw, like I did, and you have any flair for it at all, like I did, you eventually become fairly decent at it. At least, decent enough to get past the stage of making a five-pointed stick with a ball on top and calling it a person. I stayed in my room and drew because I wanted people to be impressed with what I showed them when I emerged. Problem is, they were, or at least they said they were, and they've taken advantage of me ever since. Pretty soon I was staying up late drawing dance announcements, birthday cards and caricatures of people for the yearbook. Word spread fast, too. I had helped Barbara Petrie do a program cover and suddenly news of my miraculous abilities had reached the hoi palloi of PCPA.

"This is very generous of you," I said.

"You would only be required to set aside five dollars a week," Bronson said. "Because you would be admittedly shouldering most of the production work."

"We would create the slogans," Lloyd said.

"And I would be the third partner?" I asked.

"That's right. Well, the fourth, actually," Bronson said. "We have a silent partner."

45

"A silent partner? Is this they guy who did your research down at the county courthouse?"

"Yep," Bronson said. "Same guy."

"You mind cluing me in as to who this guy is?"

Lloyd and Bronson looked at each other again. "He wants to remain anonymous," Bronson said. "We can only say that he's a local business-man."

I told Bronson and Lloyd I'd meet with them tomorrow and present my counter offer. I figured if they had Fred Norton, a wanted felon, act-ing as their Daddy Warbucks, they didn't need my hard-earned fifty bucks. But they did need my talent. I figured I'd sell them my designs and actually make some money rather than get embroiled in some un-derworld crime ring financed by stolen cash.

Besides, I had more pressing matters to wrestle with. I decided to pass on wearing the hairpiece during *Salesman* rehearsal that afternoon to give me one more day to consider the option. The guy playing Hap and I were rehearsing our bedroom scene, where the two brothers lay in their beds in their childhood bedroom and hash over old times while their parents are downstairs talking about what great promise Biff has. Here's Biff, home again after yet another career failure. Here's Hap, his philan-dering brother. Both lost in their own way, unable to leave the nest.

I was hoping that, in this case, life didn't mimic art. Here I was with three more months left in my contract, and then I had no idea where I was going to go or what I was going to do. Chances of getting on at PCPA in the winter were slim; they pared their actor ranks down from 75 to only eight paying Artist-in-Residence positions. But these were covet-ed assignments, because after what they paid an actor during the summer, an AR's salary was like landing on Easy Street. ARs were paid exactly half of what a beginning teacher at the college made. Noah Manning was a pretty smart guy and he had convinced the college board to let him hire eight actors in the four teaching posts the drama department was custom-arily allowed. He sold the idea on the concept that a professional actor's experience was far more valuable than a teaching credential, and it would benefit the students by exposing them to this expertise. The benefit to

Manning was that he could cast his shows with real actors in key parts and double the number of paying students in the conservatory, thereby doubling the spear carrier ranks in his shows as well. An AR was a great gig if you could get it. You taught classes during the day and rehearsed the main stage shows at night at a much more manageable pace than in the summertime. Plus, there was all that money.

But I couldn't count on being asked to stay on when the fall came. October first I would hit the street with everybody else, flooding to N.Y.C. or L.A. to waft headshots under the noses of casting directors. It was enough to make me want to fall back on my art skills and seek a career in advertising. I had no desire to be as uncertain about my next career move when I was 40, with no idea where my next paycheck would come from.

For the time being, however, I was cocooned in a supportive environment where my biggest worry was whether or not to try to convince the audience that a fourteen-year-old would have a sizable bald spot.

"So what do you think?" The guy playing Hap asked me.

"About what?"

"You going to wear the rug or not?" His name was Ephrem Byrd, and all I really knew about him was that he carried a shivering chihuahua named George with him everywhere he went. George slept in Ephrem's gym bag when he was in rehearsal.

"I haven't decided yet."

"You think we look like brothers?"

"I think we look enough like brothers."

Ephrem was dark, I was fair. Ephrem was a Jew, I was not.

"Are you circumcised? I guess we would both be. Or not. Being brothers," he said.

"Circumcised," I said.

He smiled. "There you have it then."

The costume lady stood in the back of the room for a few minutes. I'm sure she noticed the Biff Wig still perched atop its styrofoam head and was there to smack her lips in disdain. Mr. Manning was respectfully mute on the matter. I didn't want to think about it while I was rehearsing.

Richard Siebert asked both Ephrem and I out for dinner, but he forgot I had to catch the bus to Solvang. It was the cast of *Hank V's* last rehearsal before a preview audience. I would have relished the chance to talk shop with Richard but was in a way relieved because I thought I might be so in awe of the guy I'd clam up and not know what to say. Richard and Ephrem left together, Ephrem's green gym bag open slightly so George could stick his quivering head out the top.

Someone decided the entire bus should join in singing songs from musicals. Do people in the theatre actually LIKE those songs? I grew up teaching myself riffs from rock guitar heroes. But Ethel Merman held no allure, and I couldn't figure out why she or any of the other musical stars left the guys in my undergrad program breathless. That hammy showboat bullshit, those ridiculous lyrics. I suppose when *A Chorus Line* came out I appreciated the musical form a bit more, but mainly because of the women-in-spandex angle. I had always fantasized about having sex with a woman in a top hat and tails. But 17-year-old guys knowing all the lyrics to *Gypsy?* That was something that was not in my orbit.

As I sat there trying to drown out the singalong by hearing Humble Pie's "I Don't Need No Doctor" in my head, it occurred to me that, perhaps, there might be some homosexual people involved in theatre (!). In fact, homosexual people might actually be drawn to theatre as a profession (!!). There might have even been one or two homosexual people on the bus at that very moment (!!!). Knowledge of musicals was pretty much a litmus test as to whether or not a person was gay. In college I was clueless of gays. I may have suspected somebody might be *that way,* but it was never discussed, and it never mattered. But I knew and everybody knew that if a guy could break into all the verses of "Easter Parade" at the drop of a hat, it was a safe bet his sexual orientation was different than mine.

So when the esteemed Verden Price stood up on the bus and tried to lead us all in "Shapoopie," my suspicions about him were confirmed.

Ripley and I looked at each other.

"So That's why Wanda Dare pals around with him," I said.

"No sexual threat," Ripley said.

I'm sure even Verden winced when somebody tried to start a round of "The Farmer and the Cowman Should be Friends." That effectively killed the rally and the bus fell quiet.

Wanda Dare had actually deigned to ride the bus that evening and I noticed Ripley had his eyes glued to her the whole trip. My jaw hit the sidewalk when Ripley accosted her on our way to the dressing rooms in Solvang. I saw the whole thing in dumbshow as I lingered just out of earshot. I half expected Ripley to haul off and slug her in the face, but instead he approached her apologetically, practically slumping toward her like a bad puppy. Wanda Dare didn't snub him at all; Ripley's meekness seemed to mollify her. She tipped her head in a way as if to say "Awww, look at that cute puppy," and she smiled openly. Ripley went on for awhile, bobbing his drooping head back and forth. And Wanda Dare did the most uncharacteristic thing: she put her hand on Ripley's shoulder. I saw Ripley actually swell up when she did this, as if the diva had inflated him magically. And she left her hand there, rubbing it gently up and down his shoulder, tipping her head the other way this time. Finally, Ripley, puffed up almost twice his normal size, jerked his arms spasmodically wide open, like Tony Bennett opens himself to the audience to say "Ain't it wonderful, folks?" and Wanda Dare rushed into his arms. It was a brief embrace, but significant, as Wanda Dare let her fingers trail slowly off the small of his back before she turned, her hair swinging buoyantly, and walked to her dressing room.

I waited for Ripley. Kathy Bishop and Peter Ross passed me arm in arm, Kathy shooting me only the slightest glance as she babbled in Peter's ear.

"All made up?" I asked Ripley. "All better now?"

"She deserved an apology," Ripley said.

"You astound me, pal."

"I think she's a good person. I should have been paying attention. She apologized to me for making a scene. And she says she's going to apologize to Lou."

"Wonders never cease," I said.

Rehearsal that night was tame compared to the night before and the company actually pulled it off without stopping. Wanda Dare had accepted the revisions to her dress and presented one red rose apiece to the costume girls, who nodded their heads and slunk away into the shadows without a word. The running time of *Henry V* was three hours and nineteen minutes, not counting intermission. Director Mario seemed pleased that his vision was taking shape.

Mario's vision, I might mention, was what Mario would describe as "groundbreaking," theatre management would describe as "risky," and most of us in the cast would describe as "fruity." Mario had explained to us that he was dissatisfied with the message of the play and felt that it was among the weakest in Shakespeare's canon. So he set about to re-shape it into a piece that he felt would speak to a modern audience. It might have had a shred of a chance in New York, but we had our doubts that tourists who came to Solvang and spent the day eating Krumcakken and watching oom-pah-pah bands prance around in lederhosen would truly appreciate the extent of Mario's genius.

Shakespeare portrayed Henry V as a straight arrow, good and true, and his campaign to exterminate the French was shown as being the will of God. Mario called this "horseshit." For one thing, he claimed, no man, even if he was a king, could be so sure of himself. Where were the dark thoughts that plagued Hamlet or Macbeth? The result was, Mario attested, a pretty boring play. So Mario decided to augment the text to explore Henry's dark side. Shakespeare hadn't supplied the words, so Mario created passages in pantomime that he felt brought out the hero's fears and doubts. The play would go along as written for awhile, all of us speaking the familiar text, hamming it up in our pantaloons and embroidery. Then out of nowhere the stage would become washed in blue light and this "progressive" music would herald an exposé of Henry's innermost fears. Old Verden Price would shuck off his cloak and reveal himself in his underwear, actually beige tights that made him look like a naked store mannequin. The spear carriers and I, who had stripped down to our fruity black tights, would slink on stage all slow-motion-like to point and jab at poor Henry like some demon tribunal, which is what Mario had dubbed us. We, apparently, were portraying Henry's conscience. Verden would

shudder visibly as he saw us. He'd do this exaggerated freak-out movement which looked like an opera singer trying to dance to the Grateful
Dead. Meanwhile, we demon-types would slink along, hissing, making
low guttural sounds and other noises that I imagine you would make if
you were a demon. Then we'd assume some taunting position the chore-
ographer had told us to assume, leaning towards Henry threateningly.
Mario said we looked like a large black spider. Verden Price would run
around for awhile, gesticulating wildly, and sometimes Wanda Dare
would come out, relying heavily on her ballet training, and do this soothing pas de deux with Verden. She was in a beige body suit like Verden's
and was pretty hot-looking except I suspected her boobs were augmented
somewhat. So the two of them would end up like that statue of the
Madonna and Child, Wanda cradling Verden's sweaty form, and then the
lights would change, the demons would slink off, Verden would put his
clothes back on and go on with the play. Mario had spaced several of
these pantomimes throughout the evening, and to keep from repeating
the same device over and over, he had us throw in snatches of Shake-
spearean dialect later on like "Kill the French," and "By my troth." We
demons would vary our movement and Verden would freak out in different choreographed ways. All this fal-de-ral added a good chunk of running time, but at the end of three and a half hours, Mario had words of
praise for everyone.

"Very exciting, darling. Truly exciting."

He had come into the men's dressing room and was shaking everyone's hand.

"Thank you, Robert, good job. Nice work Bill. I think we're ready
for an audience."

Hanover and I looked at each other.

"At least he thinks so," Hanover mumbled.

Mario moved on to the women's dressing rooms, and Peter Ross began slapping on some horrible aftershave, no doubt greasing up for a big
night of unbridled lust with Kathy Bishop.

"Jesus. Do you have to do that here?" Hanover said. He was a little
stocky guy with wide shoulders. "What is that? Patchouli? I thought they

quit making that shit in 1970."

"What are you? Jealous?"

Leave it to Peter to come up with a terse and cutting reply. Surprisingly the two of them got into it a little bit, in a clumsy verbal exchange that included the word "pussy" in a slanderous reference (by Hanover) to Kathy's genitalia, and then in reference (by Peter) to Hanover's lack of ability to defend himself. But I figured if it came down to it, Hanover could take the tall but gangly Peter Ross fairly easily. I felt he wasn't above doing it either. Peter Ross was someone who just naturally pissed people off. You felt compelled in some sort of primordial way to jump on him and beat him up.

It was almost midnight. I was looking for Ripley on my way to the bus when I heard Angie's voice.

"Hey Bob," she said. I turned around and she got me in a choke hold.

"Jesus Christ, Angie." I had to drop my gym bag. "What are you doing here?"

She let me go and tenderly smoothed my shirt. "Ronni and I decided to drive down and bug you guys." Angie rehearsed *Fiddler on the Roof* at night in Santa Maria. Still two weeks from opening, they had wrapped up on schedule at eleven o'clock. Three paces off to her left Ronni Flowers was absentmindedly tracing a pattern on the sidewalk with her toe. Nathan Trask got her attention, hanging out the bus window, and Ronni skipped over to flirt with him.

"We figured we'd give you a ride back. I drove the bug," Angie said.

"Some people are getting together at Candice and Mark's house," I said. I hadn't planned on going.

"I know. It's called a party, Bob. We'll take you there." And she pulled my hand toward the parking lot. "Ronni? We're leaving!"

Ronni Flowers waved goodbye to the bus and trotted up behind us. She had straight, dark hair and chestnut eyes, was dressed head to toe in denim and reminded me quite a bit of Linda Rondstadt as she looked on the cover of *Hasten Down the Wind*. That record, by the way, had wound up in Gina's half of the collection, along with the Cat Stevens, most of the Dylan stuff and the Wishbone Ash. I told her she could take all the

Dan Fogelberg she wanted.

But Ronni's lips weren't quite as pouty as Linda's. And she was gawkier and flapped a little as she ran.

"You two know each other, right?" Angie asked.

"Yeah. Hi Ronni."

"Hi Bob."

"How was *Fiddler* rehearsal tonight?"

"Okay, I guess," Ronni said. "Did Angie tell you that Jean Martine is out with the flu?"

And we made small talk like this as we bent ourselves into Angie's red VW. I found myself chatting mostly with Ronni, who draped herself over the passenger seat a lot to look at me. One thing about Ronni, she really looked at you. Not just gave you a passing glance, but practically bored into your eyes like she had been given a key to a new house and went in and started looking in all the closets. It was almost scary. And when she pulled away it was like she knew more about you than you really wanted her to. I found myself staring back into her eyes much longer than I would with anybody else, just so she wouldn't think I was hiding anything. Fact is, I was doing a pretty good job of covering up, making inconsequential stuff seem like it was important, telling her about Mario's vision, the mercurial Wanda Dare, the hambone histrionics of Verden Price, when what I really wanted to say was "Hey Angie, where's Willie tonight?" and "Are you really interested enough in me to drive all the way to Solvang to pick me up?" and "Do you think I should wear a hairpiece for this play?" But halfway back to town I realized that Angie was setting me up. She would throw in an occasional line or two, but mostly she just drove. Every now and then I'd catch her eyes checking on me in the rear view mirror. I could almost hear her voice saying "Ronni has been asking what you're like, so I thought I'd show her what a decent guy you were. Go on, Bob. Have a good time." I should have been flattered, I suppose. Instead, the familiar lump rose in my throat. I felt lonely.

We beat the bus back to town and knew we had time before things got started at Mark and Candice's, so Angie drove the three of us back to the apartment so she could smoke a joint. The place was dark and it looked like Willie hadn't been home. Ronni pulled some thick, gooey dope from a plastic bag in her backpack and loaded a pipe. She offered it to me first.

"I don't have any dope," I said. "So we need to stop so I can buy some beer."

"This stuff isn't going to the party," Angie said. "It'd be gone in the morning."

"This is just for us," Ronni said.

"Then you won't need any beer." Angie smiled and flicked her lighter.

Mark and Candice were renting a 1950's stucco tract home on the east end of town near the freeway and the Holiday Inn. It was familiar, their house. Not that I had been there before. But I had seen many like it in the last ten years, briefly inhabited by nomadic students and actors on their way to Someplace Else. It was unfurnished and they hadn't afforded to furnish it with anything besides a cable spool coffee table and four folding chairs. Against one corner in the otherwise empty living room was an expensive looking stereo phonograph which was blasting the Rolling Stones' *Some Girls* through two huge speakers. I cased the stack of lps: Average White Band, Tower of Power, Steely Dan, Little Feat. Mark and Candice's tastes ran a bit toward disco/funk, but Hanover had brought some Foghat and Allman Brothers and laid them nearby, which made me happy. There were two bedrooms with nothing in them but a few boxes and two bicycles. In the master bedroom, which opened up onto the patio, they had thrown down sleeping bags on two large pieces of foam rubber. Their pillows were covered with Oscar Meyer Wiener slip covers, all yellow and orange, probably thrift store purchases or sentimental artifacts from Mark's boyhood. The only adornment in the entire house was a map of "Santa Barbara and the Central Coast" tacked up on their living room wall, presumably to help them map bike routes. Everything inside was painted white with a thin walnut-stained baseboard, and the omnipresent green brain-pattern carpet covered everything. Most people had crammed into the kitchen, shouting above the music, but I didn't see our hosts anywhere. In the back yard there was a keg with a coffee can on top for donations, and a bathtub filled with ice and contributed bottles of beer.

"I told you I should have brought some," I said to Angie. She pushed me and made me lose my balance, so I had to steady myself against a wooden planter. It wasn't because I was high. For whatever reason I had decided to go light again, sucking mostly air instead of smoke, putting on a show for Angie. We had migrated through the house to the backyard. It was quieter outside and you could actually hear yourself shouting, but it was chilly and I wished I had worn something heavier than flannel. Ronni was standing in a group from *Fiddler on the Roof* that included Ephrem and George the chihuahua, completely concealed but shivering noticeably beneath Ephrem's sweater. Ronni had a beer in her hand and was bouncing on her heels now and then to stay warm. She smiled at me to join them but I made like I had to take a leak and went back into the house.

There were a lot more people at the party than I think anybody had figured there would be. It was Sunday night, and Monday was the company day off. I hadn't planned on getting up until noon, but I figured it might be even later since it was 2:00 a.m. and the party was still ramping up. Peter Ross was skulking around, brooding. Kathy Bishop was in the living room dancing all by herself, gyrating slowly in some sort of hallucinogenic trance. Elite ACT actors, the ones that had wound up with large parts for the summer, like Wanda Dare and Verden Price, were standing around in tight, closed circles that let you know they were discussing topics that wouldn't be of any interest to spear carriers and anything spear carriers had to say couldn't possibly be of any interest to them. I didn't even attempt to encroach upon a haphazard *Once in a Lifetime / Country Wife* clique that included Richard Siebert and Curt Harnick, even though Richard caught sight of me out of the corner of his eye and lifted his chin in greeting. The only director present was Mario, the others being too domesticated and sensible to be out so late. The remaining groups were more fun: Rita Tasner was teaching Bronson, Marla Spencer and Cal Munson a disco line dance to "Shattered"; Harold

Becker was telling Lloyd and Trish Coleman an obscene "true" story about a naked woman, a can of dog food and a surprise party; Ann Peters and Laura Finn had gathered a crowd and were having an impromptu seance to speak with Ann's brother who had wrapped his car around a tree; Wally Messenger and a girl from the costume shop were making out; Stage Manager Lou had temporarily forgotten she was supposed to be intimidating and was doing tequila shooters in a group with Ripley and Hanover.

It's hilarious when people who don't know you very well decide they want to go to bed with you and make that first move toward being physical. Like when Ronni accosted me when I went back out to the yard. She grabbed me and said "brrrr," using the old "Hold Me It's Cold" trick. I took the bait, rubbing her as sensually as I could through her denim jacket. She worked her hands inside my flannel shirt and massaged my ribs through my t-shirt, lowering her head to my chest so I could rub my nose in her hair and kiss the top of her head if I wanted, a move women usually interpret as a sign of affection and tenderness. Often this move is followed by the female raising her head to stare into your eyes, lips wet and slightly apart to invite that crucial first kiss. But Ronni broke off our embrace suddenly and without looking at me took me by the hand to the unoccupied breezeway. Then she resumed the ritual, locking her eyes to mine in the prerequisite gaze of seriousness and longing.

Here's where that part of me, the critic who usually perches somewhere outside my body and judges my actions, said "what the hell" and jumped back inside my body to enjoy the moment. As we kissed I wasn't second guessing standard mating procedures at all, I was completely engulfed in Ronni, with this surge of energy that shot through her lips and into my chest and my groin. I felt the bass of the stereo pounding into my back through the cold stucco wall, and I felt Ronni's body in front of me, all warm and melty. She had small, taut breasts, and she pushed them against me teasingly. I lifted up her shirt and caressed her back, and worked my fingers under the elastic of her underwear. Her tongue was in my mouth and her hand was beneath my shirt, gently pulling at the hairs on my chest. She brushed her hand coyly over the front of my jeans and lightly caressed my erection. She began to make little gasping noises with her breath as my fingers brushed the soft skin of her armpit and encircled her breast.

And here's where the cynical part of me jumped back out of my body and resumed his familiar perch in that dark corner, judging every move I made. In the long moments between Ronni's teasing of my erection and the second she started toying with my belt buckle, all the electricity that had been coursing through my body, into Ronni's body, into my dick, flowing through my fingers, all of a sudden decided to suck back into itself, like a funnel cloud that decides not to become a tornado, like the wizard dispersing the water at the end of *The Sorcerer's Apprentice*, like a storm dissolving in time lapse, and I knew if Ronni successfully navigated the simple clasp and zipper apparatus of my pants her fingers would encircle a soft, diminutive organ that did not in the least convincingly convey my desire to penetrate her soft recesses.

So I had no choice but to take her hand away before she discovered how flaccid I was.

"Oh, I know," she said apologetically. "It's too cold out here. Should we go inside? Or let's just go back to my place."

"Ronni," I said. "I don't know if I'm going to be able to do this." In the darkness I could tell her eyes had narrowed slightly.

"Do you want... is it me?"

"No, no. It's..."

And then I realized that for whatever reason my body wasn't allowing me to manifest my passion, I had an alibi.

"You know, I'm married," I said.

Her eyes grew rounder again, as if with a few words I was once again able to validate her womanhood.

"I'm emotionally unavailable," I said.

"Well I knew but... I thought..."

"It's really tricky for me right now. I'm sorry if I led you on or made you think..."

"Oh please. Are you kidding? I nearly attacked you. I'm so... I just... I shouldn't have smoked all that weed. It just makes me get like this."

"I'm glad that you felt comfortable enough with me to want to, you know, get to know me and all."

"Bob, I feel so bad. I mean, I'm sorry to leave you all... like this."

I had always dreamt that a girl as sexy and exciting as Ronni would single me out and maul me and that I could be involved in one of those Penthouse Letters scenarios where I drop trow and nail her in the bushes near somebody's garbage cans, just around the corner from where people are standing. Then we'd brush ourselves off, go back to the party for awhile, and adjourn to her apartment at the first light of dawn. I was sick that I had missed the opportunity and mad at myself for lying to Ronni, for blaming my marital condition and not fessing up to my dysfunctionality. The worst thing is, there's no excuse for impotency. You can't blame anybody else or explain it in a way that someone who wants to have sex with you would understand. I still felt aroused, but I felt between my legs and there was not a chance that Ronni and I were going to make the pages of *Penthouse* anytime soon. It was all mixed up. I had to get out of there.

We wound up at the Denny's near the 101 interchange, Ronni and I. We picked an out of the way table and I tanked up on turkey and mashed potatoes, thinking that maybe, if I was given another chance, the food would kick in and supply the fuel I needed to make my dick work properly. But I knew, and I knew she knew, that the moment between us had passed, and that we would slither off to our separate beds and say hi to each other in the hallways, at picnics, share a caring embrace on opening nights, and then wish each other well in October, mean it sincerely, and never see each other again.

"How can you be an actor with no life experience?" Ronni was staring at the tabletop through half-lidded eyes, her head in her hand. She was drinking decaf.

"You don't think I have life experience?" I asked.

"Oh you do, probably. You've been married at least. I mean anybody. I mean me. All I've been through is school. I haven't been to Vietnam. I haven't been to New York. I'm 23 years old. I grew up in a San Diego suburb. I've never known poverty. I've lived a sheltered life. My dad thinks the acting thing is just a phase and that I'll grow out of it and marry a doctor."

"Is that what you want?"

"My sister works in a legal aid office. They help homeless people. She wants to go into politics."

I was going to confess to her about the impotency thing. "Ronni," I said.

"But then nobody's asking me to do anything difficult that really requires life experience. I'm trying to bring some depth into the roles I play, but there's not much room. What does it matter if you've never been addicted to heroin or lost a child or killed someone in the line of duty when all you're asked to do is look pretty and sing?"

She sighed and looked out the window at the parking lot. "I did almost drown once," she said.

"You almost drowned?"

"At Lake Castaic. I guess that constitutes some life experience."

"I would say," I said.

She looked at me then, this quiet girl with Linda Rondstadt eyes, in one of her deathgrip eyelocks. I was able to look back without flinching. In that moment I had an image of growing up with Ronni in Escondido. I saw her riding her blue Sting Ray with the plastic tassels streaming from the handlebars. I was spraying her with the garden hose in the summertime, ditching her in the canal, making fun of her haircut, hiding her training bra, spying on her as she kissed some boy. I saw her room, with the Partridge Family and David Cassidy posters on her wall, her Love Bug notebook and her Tammy hair curler set. We walked home from the store together with jawbreakers and Tootsie Pops and played tag on the lawn. I drove her home from cheerleader practice, she drove me home from the swim party when I sprained my ankle.

I loved Ronni deeply in that moment.

"Bob? Are you all right?" she asked.

The sun was starting to come up.

"I'm great," I said. "Thanks for asking."

JULY

6

PCPA was a theatre that ran its productions in true repertory, which meant that once, say, *Henry V* opened, it rotated in the lineup with the rest of the plays for the duration of the summer. Opening nights were staggered between Santa Maria and Solvang over about four weeks in late June and mid-July. To keep the set crews from storming the gates, they let a show run two or maybe even three nights in a row in Solvang. But in Santa Maria, where the indoor theatre allowed the scheduling of matinees, they could run, say, *Fiddler on the Roof* on a Tuesday night, have a *Fiddler* matinee the next afternoon, then strike that set and throw up *Henry V* for Wednesday evening. Meanwhile, the *Fiddler* set would be on the way to Solvang. It must have been a nightmare in the Admin Office trying to figure it all out. It was great for tourists, who could bounce back and forth between the two towns on any given week and see most of the plays in the season. It was great for actors, who admittedly worked pretty hard to get the season open, but, once the middle of July rolled around, had most of their days and even some of their nights free to do whatever they wanted.

We hadn't gotten to that point yet, but we were five days away from running in full rep. The first two shows to open had been *Brigadoon* and *Henry V*. I hadn't seen *Brigadoon* but I heard it was fine; standard issue, really. Give 'em what they want. Pretty girls and guys with muttonchops singing fruity songs about shamrocks and leprechauns and pots of gold.

Henry V had opened to a resounding "Whhhaaaaattttt?" from the befuddled crowds. Some people who didn't know any better must have thought Shakespeare had something to do with those strange interpretive dance sequences in the middle of the play and it probably lowered the reputation of the Bard substantially. There was a very positive review in the *Santa Maria Times,* which was fishy because it actually appeared in the paper the day before the play opened. The writer, Harold Feiss, was at one time a student in the conservatory, had some knowledge of the leading actors' credentials and probably wrote the review from a press release. Verden Price was praised for being "stolid and heroic" and Wanda Dare was singled out as "fetching" and commended for her beautiful voice.

Once in a Lifetime was in my book one of the strongest offerings in the lineup. It opened in Santa Maria to a moderate but enthusiastic crowd. Richard and Curt and Barbara Ledbetter were doing fine work, and Mr. Lark had kept the pacing brisk and the timing razor sharp. I enjoyed being a part of the cast. Ripley, Lloyd, and Bronson and I were having a great time throwing in our one-liners and cagey zingers and making all of our entrances and exits.

Before he left to go back to Texas A&M, Mr. Lark took me aside, squeezed my arm and said "Keep telling that Ripley to stand up straight."

"Yes sir," I said.

"That boy has got to learn to walk across the stage without apologizing for it."

"Bad self image," I said. "He's Catholic."

"So am I," he said.

Oops.

Fiddler was by far the most popular show and word had it as being quite solid. Angie said the guy playing Tevye was an asshole to work with but he was wonderful on stage, with a deep voice like what's-his-name who did it on Broadway. Ephrem also had been praising the production, saying Angie and Jean and Ronni as the daughters were quite good. I was anxious to see the show on a night off.

Major Barbara was the show that had most recently opened, and it appeared in the lineup for no other reason than to showcase the talents of Wanda Dare, who was admittedly an audience charmer and major attendance draw. Ripley was in that show with her too, in another minor supporting role. I plied Ripley for stories from the trenches every day, and he had been quite forthcoming with gossip at first, but as rehearsals wore on he became less and less willing to spill any dirt. He would only spout claptrap like "I have to work with Wanda (he called her Wanda) in two shows, so I owe it to the productions to respect her and her work." I had never known Ripley to be such a kissass before and I wasn't sure what had come over him. I had even seen him pal around with Wanda on occasion. They had dinner in Solvang one night, not just the two of them, which would have been too much like Eleanor Roosevelt having dinner with Jed Clampett, but in a safer double date situation with Kathy Bishop and her *new* guy Rob Banister (who took the place of Peter Ross after Kathy had decided Peter was too dark and moody). I had to hand it to Wanda – she was trying her best to shed her prejudices and mingle, however carefully, with supporting actors whose entire combined line count couldn't have whet her appetite in a lean season.

The last two shows scheduled to open within a few days of each other were *The Country Wife* and *Death of a Salesman*, and the entire company was pitching in to get the shows up. Because her role in *The Country Wife* was so small, Angie had been working extra hours in the costume shop. I hadn't seen her in days so I wasn't able to get her take on that show, but I was excited about *Salesman*. Ephrem said that several theatre bigwigs were traveling great distances to see the show, because they wanted to see Richard Siebert play Willie Loman. Richard was breathtaking. Ephrem, who had a tendency to wear his emotions like a red sweater, was having trouble breaking character and bawling onstage. In one recent runthrough he didn't show up for the final scene at the gravesite because he couldn't control himself. He said when Biff confronts Willie with the suicide hose and Willie rages at his son, calling him a "vengeful, spiteful mutt," he would lose it every time. And the gal playing our mother Linda was a basket case at the end of each rehearsal. She was a real sweetheart, it turns out, and a very fine actress. Her name was Brenda Bodwin, and she was an acting professor at Cal Poly Pomona. She was having a little holiday from the entanglements of her kids and her ex-husband, had spent the summer rooming with young women half her age and was showing definite signs of rejuvenation. She dropped some weight, painted her toenails and around about the end of June she surprised us all by buying a Harley.

By the way, the hairpiece thing got resolved. I walked into rehearsal one day and told Mr. Manning and the costume lady definitively that I wasn't wearing it. I didn't say it like that, exactly, more like: "I'd *prefer* not to wear it," or maybe "If it's all right with you guys, I'd prefer not to wear it." I might have added "at least for now," at the end of the sentence but whatever I said it got the point across. Mr. Manning said congratulations and the costume lady gave me a tight-lipped nod and that was that. Ephrem said I had made the right choice. I was quite proud of myself for putting my foot down. I never got Angie's opinion on it and frankly, after the issue was resolved I preferred not to mention it.

I felt alive in the role of Biff. I've heard songwriters talk about how they channel a song – that they don't write it so much as serve as a conduit for the song to come through them. That's how I felt. All I had to do was step aside and let Biff Loman come out. I wasn't sure where he was coming from, but it felt like some other part of myself I could dial in if I found the right frequency. I was spent but truly high after rehearsals and it was sometimes hours before I could come down.

I had been hanging out after the evening shows at the Santa Maria

Inn, which the company had practically taken over for the summer. We would descend on the place in two waves; first when the in-town shows let out, the second an hour later when the bus arrived from Solvang. I didn't drink much and I couldn't afford it anyway, so I went mainly to soak up the energy and continue the high, watching Rita Tasner dance on the tables and Hanover do his Elvis impression. Topics of conversation varied, but never strayed too far off of theatre and the people in it. Talk was pretty narrowly focused because, like most of the other actors, I had no idea what was going on in the rest of the world. I hadn't seen a newspaper in months and I never saw any news on tv or got anywhere near a radio. I didn't care. My world had no room for politics, famine in the third world or labor strikes at General Motors. I didn't care about taxes because I hardly made enough to pay any. *This* world, the one that rehearsed together and packed the Inn after performances every night, was much more interesting. These people had quickly become what mattered to me the most.

I hated to see the day end. I refused rides home. I liked to walk, usually bought some onion rings at Jack In The Box and watched Angie's little Japanese seven inch tv until I fell asleep. Angie and Willie were coming home at about three thirty every morning and I was usually in bed by then.

Except sometimes I found myself waiting up.

I lay there in the dark in my little spare bedroom and I heard them come in, heard the screen door slam, heard their bedroom light click on, heard their backpacks being dropped on the bed, heard Willie putting the toilet seat up, heard Willie peeing, heard Angie putting the toilet seat down, heard Angie peeing, heard the shower turn on, heard the soap dropping, heard teeth being brushed, heard the bedsprings creak, heard the bedroom light click off.

Heard the refrigerator door close.

That meant one had gone to bed and the other was hungry.

But which one?

I heard the kitchen chair moan across the linoleum, heard the air rush out of the seat cushion, heard the kettle begin to boil the tea water.

Angie.

"Oh I'm sorry," she said. "I didn't mean to wake you up."

"I haven't been in bed for very long."

I hugged her. It felt good but I yawned to make it appear nonchalant. She was in her white nightgown, I was in my boxers and undershirt.

"I'm making tea. You want some?"

"Sure. Aren't you exhausted?"

"Yeah," she said. "We're almost ready for your tech tomorrow. I like the extra money but tonight was my last night."

"That's good. You can enjoy being an actress again."

"It's good to see you. What did you do after *Lifetime* tonight?"

I told her about Rita Tasner dancing on the tables. I told her about the rerun of *Mr. Ed* I watched on her seven inch. Then I told her about *Salesman* rehearsal and how exciting it was to be opening the show in a few days.

She put her hand on my knee. "I'm glad for you," she said. "I can't wait to see it."

"Not that it's anything special or anything. Ephrem says you're tremendous in *Fiddler*, Angie. You and Ronni and Jean."

"Ronni talks about you a lot," she said, looking square at me, smiling. She must have seen me turn three shades of red.

"You've just turned three shades of red."

"I think she's great. I wish it could have gone differently between us."

"Because of the Gina thing?"

"Just not the right time for me."

She sipped her tea.

"I won't set you up anymore then."

"Okay." I wanted to change the subject. "How's Willie doing?"

She looked down and shook her head. "Bad. I mean he's fine. Us, I don't know. It's pretty screwed up right now, actually."

"Sorry to hear that. I'm sure it'll get better once the shows are open."

She looked at me with that tight-lipped smile, really a grimace, like people give you when they can't muster a genuine smile. Kind of a stopgap expression, signaling nothing but acceptance of one's lot. She put her hand on my knee again, nodded her head, looked at the floor.

"Give me a hug," she said.

7

Since *Once in a Lifetime* had opened, my mornings, which had been occupied with those rehearsals, freed up. But I needed to wake up at a reasonable hour because it was important that I finish up some button art for Lloyd and Bronson. I had drawn four circle templates double size on some illustration board and had very carefully inked cartoons inside the circles. Those particular designs featured a character we had dubbed Mr. Happy, who was the ubiquitous yellow "Have a Nice Day" character, with a curved-line smile and two dots for eyes, which had recently swept the nation and appeared on everything from buttons to t-shirts to lunch-boxes. I had given the obnoxious guy some dimension, so he could flatten or stretch out like a rubber ball, and I had given him some Mickey Mouse type arms and legs, with three-fingered gloves and spats. Mr. Happy was depicted in the four panels as being in dire circumstances, getting squooshed by a truck, chased by a dog, sat on by a German oompa-pa tuba player (inspired by Solvang) and dropped from a plane without a parachute. Lloyd and Bronson had come up with the idea. They hated the yellow smile buttons and said this would be a fitting counterattack. It was just the thing their customers would want, they said. I met them in the lobby an hour before rehearsal.

"Fantastic," Lloyd said.

"These buttons are not just words, like 'Keep on Truckin'," Bronson said. "These are little pieces of art."

"Each one is truly unique," said Lloyd.

"We're making a real statement with each one."

"Nicely done."

"How are the bumper stickers coming?" Bronson asked.

"I think you guys should rethink those bumper stickers," I said. "You want to be able to read them from a ways off. There should be some catch phrase in big letters. These little drawings... people won't be able to tell what they are."

They both nodded their heads. Lloyd's brow was furrowed.

"What about 'Have a Fucked Day'?" Bronson said.

"With Mr. Happy sticking his tongue out or something," Lloyd said.

"Or his dick," Bronson said. "'Have a Fucked Day.'"

Lloyd cracked up. I was not amused.

"I don't know," I said. "Every time I see a bumper sticker like that I want to pull the guy out of his car and beat him up. You gotta get more clever than that."

"Not so off-putting, perhaps," Lloyd said.

"I don't want to add to all the sight pollution out there," I said.

"But the spirit of the novelty industry is pretty risqué," Bronson said. "You gotta have stuff like that to get noticed."

"Maybe so, but I think it's just stupid."

"I think Bob is right," Lloyd said.

"But instead of 'Have a Nice Day'?" Bronson said. "It's great."

"It's been done before," I said. "Besides, I don't want to be drawing any penises on Mr. Happy. It's obscene. And nobody but low class illiterates will buy them."

"That's not a bad demographic to shoot for though," Lloyd said.

"I mean why not just do Makin' Bacon? It's disgusting."

"Blue had one of those bumper stickers on his truck," Bronson said.

"Back in 1972 it might have been amusing for fifteen minutes," I said. "This is the next decade. This is the age of enlightenment."

"But we're talking about making money," Bronson said. "It doesn't matter if you or me or Lloyd thinks it's great, it just boils down to 'will it sell?' That's all we should be askin'."

"Aesthetics be damned," Lloyd championed.

"Well, you can make money by selling drugs or selling your ass on the street," I said.

I might have stepped over the line there. Bronson shifted his weight and actually appeared bigger. Before he could speak, Lloyd said:

"Okay, look... it's no big deal or anything. We know the buttons work. Let's just rethink the bumper stickers."

"I'm not sure about those buttons anymore," Bronson said.

"Well a while ago you thought they were great," I said.

"Since when did you become so artsy fartsy?"

"If you want to publish cheap crap you guys can get somebody else. I want to do decent stuff that makes people laugh, not make them puke."

We went around like this for awhile. In the middle of it all I thought about trying to write a screenplay with Darrell Bobo when I was six and I was pissed that at age eight, he could write better than I could, and I had to give in on the really important stuff, like whether the dinosaurs should be real dinosaurs or whether they should be some sort of mutated lizard beasts. But in the true spirit of collaboration, we triumphed, and emerged with our two-page screenplay (single spaced), and preproduction was running on schedule until we realized that in order to shoot the movie, we needed a camera. And in order to shoot the dinosaurs, there needed to actually BE dinosaurs that moved and roared and stuff. This, at my tender age, was a dose of reality that was hard to swallow. But the point is, we collaborated, and we collaborated successfully because instead of holding out for the mutated Tyrannosaurus, I settled for Darrell's wimpy normal version. The key to winning battles, I thought, was choosing your particular hill to die on. And this battle was not worth losing it over. I eventually calmed down. It seemed to have a soothing effect on Bronson as well.

"Look, let's shelve the bumper sticker idea until we can all agree on which way we want to go," said Lloyd. And when they remembered their silent partner, who would have veto power over everything the boys did, the argument became moot. "It's his call anyway." "It's not really our decision to make." And I said I didn't mean to infer anybody was a prostitute, and they said they were concerned about quality as well as the novelty of the idea. After it was all said we agreed it was a pretty stirring debate about art versus commerce. I agreed to let them show my work to their "partner" so they could get some "feedback."

It was our first tech for *Death of a Salesman* that afternoon. That meant instead of throwing our stuff down in a corner of the rehearsal hall, we reported to our dressing rooms and threw our stuff down in there. Angie had said the costumes would be ready, and sure enough my Biff clothes were on the rack. I looked forward to getting into costume because at that point in the rehearsal process, little things – like having the right shoes, the right tie, the right shirtsleeves to roll up – gave us that added feeling of what it was really like to embody our characters. Ephrem and I shared a dressing room. He was already in his clothes and chihuahua George was pacing nervously across the makeup table, his claws ticking across the formica.

"What's George upset about today?" I asked. Ephrem was examining a prop briefcase.

"Maybe it's your little furry friend."

I wheeled in horror. There, sequestered meekly away behind the hats, was the noxious, offending rag of a hairpiece, squatting grotesquely on its styrofoam perch.

"What the fuck is *that* doing here?" I said.

"Don't spook it," Ephrem said, "It might attack."

"Jesus Christ! I told her I wasn't going to wear it. Did she hear me? I thought we had this whole thing settled. I told her once and for all the fucking hairpiece is out!"

"Maybe you need to say that to *him*." Ephrem nodded to the rag.

"This is ridiculous. No note or anything, just 'Here it is. Just think of it as part of your costume.' Fuck this."

"Maybe it walked in here by itself."

We both looked at it, half expecting it to move. George was trembling.

"We could burn it," Ephrem said.

"Do you think she's expecting me to wear it, or what?"

"I think she wants you to wear it, that much is clear."

I picked it up.

"Why don't you talk to her about it again?" Ephrem said.

We had twenty minutes before we were due onstage. "Forget it," I said, exasperated. "I'll just wear the damn thing for one day. What could it hurt?"

Ephrem didn't say anything, even when the costume lady, all cheery and nonchalant, came in to help me with the wig. I told her I was willing to give it a trial run for one rehearsal only, and she seemed fine with that, saying that she just wanted to give Noah Manning a chance to see it on stage.

To give the thing credit, it was something you didn't notice right off. I walked out on stage for a pre-tech pep talk and Richard Siebert looked at me funny.

"Why do you look so different?" he said.

I turned around to show him the back of my head.

"Ohhhhh," he said. "Well, it looks... very good. I never would have known."

"Look at you!" Brenda Bodwin hustled over in her motherly way from the other side of the stage. She grabbed my shoulders and stepped back to examine me thoroughly. "Biff! It's really you!" she said.

"It really does look excellent," Richard said.

I pretty much wanted to melt right there on the spot, turn into a little puddle of ooze and drip away under a seat. Mr. Manning and Stage Manager Lou were seated at the temporary command center in the middle of the theatre, and the stage lights shining on us prevented us from seeing them. Mr. Manning said a few words, and then the comforting tenor of Lou's voice with its familiar Texan accent boomed across the auditorium.

"Good afternoon everybody. This will be a stop and start day. It's mainly to set light levels and give our board operator the feel of the light cues. We want to see how your costumes look on stage and we want to give you a chance to get used to the set. We may run back over some things several times..."

In other words, as expected, no acting required. It was a good thing, because everything felt entirely different. Probably because the top of my head felt like it was wrapped in paper maché, and the lights and the set with actual stairs and wall units were new and oddly disconcerting, the day felt like I was swimming through Jello. When I opened my mouth somebody else's voice came out. I had never felt so discombobulated, so wooden. Every bit of progress I had made in rehearsals seemed to vanish and I found myself at Day One all over again. By contrast, Richard, Brenda and Ephrem seemed to thrive. They seemed energized by having real props, real doorways, real clothes. At the end of the day they were galvanized, joking and upbeat, and I felt completely lost.

My mood did nothing to perk up the atmosphere in the dressing room after rehearsal. Ephrem walked in and clammed up immediately. Lou knocked on the door and opened it a foot, steadying herself on her cane.

"Bob? Noah says he likes the way the hairpiece looks and he wants you to try wearing it in the runthrough tomorrow."

The costume lady had won.

Instead of being fueled for the rest of the evening I felt like somebody had flattened me with a steamroller. On the bus to Solvang I could barely carry on a conversation with Ripley, who seemed uncharacteristically happy.

"Wanda and I are going to Santa Barbara on our first day off."

There used to be an Excedrin commercial on tv that had a guy describing his own, unique headache as if "two bull goats" were butting their heads together inside his skull. If my headache could talk, it would have called me a piss ant and eaten me alive.

I walked through *Henry V* that night and couldn't wait to get back to the Santa Maria Inn and get plastered. I wished Ripley had ridden the bus back with me because, with a slightly clearer head than I had after *Salesman* rehearsal, I wanted to ask him questions: *What do you see in Wanda Dare? What is she really like? What do you talk about? Are you dorking her yet?* But questions would have to wait as he was, at that moment, sitting in the passenger seat of Wanda's red Mustang convertible, fiddling with the control knobs on her FM radio, dialing in that Oxnard station that played "cool, soft hits," gliding up Pacific Coast Highway while the strains of "Girl From Ipanema" stoked the fires of their passion under a mantle of stars.

Angie and the rest of the *Fiddler* cast had commandeered the Inn a good hour ahead of our group pulling in from Solvang. She and Ronni were at a corner table drinking beer. Ronni was in jeans and a sexy suede cowboy hat. The place was packed, and almost everybody was a company member. Angie smiled at me and pulled out a chair for me to sit down.

I sat. Ronni and Angie looked at me.

"What's the matter with you guys?" I said.

"Nothing," Ronni said.

"Ronni's trying to figure out if she wants to date Nathan Trask," Angie said.

"Big decision, huh?"

"He's cute. But he's just such a weirdo," Ronni said. "I think he might be a child molester or something."

"What makes you say that?" I asked.

"He looks like he's permanently stoned."

"And then that huge shit-eating grin he wears," Angie said.

"Total nutcase. Too bad I can't find anybody *nice* to go out with."

"Or like, somebody nice won't go out with *you*," Angie said.

"It must be because all the good ones are taken."

"Or *married*."

"Yeah, too bad," Ronni said. And then they both sighed theatrically, and their sighs dissolved into ridiculous giggles.

"Look Ronni," I said.

"No, Bob. Don't try to sway me. I've made up my mind. Nathan it is!" And she stood up like Desdemona, looked to the ceiling and thumped her hand against her chest. Then she looked at me. "How was that? Convincing?"

"Just let us meet her sometime, okay Bob?" Angie said.

And Ronni leaned into the table and said to my face "Your WIFE."

"Okay."

"I've got to pee," Ronni said. "And on my way back, I'm going to jump Nathan and blow his mind." She made her way across the bar.

"You go get him, girl," Angie called.

Then there was a silence that was fairly thick.

"I guess she's pissed at me, huh?" I said.

"She'll get over it."

I wanted to get off the subject of Ronni. "You started drinking without me," I said.

"I couldn't wait to get here tonight."

"Neither could I."

"Life is seriously catastrophic sometimes."

"Tell me about it."

"Have you been home yet?" she asked.

"No."

"It's kind of a mess. Don't look in our bedroom."

"I don't care," I said.

She rubbed her nose. "Willie might not be back tonight. He's really pissed at me."

"Why?"

"For throwing his clothes around I guess."

"Why did you throw his clothes around?"

"Because I was pissed at him."

This was a game. Angie was being coy, and I was tired of it. "Look, I've had a bad day, okay? Do you have something you want to tell me about you and Willie or not?"

My bluntness surprised her. She took a thoughtful breath. "You know, I've had it with men who are impossible to read. Like you know something's going on with them but they won't tell you what it is."

"Are we talking about Willie now or are we talking about me?"

"Frankly I don't know you well enough to know how much you hide from people."

"You've said that before. That's too easy."

"Okay. You seem all right. But that doesn't mean you're honest. You're an actor. You sure as shit have the same evil thoughts as everybody else but you just don't fess up to having them. So nobody sees the real you. And then all the stored-up shit comes out later, and it's not pleasant."

"So you don't trust me then?"

"No. I don't believe you."

"You think I'm too nice?"

"I think you're too fucking 'nice' to be trusted."

So far, the day had not gone well. On top of having to endure arguments about true art versus popular culture as influenced by the novelty business, showdowns with maniacal costume ladies and pointed jibes from jilted potential sex partners, Angie was challenging my God-given right as a male to lie my ass off. I wanted to say "Are you kidding? The whole structure of male-female communication is built on guys not telling the truth." Guys will say anything to get laid. Guys will say anything to keep the peace. When I lied to people, I always told them something I assumed they wanted to hear. What was wrong with that? What was wrong with making people feel good? Why seek conflict in the world by engaging in truth-telling? Telling the truth had only gotten me in trouble. But I decided in that moment – you know what? I didn't care about saving Angie's feelings. What about *my* feelings? So I just backed up and got a running start at that cliff, flung my arms out, and as my feet left the ground and I arched back into position for a huge swan dive, I said the most honest thing I could say in the situation:

"Well fuck you then, Angie."

And I got up and left.

I was immediately accosted by Nathan Trask.

"Hey Bob," he said. "What are the words to that song about the pig?"

"What pig?"

"You know, something like: there was a pig and something was his name-bo."

I maneuvered him into the middle of the floor to put more distance between myself and Angie. Nathan had ruined my clean exit. Hanover was hovering, waiting to hear the words to the pig song.

"Jesus. I don't know. Isn't it about some dog who wished he was a pig or something?"

"That's it!" Hanover cut in. "He had a pig."

"There-was-a-dog-who-was-a-pig," Nathan sang.

"*Had* a pig," Hanover corrected.

"There-was-a-dog-who-had-a-pig-and-Embo-was-his-name-bo!"

They had forgotten about me and I headed for the door as a small group sang "E-M-B-O, E-M-B-O, E-M-B-O and Embo was his name-bo."

I had no idea why they were calling the dog Embo. Before I could extract myself further, Angie grabbed me by the arm.

"Let's go to the beach," she said.

"Let go of my arm, Angie. It's been a bad day and I don't feel like going anywhere."

"Come on. You were right to tell me to fuck off. I deserved it."

"I'm probably the lyingest sack of shit you ever met. So leave me alone."

"Come on Bob. I'm sorry. I'm apologizing, see? I need you right now. I need you to give me the male perspective on this Willie thing. Because I am at my wits' end with him and I don't have a clue about what to do. Please go to the beach with me. Please."

Normally I would have leapt at the chance to be alone with Angie on the beach. But the thing was, I really felt like I had to go home and check the thread count on my bedsheets. For lack of a more definitive response in the moment, I nodded my head and didn't say anything, thinking that when we got away from the high visibility zone of the open floor and reached the serenity of the parking lot, I would explain to her once again how badly I needed to watch *Mr. Ed*, because the previews from the night before had looked really good. Angie went back to the table to get her coat and said something into Ronni's ear. Ronni looked at me. Angie waved goodbye to Ronni. Ronni looked at me again. Nathan Trask even looked at me.

Outside a light mist from the ocean was rolling in. Angie stopped us halfway to her VW.

"So tell me the truth then, okay Bob? Promise."

"What do you want to know?"

"I want you to be honest with me. If you can do it."

"Hurry up. Just ask me before I chicken out."

"I need to know this before I can go any further."

"What?"

"Are you attracted to me?"

I blanched and started to make a noise like "Ah..."

"Saying 'Why are you asking?' is not acceptable. You can't answer a question with a question."

"I wasn't going to!"

"So what's your answer?"

"Yes," I said.

"Okay. Second question. Are you gay?"

"What?"

"Don't answer a question with a question. What is it, yes or no?"

"No!"

"Because Ronni thought you might be having a crisis with your sexual identity or something."

"Oh for God's sake. Did she tell you that?"

"Don't worry. It was just between us."

"Right. You and the rest of the company."

"I swear to God it was just between us."

"No I'm not gay."

"Can you be my friend, really, or will you just be thinking that you want to fuck me all the time."

"I can't really be your friend because I'd just be thinking that I wanted to fuck you all the time."

"Honestly?"

"That's as honest as I can get. I fantasize about you, since we're telling the truth here. I'm not embarrassed by it."

"No, no. You shouldn't be."

"I go home every night hoping that something will happen between us."

"Uh huh."

"That's the way I feel. I want to know when it's okay to start asking you questions."

She was looking at the pavement. I think she was actually speechless. I was enjoying this honesty business. Finally she took a breath and looked up at me.

"Not quite yet," she said. "First you have to give me time to respond to what you said."

"Okay."

"I'm attracted to you too, but not to the point where I want to ruin my marriage or anything. If you and I went to bed it would only be because I'm mad at Willie and I really wanted to hurt him. It would be something I would confess to him and make him get over. Because I needed to hurt him to get his attention. So by doing this I would in a sense be using you. If you just wanted to get laid or something you might be able to handle it. But if you think you have real feelings for me, like you think you might be in love with me or something like that, I wouldn't recommend you getting involved with me at all, because I'm not going to leave him for you. I might leave him, but not for you. Understand?"

"But you don't know me very well."

"Ooh. See there? I hurt your feelings when I said that, didn't I?"

"It stung a little."

"So you *are* in love with me then, or think you might be?"

"As much as... Yes. I guess so. A little."

"So I guess the question I have to ask myself would be whether I can handle our relationship, you being in love with me and like that."

"I guess you could ask yourself that."

"How bad is it?" she asked.

"It's my turn now," I said.

I told Angie I didn't have it for her that bad, that if she told me to get lost I wouldn't feel like I even had to move out or anything. I told her what I found attractive in her, aside from the way she looked, like her candor and the way she handled herself, even the way she was when she was stoned. I said with my best attempt at searing self-analysis that it probably had something to do with the fact that I found her so different from Gina, and I was projecting or acting out or some Freudian mumbo-jumbo. I could sound pretty self-analytical when I put my mind to it. Angie seemed to buy it. I wasn't embellishing anything for effect. I didn't feel like I had to say the right thing to spare her feelings about anything. And I didn't feel like she was judging me. I felt pretty good, better than I had all day. All this took awhile, and while we were talking, people from the company started dribbling out of the bar to go home. Angie and I were leaning up against the passenger side of her VW, our arms crossed, not looking at each other much, kind of like we were talking to the night and the other person could listen if they wanted to.

I ran out of things to say and she let several minutes go by before she spoke.

"Do you think you can be objective enough to help me with my old man problem?"

"You still love Willie?" I asked.

"Sure. That's not the problem. I just think he finds me boring. I feel like he's ignoring me."

"It's common," I said. "It's what men do. It's a manipulation thing. He's pissed at you for some reason so he's trying to control you by putting you down."

"But I don't know what I did."

"You didn't do anything. It's nothing you can change, believe me. He's just pissed at you in general, because you are what you are. It's just immaturity. He doesn't know how to express himself properly. He's passive aggressive." And I told her about Gina and me, how I felt that I probably drove her into having an affair by trying to control her too much.

"For a guy who doesn't talk much you seem to have something going on in the insight department," she said.

"Gina and I went through counseling for fourteen months. Plus I read *Psychology Today*."

Truth: Gina went through counseling, more like four months, from some lady doctor in the psych department. I just heard it all secondhand from Gina when she got home. I *did* read *Psychology Today*. Occasionally.

"Here's the deal Bob," Angie said. "Even though you want to have sex with me I still want to be your friend. I think you could be a very good friend. And don't get me wrong. I'm flattered. I love the turn-on factor you know? Because I said I was attracted to you too, and I am I guess. Do you know what I'm saying?"

"Yeah."

"Is that good enough for you? Do you feel abused or anything?"

"You know what? That's fine," I said. "I'm kind of over you now anyway."

"Seriously?"

"Well, you know how it is when you have a romantic situation; this unspoken chemistry thing happening between two people? There's all this electricity because there's so much mystery to it. You don't know that much about the other person and they don't know that much about you. And it makes it all, I don't know... exciting because of the unsuredness of the situation."

"I know what you mean."

"And the second somebody turns on the lights or opens the window and airs the thing out, it's like all the mystery goes away. So I'm glad you aired this one out, Angie. You just allowed it to be more real between us. Not so cloaked in romance and intrigue, you know?"

She nodded her head.

There were two other cars left in the parking lot. Another light blinked off in the bar.

Angie hunched her shoulders and zipped up her jacket. "That reminds me, I asked you to go to the beach," she said.

I'm not sure if either of us felt like it, but out of a sense of obligation we got in her car and headed west on Main until the buildings faded away behind us. The headlights shone on an increasingly thickening gray bank of fog, and after a few miles we decided to turn around and drive home. I think we were both relieved that we didn't have to stay up any later. Santa Maria was completely still as we drove back through town. I made a conscious effort not to look at the time on Angie's funky dayglo digital clock stuck to her dashboard. We were all talked out, and neither of us said anything as we pulled in to her parking space and trudged up the stairs. Willie had left a lamp on in the living room and a note pinned to their bedroom door. She read it in silence. I didn't ask. She looked at me, gave me one of those noncommittal tight-lipped smiles, twiddled her fingers at me, and quietly disappeared inside the bedroom, shutting the door behind her.

8

In fact, I don't think I said one word to anybody in the morning until I opened my mouth in dress rehearsal to utter my first Biff line. I might have said hello to Ephrem in the dressing room, but I didn't see much of him, as he was customarily preparing for his role by getting there early, getting dressed and heading out to the stage to do some utterly annoying warm-up exercises, the kind where you open your pipes and emit the most horrible noises, like farting out your mouth, and slide up and down your register at the top of your lungs like an air raid siren had been stuck up your ass. It was all very yoga-like and freeing and all that, but I saw it as a futile attempt to dispel pent-up tension. I felt that a better way to combat tension was not to be tense. I wasn't tense as I sat silently in my makeup chair, the costume lady squeezing my scalp like a ripe lemon. I was sullen to the point of being comatose, but I wasn't tense. I knew I could do the role justice, but whether I could perform it in the fright wig remained to be seen. The costume lady left. George stuck his head out of his gym bag, looked at the strange hairy thing that had attached itself, leech-like, to the top of my head, sighed once and shakily curled down into Ephrem's sweat clothes.

Lou knocked on the dressing room door and opened it.

"Bob? I'm keeping valuables with me in the booth. Don't forget to take off your wedding ring."

I took off my wedding band and chucked it and my wallet into Lou's Chock Full o' Nuts can.

"Have a good show," Lou said, trying not to look at my toupé.

It was our first runthrough with lights and costumes. My performance aside, the show was going to be first rate. The set designer had built a marvelous abstract realist set, dollhouse style, its outside wall removed to reveal two stories of the venerable American home, the kind that kept watch over the crumbling infrastructure of America's inner cities as newer, shinier houses sprawled into the suburbs after the war. This was the Loman House as Arthur Miller had envisioned, with an expansive front porch and exquisite realistic details inside. Noah Manning had directed the show masterfully, prodding us all to deliver the most honest work we could. His choices always opted away from sloppy sentiment yet seemed to wring every ounce of drama from the script. And then there was Richard, who had crafted his Willie Loman as the familiar Everyman, lumbering, downtrodden, yet full of hope and false optimism, bursting with pride for his sons yet terrified that they would end up to be just like him.

We started the runthrough. David Shuster's evocative theme, written for the production, a lonely oboe melody weaving through a cello accompaniment, filled the stage as the lights dimmed to black. Ephrem and I took our places in our twin beds upstairs. Below, Richard and Brenda started the first scene:

[Willie has aborted his sales trip and has come back home in the middle of the night. Linda tries to soothe him. He confesses to her that he nearly ran off the road, and complains about how unsympathetic his company is. Then he complains about Biff, who has come back home after leaving another dead end job. Linda humors her husband awhile, kisses him tenderly and then goes off to bed. Happy and Biff wake up and listen as Willie continues talking aloud to an imaginary Biff as if he were

a young boy. The lights ease up slowly on the boys' room, and the boys talk about their Pop for a bit.]

So, we were acting away, up on our platform. Hap tells Biff that Willie's been flipping out. We were smoking our cigarettes and reveling in our masculine prowess, brother to brother. It was all going fine. I was feeling pretty good, Ephrem was into it. We were talking to each other. So just as I was about to launch into some lines that talked about what a stud I was, and how many women Happy and I had porked, I looked over at Ephrem and he wasn't meeting my eyes. He was gazing over my head, or at least above eye level, kind of lifting his chin to indicate something beyond my sight. Really, I had been doing all right up until this point. I had almost been able to forget about the top of my head and concentrate on my work, but Ephrem was trying to indicate something, and I immediately thought it must have something to do with the hideous hairpiece. I brushed my hair back, in character I might add, and it didn't seem like the wig had shifted at all. So I tried to burrow into Ephrem's eyes for a better clue, all the while saying my line about the big Betsy something over on Bushwick Avenue, but Ephrem was still looking over my head, and worse, he had an expression of utter incredulity, which had nothing to do with what his character was thinking in the moment. Ephrem was so distracted that he was not saying his next line. So somehow I rationalized in that moment, the consummate actor that I am, that perhaps Biff could turn around and look behind him as well, at whatever Happy was looking at.

I was aware as I turned and gazed out into the audience that I had been hearing some sort of commotion for the past several moments, and I realized that it was actually a frantic shuffling of feet that seemed to be emanating from the top row of the auditorium. I couldn't see anything with lights in my face and the auditorium in darkness, but I determined that the sound was being made by at least two people who were struggling with each other, perhaps even fighting, as occasionally there would be a breathy grunt or groan accompanied by more shuffling and falling down sounds. Abruptly the combatants spilled down the center aisle, and I could discern movement and people running and I recognized the unmistakable sound of feet hitting the stage. I could see one figure in some sort of uniform tackling another man in jeans and a black t-shirt. The t-shirted man then kicked the uniformed man furiously, enough to break the man's grip, and send some sort of canister bouncing off the lip of the stage. Ephrem was waving madly, signaling distress to the light booth. The man in the t-shirt scrambled to his feet and raced up through the auditorium as the house lights came up. The uniformed man squirmed on the stage floor, seemingly dazed, and smoke began to billow in a hissing cloud from where the canister had been dropped. We heard the BANG of hands hitting the exit bar on the lobby doors, and the t-shirted man disappeared into sunlight. The man left on stage struggled to his feet, covering his face with a handkerchief.

"Clear the auditorium," he said, as the hissing cloud of smoke grew larger. Ephrem and I clamored down the escape and didn't stop running until we were outside. The rest of the cast and crew were streaming out various exit doors, some were bent over, coughing. Brenda Bodwin seemed to be overcome a bit and collapsed to one knee, but she promptly waved that she was fine. Ephrem and I trotted over to her.

"That was tear gas," she said. "I recognize it from Berkeley."

Several squad cars roared into the parking lot, sirens screaming, and policemen drew guns and took cover behind the cars. A voice came over a bullhorn telling us to clear the area, and as we all dispersed I saw some cops make a run for the lobby doors. A medic alert truck, its siren wailing, skidded up to the front of the building. Most of us collected in the middle of the football field, Ephrem and I in our Biff and Hap pajama bottoms, shirtless, Richard with his Willie Loman shirttails hanging out of his suit pants, Brenda in her Linda robe and curlers, others in the cast in various states of undress. The costume and scene shops had all emptied out. Noah Manning, Lou and the light crew were looking back at the melee. Everybody was completely bewildered. A light wind blew in from the sea. A few Mexican guys were playing soccer at one end of the field. And we all tried to piece together what had happened.

I had not even known what Fred Norton looked like, but that was him apparently, in the black t-shirt. The riot-ready officer was Officer

Wadleigh, the Barney Fife of campus security. We speculated that the jumbo tear gas canister was unauthorized, and was probably a vigilante item that he had picked up at an Army surplus store just in case he had to quell a restless student body. Why Fred was hanging around the auditorium was cause for wild speculation. Perhaps he had flipped his nut and had been living in the bowels of the theatre like the Phantom of the Opera, waiting in the wings for the right moment to kidnap Wanda Dare. Perhaps he had returned to exact some terrible misguided vengeance on Noah Manning. Maybe he had concealed his fortune in the basement and had come back to claim it before he left town for good.

Noah Manning was shaken and obviously disappointed that the incident had robbed him of valuable rehearsal time. Unable to remain idle, he and Lou hustled off to the admin building to do something important.

"Everybody just stay put until we tell you what to do," Lou said as she left. "Actors do not get your costumes dirty!"

So we stood in the field. The Mexican guys had scored a goal and were making some noise about it. Planes from the Air Force base flew overhead. I had a feeling somebody was looking at me behind my back. I turned around. Ephrem was watching me warily, frozen like a statue, his white chest gleaming in the afternoon sun.

"What's the matter?" I asked.

"You know."

"No I don't. What's the matter?"

"You know. It's the wig. It's cursed. It's voodoo."

"Don't be an idiot."

Ephrem nodded his head and moved away slowly.

After an hour or so we had all migrated to the shade of some trees, and Lou eventually returned and said we had no choice but to cancel rehearsal. With a SWAT team in gas masks swarming through the theatre and an escaped felon at large, it seemed the most appropriate choice, but leave it to Noah and Lou to hold out hope until the last possible moment. It was getting late. Lou told us actors we should just wear our costumes home that night and take good care of them. The theatre was cordoned off with yellow tape, which meant we couldn't even get our street clothes, our wallets, our keys. That stuff would have to spend the night in Lou's Chock Full o' Nuts can, locked away in the gas-ridden confines of the theatre. It looked like they might have to cancel that evening's performance of *Brigadoon*, but the actors and crews for *Henry V* were already making contingency plans for getting to Solvang. Some tech guys who had their car keys were shuttling the actors home so they could change. Ephrem wrenched his bicycle out of the rack and rode off in his pajama bottoms. Without my apartment key there was no use even going home. I looked around, thinking I might find Willie, but he was in Solvang all day, working. I could call Angie, I thought, but as I hesitated, standing there half naked, I realized I was practically alone. There had been security in numbers but now the volleyball guys were beginning to look at me funny, so I hurried off to the admin building to use the phone. I sat at Lou's desk and dialed. The office was buzzing with frantic activity. Angie wasn't home, so I called Ripley and asked if he and Wanda were driving to Solvang that evening. He said they were just about to leave and would swing by and pick me up.

Lou came by with a stack of papers. I hung up the phone, stood up and offered her the swivel chair. she swung her bad leg into her chair and hung her cane over the armrest.

"Thanks," I said to Lou, "for the phone."

She looked at me like she was a mom about to tell me the facts of life. "Bob," she said in her best midwestern drawl, "You might need a shirt for later. Why don't you take my jean jacket?"

"Won't you need it?"

"I've got others at the house."

"Thanks," I said.

"And... maybe you should leave that toupé here. You can keep it in my desk overnight." She slid her top drawer open and nodded to me. "Hurry up before someone thinks it's weird."

I sought the deeper seclusion of Lou's cubicle to remove the thing from my scalp. I tossed it in her drawer and she closed it quickly. Then she smiled at me.

"Have a good show," she said.

I smiled back and folded myself into the bustling throngs of volunteer office workers, and went out the back door.

9

I met Ripley and Wanda at the back entrance to campus. Ripley was driving Wanda's Mustang.

"Ripley! You're slumping!" I said, imitating Mr. Lark. "Sit up straight. Square those shoulders!"

He ignored me. "Hmmm. It's a look, I guess," he said, referring to my pajama-bottoms-with-jean-jacket fashion statement.

"Always on the cutting edge," I said.

They were both rabid for my take on the Fred Norton story, which by this time had circulated so thoroughly around the company, they actually knew more facts than I did, like the fact that the police had cornered and subsequently lost Fred in a soybean field about three miles out of town. I was able to captivate them thoroughly, however, with my on-the-scene report from the best vantage point possible. Speaking to people from the back seat of a convertible doing sixty is tricky though. I wasn't sure how loud I needed to speak, because with all the wind in my ears I couldn't hear myself all that well, and I thought it might be possible that they could hear me better than I could, because when they replied, I could barely hear them. They probably thought they didn't have to strain to be heard because the windshield and dashboard acted like a cocoon and they could hear themselves just fine. But all I heard was the wind shooshing in my ears. So to make up for it I had to practically scream at them. It went on this way for twenty miles, me screaming at them, them practically whispering back at me. Then I became self conscious because I thought that by practically whispering at me, they were really telling me I didn't need to talk so loud. Then I felt like an idiot, and started to get mad that Wanda had such a stupid car. I was at the point of refusing to speak anymore when Ripley pulled off the freeway at Buellton and the lower speeds of the back roads helped mitigate the situation immensely.

The trip didn't really help me get to know Wanda any better, because the information exchange was so one-sided. The two of them mainly asked questions and I replied. But once I had run out of Fred stories and we tooled along at 35, I could observe them a little more thoroughly. They weren't into lavish displays of affection at all. Wanda was actually very respectful of Ripley, and was behaving very genuinely towards him. I would have thought she would be the kind of woman who went absolutely silly when she found a man, but Wanda seemed to have settled down, become more confident, as if Ripley's interest in her made her feel as if she didn't have to work so hard.

"Hey Wanda," I said, "I wonder if I might be able to talk to you about something. I need your advice."

"Well, I'd be happy to help any way I can," she said in her perfectly studied ACT-trained voice.

"Not right now, of course, because I know you have to prepare for your role and all."

Ripley shot me a glance over his shoulder. "We're spending the night here at the Viederschlossen Inn after the show," he said.

"Is this something that Jake could be privy to as well?" She called him Jake. I had to remember that Ripley's first name was Jake because I hadn't called him that in years. "Because we could talk about it now, if it doesn't take too long."

"Frankly, it's a bit of a touchy subject. If you don't mind, I'd just like to get your take on it. Maybe five minutes of your time. No offense, *Jake*."

Ripley gave me another look. Wanda and I arranged to meet for coffee at the Hamelskraaken before the show the following afternoon. I'm sure Ripley thought I wanted to bore Wanda with some sob story about my marriage, and he was probably all uppity because he was worried that

I was going to implicate him in my past somehow, make references to his wimpyness and expose his true paranoid self. But I had no intention of discussing him or my marriage with Wanda Dare.

They *had* cancelled *Brigadoon* that night in Santa Maria, and some cast members who hadn't yet seen *Henry V* took advantage of the opportunity and showed up in the audience. They didn't have much to say afterwards. I think some even left before it was over. I would have. We customarily lost three to five percent of the audience on any given performance of *Henry V*. Verden Price had become sullen and withdrawn because of the show's lukewarm reception, and several witnesses claimed that he confronted director Mario in the Allen Hancock parking lot the night after opening and screamed at him for a couple hours. Mario apparently just escaped being pounded. I know how Verden must have felt, having been duped into a false confidence by one or two Directors With A Vision myself, and would have felt sorry for the guy if he wasn't such a vain, clueless ponce. Verden was experienced enough. He should have seen this one coming.

I noted the conspicuous absence of Angie, who, had she been at the show, would have at least waited until it ended, pulled me aside and told me how putrid she thought it was. I missed talking to her about it.

The bus let us off in the Allen Hancock parking lot around midnight. I bummed phone money from Hanover and called home. Still no answer, no Angie, no key, no way to get in, unless she left the window open in the bedroom, which she probably did.

"You need a ride somewhere?" It was Kathy Bishop. She was on her bike.

"You have a car?" I asked.

"No. Do you have a choice?" she said, referring to my attire. "Get on. Walk home like that and you're liable to get mugged." She had a Schwinn Stingray with a banana seat.

"Where'd you get this bike? I had one like this when I was a kid."

"I'm still a kid," she said. She was right, I thought. She dipped the bike to one side and I swung one leg over the seat. I wasn't sure where to hang on. "Are you on? Where are you going?"

"Home. I'll show you."

She started pedaling and I had to quickly reach forward and grab her to keep my balance. She stood up to put some power into it, and I grabbed her thighs just below her hips. She sat down and I shifted my grip to the small of her waist.

"Good thing Santa Maria is flat," she said. "I haven't seen you in awhile. Where've you been?"

I gave her some answer about trying to open *Death of a Salesman*. She was such a bullshitter. She saw me practically every day. She had been snubbing me as a way of punishment for my not wanting to pursue a relationship, and this was her ice breaker, laying the responsibility for our lack of communication at my feet. She was cute though. She was no ballerina, but she was as sexy as she was shallow, well-proportioned, with breasts that I had admired since our French lessons on the grass. She was wearing jeans patched with paisley fabric on her butt cheeks and knees. Her t-shirt had pulled out of her pants with her pedaling, her buckskin jacket rode up the small of her back and I felt the warm skin of her waist under my hands. She had to stand up occasionally to pedal, and when she did, her legs pumped like pistons, and I felt like I was fucking her from behind.

"Where's your boyfriend tonight?"

"What boyfriend?"

"Rob Banister. I thought you were going out with him."

"Occasionally. Not tonight though." She shot me a smile. "What do you care? I thought you were gay."

Here we go again, I thought. "Where'd you get that idea?"

"I have my sources."

Women must talk about nothing but sex. But at that moment, I wasn't going to get into a discussion about what she may have heard from Ronni or what conclusions she may have drawn to protect her ego. I didn't care what Kathy Bishop thought of me.

"You think us gay men aren't interested in women?" I said.

She was breathing hard as she pedaled, and she gave a breathy exhalation which was meant to be a laugh, but it got away from her a little bit and it sounded orgasmic. I started to get a hardon, which could have been very embarrassing in my pajama bottoms even though I was wearing briefs under them, and I had to think about asparagus, which I found disgusting, to keep from giving Kathy a surprise when she sat down. Her shoulder length hair was blowing in my face. The night breeze was cool.

"You're too big," she panted. She meant I weighed too much.

"You can handle it."

She laughed again. I let her go a couple blocks out of the way so I could savor the experience, but she caught on to that ploy easily.

"You creep," she laughed. "You're enjoying this aren't you?"

"We're almost there. Let me steer."

I leaned into her, took hold of the butterfly handlebars and steered us down the alley. She let go and relaxed against my chest, still panting.

"You pedal, too," she said.

She lifted her feet off the pedals. I replaced hers, then she put her feet on top of mine. Some dog let us have it loudly, throwing himself into his owner's chain link fence. We coasted up to the garage apartment. The place was completely dark, and there was no car in Angie's space. I disentangled myself from Kathy and pushed off the back of the bike.

"Nobody home," Kathy breathed. "They're at the Inn, I bet. Hop back on and I'll take you there."

I was attempting to shinny up the carport pillar to get to the open bedroom window. "I think I can get in," I said. "I'm not really dressed to be out on the town."

"I like it. I think you ought to wear that outfit in *Henry V*." She rolled her bike into the breezeway and let the kickstand down. Then she cupped her hands to boost me up. I thought this was a thoughtful gesture. She pretended she was a traffic cop, doing all these bogus moves to guide me up the side of the building. "A little more to the left! Back up! Don't fall! Easy does it!" Finally I reached the sill and squirmed through the window. I picked myself up and craned my head out the window but Kathy was gone. Then the doorbell rang.

"Hi," she said as I opened the door. And that was that.

I will say that the problem I experienced with Ronni that night was not a factor with Kathy Bishop. It was the first time I had been laid since splitting with Gina, and Kathy was the only other woman I'd had since my wedding night. Not that I was a saint or anything.

Angie's intuition had been right. I'd had a big infatuation with a student that undoubtedly fueled the fires of jealousy for Gina. In fact, the only reason that I didn't succumb to an actual sexual affair with the student was because she had moral issues with the fact that I was married. We never got very far. She quit school and went home to live with her parents, disappearing one day without a word. Needless to say, it was never the same with Gina. She sensed it. Women sense things. I never confessed the true depths of desire I had for this young woman. I just made out like there was nothing to tell.

If I had thought of this episode at that moment, it may not have gone well for me. But I wasn't thinking about Gina then. Maybe because I didn't feel anything for Kathy except lust, I was able to ride a wave without my head getting in the way.

I did stop and think once, very late in the night, which had been a blurry, wet fever dream of rolling and thrusting, while I was buried deep inside Kathy and had my fingers in her mouth and was watching her, mesmerized, as she sucked on them, her eyes closed and about to come, that it was the first night I had spent without my wedding ring, which was lying in Lou's coffee can in the dark theatre. Somewhere in the back of my consciousness I thought this might be significant. But it was a fleeting thought as Kathy arched and convulsed and made wonderful female noises beneath my body. I thought that maybe Ephrem had been on to something when he talked about the wig being cursed. Maybe the ring had been bringing me bad luck, too. Here it was my first night without it and I had definitely, as they say, gotten lucky.

I was aware of one other thought during an especially verbal outburst from my guest, as I heard the screen door close and heard the footsteps and bedtime noises made by Angie and Willie:

Maybe, that night, they would be listening to me.

10

The next day was a circus. The admin office was furious with the police, who by eight a.m. would still not admit entry to the theatre for security reasons. Noah Manning had to threaten to pull his conservatory out of Santa Maria before City Hall relented, and at about 11:00, the doors swung wide open to air the place out. The tech guys rented huge fans and aimed them at all the doors. Swarms of cleaning people had to swab everything down fifteen times to prevent patrons who might be allergic to some substance in the gas residue from having a reaction and suing the theatre. There was no physical damage to any set pieces, but all the costumes had to be washed or dry cleaned all over again. Actors were not even allowed in the theatre, so our final dress rehearsal for *Salesman*, which was scheduled to start at noon, took the form of a line-through in the girls' gym, without any lights, costumes, props or set. It was the theatrical equivalent of eating a peanut butter sandwich after you'd come to expect prime rib. The big problem for Noah Manning and the *Salesman* cast was that the Fred Norton incident had robbed us of our last two dress rehearsals before opening. We were called for special sessions throughout the day beginning at 10:00 a.m., even though we lost the stage and part of the cast for a matinee performance of *Brigadoon*.

Ephrem was a nervous wreck because in all the excitement he had forgotten completely about George, who had spent the night in Ephrem's gym bag in our dressing room. Ephrem discovered his error when he got home and went to the refrigerator to get George his pork chop. Pleading with the administration and the police proved fruitless, as both claimed their hands were tied, and Ephrem didn't sleep a wink. He showed up at the theatre at 5:00 a.m. with six pork chops, a gallon of water, bandages and an oxygen tank. He got special permission to be among the first allowed inside, wearing a city-issued gas mask, and when he burst into the dressing room, tears of guilt streaming down his face, he found George standing up in the gym bag yawning. Ephrem must have thought of George as the canine equivalent of a canary in a coal mine, because he carefully removed his gas mask to find that our dressing room smelled only slightly of ammonia which we later determined was not tear gas residue at all, but the smell of George's pee from where he had widdled in the corner.

The *Santa Maria Times* ran three related stories in their afternoon edition. Page one led off with "Felon Escapes After Confrontation at AHCC" which gave a factual account of the incident but shed no new light on Fred Norton's motives or sudden reappearance. On page three, accompanying the continuation of the lead story, appeared an article entitled "AHCC Security Officer Reprimanded" which stated that Officer Wadleigh would have been fired for possession of the unauthorized tear gas canister had it not been for the fact that he did indeed rout Mr. Norton from concealment. Also on that page was a little three-incher: "PCPA to Reschedule Musical Performance," about how ticketholders to *Brigadoon* could see the cancelled performance on a special Sunday evening performance that was added on the last day of the season.

The whole company spent every spare minute working to return the theatre to normal. By the middle of the afternoon everyone forgot about the lost *Salesman* rehearsal and started worrying about readying the house and stage for *Brigadoon* that evening. By the time the bus left to take the *Henry V* cast to Solvang, it appeared as if things had settled down.

Lou had returned our valuables. I took my wedding ring back, but I didn't put it on.

I watched Kathy Bishop get on the bus. I scooted over in my seat for her, but she only reached out and mussed my hair and continued down the aisle. Her other hand was pulling Rob Banister. She shot me a wicked glance over her shoulder. She and Rob sat in the back. He was a nice enough guy, much nicer than Peter Ross (who nobody much cared for anymore), and definitely way too nice for Kathy. She must have been using him to achieve some sort of legitimacy in the company, her own version of social climbing. Rob reminded me of someone out of an Archie comic, Riverdale letter sweater and all. Kathy was all into holistic this and that, lava lamps, incense, astrology, natural foods. She lived alone in a beat up house in the middle of a cornfield across the railroad tracks north of town. Except for the boys she corralled to have sex with her, she was a total loner. It was hard for me to think about Kathy without getting a hardon.

I met Wanda Dare at the Hamelskraaken at 6:30. I saw her give Ripley a kiss at the end of the block and send him away, and then I saw him lurking clumsily in several nearby shops, trying not to be obvious while looking at us, as we sat on the brick patio at a round metal table. Wanda had tea with skim milk and no sugar. I had a scone and coffee.

"Thanks for meeting me," I said. "I wanted to ask you about something I've been wrestling with." And before I could open the topic I wanted to discuss she said:

"Jake tells me you're married."

I smiled politely and nodded. "Yes, I am. But we're splitting up."

"Jake told me. Actor marriages are hard. Is she an actress?"

"Yeah. She's in Minnesota. We got married too young." And then I took another breath to launch into the reason I had asked her to have coffee with me when she said:

"My husband is a lawyer."

I tried not to show surprise.

"So I understand about these things," she said.

I wondered if Wanda Dare was going to turn out to be one of those women the Eagles always wrote about.

"It seems to me that it's entirely your business, your marriage and what form it takes, and nobody else's. What agreement do you have with her?"

"We don't really have an agreement," I said. "We didn't talk about it very much because we weren't getting along. We're splitting up."

"Are you involved with anybody?"

An image of Angie appeared in my head, then a memory of Kathy Bishop's breasts swaying in front of my face. "No," I said.

"Relationships are inevitable, but they complicate matters. I would get the ground rules straightened out."

"We're splitting up."

"Then who needs an agreement? If it's over, it's much more straight-forward isn't it?" She sipped her tea. "So what did you want to talk about?"

I asked Wanda what she would do if some costume lady asked her to wear a hairpiece in a play. Not that she needed a hairpiece, but if she were faced with a question about a costume that she felt was insulting or embarrassing, how would she handle it? I already knew the answer, having seen her throw her huge and infamous fit in Solvang, and I guess I just wanted to hear her side of the story, to see how she justified her behavior, and gather support.

"Let me tell you something. One thing I can do well is make myself look good. I need to *feel* like I look good up there. It gives me confidence. If you don't have confidence you've got nothing. Actors have very little control in this business, have you noticed? Look at poor Verden. He trusted his director implicitly and look where it got him. I say, we must always keep an eye out for ourselves. Forget what they told you in acting school. You need to survive, and to do that you've got to be noticed, and to be noticed you've got to make an impact, and you can't make an impact if you can't stand up for yourself. Too often, actors trust too much. We're all very gentle people, aren't we? And we can get taken advantage of very easily, because of that vulnerability. At least I can control the way I look. Sometimes, that's all I can do."

Wanda had pretty much said it. I felt that the actor's lack of control over his or her life was one of the reasons people like Uta Hagen wrote books entitled "Respect for Acting." Why would you need to be encouraged to have respect for acting if there was any question it was worthy of respect? The reason it wasn't respectful was because of that lack of control. Basically, an actor was little more than a bum. A vagrant. An addict. Theatre was the drug of choice. Once you were hooked, you were constantly on unemployment, constantly auditioning, always at the mercy of directors' or casting directors' taste. But once you got hold of some good shit like PCPA you could ride the high for three months or more. The performance was the high, the community and the friends you made, they were the high. But coming down was a bitch, and getting off it could kill you. Often the drug gave you an excuse to become lazy. Too many acting addicts I knew seemed to adapt a victim mentality, to deliver their fate into the hands of others. They put people in false positions of power, and let them make decisions for them. Like Noah Manning. Though I had to give him great credit for his talent and business acumen, Noah was famous for stringing people out as long as he could, waiting, for whatever reason, to offer them a contract. Some might say this was just good business, that he owed it to his theatre to cast the best actors he could. People would turn down other jobs waiting to see what Noah would offer them, and often it was a sucker's bet, as the actor in question would be called into the office, given a handshake and a sincere "stay in touch." And then they were jobless again.

If you choose to be an actor, it's your fault for getting hooked in the first place, so no one has much sympathy when you wake up at 40 and find yourself in yet another thrift store, looking for knives and forks that bear some resemblance to one another.

"Is there anything else you want to know?" Wanda asked.

"No," I said. "You've answered my question." And I gave one of Angie's tight-lipped smiles to Wanda, and then I motioned for Ripley to come over. He was skulking around some Scandinavian-inspired dresses in a shop window, and when he saw me wave, he ducked.

"Jake is an interesting man," she said. "How long have you known him?"

"A few years. We went through grad school together."

"What is he going to do when he leaves here?"

It was clear that Ripley's future was not her concern. I hoped Ripley understood, as Wanda had put it, the ground rules.

An actor's struggle for control was never more apparent than it was that evening in *Henry V*. After the audience had sat through two of the curious interpretive dance sequences, the ranks started to thin. Verden Price was doing his best to keep the show moving along. His task was not easy, especially since he was saddled with numerous handicaps in the area of talent. But this night as every night he floundered brazenly away. A family of four who had been sitting in the second row got up to leave in the middle of one of Verden's monologues. Verden must have reached his level of tolerance.

He broke off in the middle of a line and dropped his crown and sword.

"All right," he said, striding to the lip of the stage, "Let's take a vote. Who among you, who are intelligent enough to actually think for your-selves, want to see the end of this play? Raise hands. For those of you who don't know what your hands are, they are the five-flanged appendages at the end of your arms. See them? Put them in the air if you would like the play to continue. For those of you who don't, please do us a favor and leave now."

No one in the audience moved. For the first time all evening, the crowd was deathly silent.

"For those of you who may have been unclear as to what I said, let me explain in more rudimentary terms. This is not a football game. It is not the destruction derby. It is not All Star Wrestling. This is a play written by a fellow named Shakespeare, who uses words that most of you could not understand if your life depended on it. However, we are going to finish this play and will tolerate your attendance if you desire to be here. Now once again, raise your hands if you wish the play to continue."

Everyone in the audience shot their hands into the air.

"Then I request your respect and your silence until the play is over."

And Verden quietly donned his crown, picked up his sword and went on with his speech. No one left. No one took a breath until the end of the play. They may have been sitting in mortal fear, but when the play ended, we received the biggest ovation of our run.

I had no idea Verden could ridicule an audience with such eloquence. He was absolutely riveting, as he had been those first few days of rehearsal before he started clamming up and letting the words get in his way. Lou announced that Mario was flying back into town at the request of Noah Manning to work on retooling the interpretive dance sequences as soon as the rest of the shows were open. So we had more rehearsal to look forward to. But I didn't mind. For once I was actually interested in working on *Henry V*.

Angie was asleep on the floor in front of her tv when I came home. I made myself a bowl of cereal and sat down cross-legged next to her. I finished two bowls, very loudly, and even rinsed out the dishes before I made enough noise to wake her up.

"Sorry to wake you," I said.

"Did you sleep with Kathy Bishop?"

Ah, good! We were being honest again! "Absolutely," I said.

"I thought you were fixated on me."

"You and I talked this all out the other night. Besides, fixated is a strong word, Angie."

She gave a little laugh and pulled her nightgown over her knees. "Oh... it's just that my little Bobby is growing up, that's all. You could have kept it down. You guys were so loud! It sounded like you were doing it on purpose."

"I was glad I could still do it, period. It was my first time since Gina."

She yawned. "What have I been watching?"

"Hogan's Heroes."

"Isn't Kathy a bit – loose?"

"Exceedingly limber."

"So – what? Are you her boyfriend now?"

"No. As a matter of fact, I'm very pleased with myself. A few years ago I probably would have fallen head over heels for her, just because we went to bed together, you know? That whole self-worth thing. But I really didn't let it affect me emotionally. I don't feel much for her, and going to bed with her didn't change that."

"So you won't be taking her to the prom?"

"I don't have to hang out with her at all. We talked about it this morning. She wants to give the thing with Rob Banister more of a try.

And I told her my mind was all over the place and I wasn't in the market for a girlfriend."

"Aha!" Angie said with false courtroom zeal, "She just wanted an excuse to dump you because you were a bad lay!"

I just looked at her smugly.

"Just kidding," she said.

She got up and went into the kitchen. Then she leaned on the door-jamb and said: "And you're still in love with me a little bit?"

"Yes I'm still in love with you a little bit."

"Good. Because a girl's ego could really take a bruising around here." And she put the kettle on.

11

I met Bronson and Lloyd at Denny's for breakfast.

"We've met with a little problem," Bronson said.

"It might present a slight delay," said Lloyd.

"Our silent partner has decided to pull out."

"He feels the economic climate is not ripe for launching art-oriented merchandise into an already jaded mirth market."

"You guys are so full of shit," I said.

"What are you talking about?" Bronson said.

"Like I don't know who your silent partner is? Why don't you just tell me that Fred Norton won't be contributing any money because he skipped town? I mean, what's the big deal?"

"Fred Norton is a known criminal," Bronson said.

"I know that."

"You think he's been financing our business?"

"Yes!"

Bronson and Lloyd looked at each other. Bronson leaned across the table conspiratorially. He lowered his voice.

"Bob, what if we were to tell you that we have a line on a very big deal. It's so big that we can't really talk about it right now. It's the reason our silent partner has decided to retrench, to evaluate his assets and see if he can finance us independently, or if he needs a co-investor."

"Does this mean you won't be using my artwork?"

"The button business is small potatoes. Now if you want, we'll cut you in on a piece of the pie just for helping us out at this grass roots level and for being a good guy."

I put my head in my hands. The waitress dropped the tab. Bronson straightened up.

"Think about it," he said, pointing at me. He picked up the bill, looked at it. Then he turned to Lloyd. "You got any money?"

The afternoon was pretty frantic. Right after *Brigadoon* ended, the *Salesman* cast chipped in and helped strike the set. In less than 25 minutes from when we started, the *Salesman* set was up, and 15 minutes later we were on stage, trying to get through a full run with lights before curtain at 8:15. Noah Manning had lost serious rehearsal time, and he wasn't going to let us off easy. We all knew it was going to be tight fitting the rehearsal in, so we really cranked up the tempo. In an empty college auditorium that sat next to a cornfield and smelled strongly of disinfectant, *Death of a Salesman* crackled with life.

Ephrem said it was because I wasn't wearing the rug.

Here's how the big confrontation went: I had made no effort to retrieve the hairpiece from Lou's desk. All during Act One the costume lady had played detective, finally cornering Lou in the light booth during a complicated cue and badgering her into divulging its whereabouts. At act break she came striding into the dressing room, keys jangling. Ephrem cleared out immediately. Without a word she stood in the doorway, brushing the piece vigorously, too hard, like an insane nanny torturing some Pomeranian dog in an old Bette Davis slasher movie. She dropped the brush on the counter and turned the piece inside out, presenting it to me like a coat presented to an errant schoolboy, expecting me to walk right into it before playing in the snow.

"I'm not wearing it," I said.

She seemed prepared for my answer. "What does Noah Manning say about this?"

"Let's go find him and ask him."

But since we were in speedthrough mode, Lou had cut intermission in half, and her voice announced "places" over the loudspeaker.

"We'll talk to him after rehearsal. Both of us. But I'm not wearing it."

She practically threw the mop down onto its styrofoam head, knocking it over and sending both items onto the floor. "Fine," she said, and walked out.

I didn't pick it up.

After the runthrough we blocked the curtain call and ran through it a couple times. We had 11 minutes until the house opened. Lou announced that there was pizza backstage for dinner. I raced up the aisle to where Noah was sitting but the costume lady had beaten me there.

"Noah," I said, "Wearing that hairpiece is screwing everything up. It's so uncomfortable [Okay, this was an exaggeration] my performance is suffering because I can't concentrate on what I'm doing. I'd like not to wear it. Not today, not ever."

But the silence was so thick I added "If it's all right with you."

Noah Manning took off his glasses. "Were you wearing it this afternoon?" he asked.

"No I wasn't."

He nodded, then looked at the costume lady. "I didn't even notice," he said.

The costume lady looked skyward, flapped her hands helplessly on her broad thighs, like a beaver flapping its tail at a predator, and walked off.

"I guess you won't be wearing it then," Noah Manning said.

"Thanks a lot. Sorry if I caused any trouble."

He put his pencil in his clipboard. "Do you have any plans for the fall?"

Let's see. Should I tell him I was considering enrolling in janitorial school?

"No. Well... actually... no."

"Because if our season shapes up like it looks like it's going to, there might be a couple good roles for you. You've had teaching experience haven't you?"

"Yes."

"Do you think you would enjoy teaching here?"

Let's see. How should I craft my answer? Should I tell him I didn't believe in teaching acting because I didn't think swelling the ranks of the unemployed in an over saturated job market was a good idea? Should I tell him I didn't believe in sending more impressionable students into a world of disillusionment and heartbreak with targets painted on their backs? Should I tell him that I thought there were too many bad actors and not enough good ones, and even if I was another Stanislavski or Stella Adler there was no assurance that I wouldn't send more talentless morons scrambling down the beach like baby turtles, hoping to be one of the few to make it to the water's edge without being plucked from the sand and swallowed alive by sharp-billed gulls?

"Sure," I said.

"Well, stay in touch, and if your plans change let me know. I enjoy your work and think you would fit in well here."

This was Noah Manning's low-key way of asking me if I wanted a job.

"We're not certain, though, about the season yet. You understand."

"Sure. Thanks," I said. "I will. I mean I understand. Thanks."

Let me give you an idea of what this meant.

Think of my next year in YES or NO terms: Ready? Los Angeles, City of Grease, NO. My own apartment with cable tv and a coffee maker, YES. Canned beans and eggs for two weeks to make rent money, NO. Spaghetti and salad at Frederick's every night if I wanted, YES. Browsing the used record store in some whore-infested area off Sunset Boulevard, NO. The new Tom Petty album, YES. Working in a Carl's Jr. with

Lemmy, the zit-faced *Barbarella* fan, NO. Sleeping until an hour before teaching my first class at 10:00, YES. Public transit to 5th and La Brea, NO. Bike to the mall, YES. Spending holidays at Huntington Beach shoulder to shoulder with everyone else who lives east of the 405, NO. Spending holidays in a dark theatre in tech rehearsal with gorgeous, impressionable nineteen-year-old girls, YES.

I was beside myself with excitement, and my enthusiasm carried over into the performance that evening.

To blab on about how great we all were that night would sound like grandstanding. Believe it if you want, but I think we were pretty good. Maybe we weren't Lee J. Cobb and the gang, but for some theatre in the tulies, we were okay, bordering on not bad. The moments of the show were just moments, after all. They would never be retrieved, never recaptured, never recorded, never played exactly the same way in the 40 or so times we were to perform the show in the season. To speak of those moments in descriptive terms seems almost sacrilegious. At the very least it's futile to describe them. I can describe the images I was left with, like the tears streaming down Ephrem's face during the final scene, Richard raising our clasped hands together in victory during the curtain call, and the look on his face, of gratitude and abundance, and Brenda Bodwin practically breaking down as we all hugged each other backstage.

There were several seemingly important people crowding the hallway after the performance, severe-looking people that I had never seen before, all of them there to see Richard, who was cornered in his dressing room, drenched in sweat from his performance, modestly smiling and saying "thank you," unable to change his clothes in the crowd. Ephrem and I nodded and smiled at each other, watching through the open door of our quite empty dressing room.

"Look at him," Ephrem said. "He handles it all so well. So professionally."

"He deserves it," I said. "Every bit of it. He's a marvelous actor."

"And a wonderful, beautiful man. He never worries about having a job. He told me. He wasn't bragging, either."

"Always got offers to go someplace, huh?"

"How many of us can say that? Not me," Ephrem said, fastening George's insulated topcoat on the dog's shivering frame.

Ah, poor Ephrem, I thought. He wasn't asked by Noah Manning if he "had any plans for the fall." Some of us were fortunate. Some of us were, not "special," perhaps, but "singled out" to form the ranks of artists, teachers, mentors, the ranks of the employed, the validated, the purposeful. *Our* talent had been recognized. But I vowed I would keep my conversation with Noah Manning to myself. It was never good policy to flaunt one's good fortune in the face of other actors, especially good fortune that pertained to matters of employment.

I got dressed quickly. I didn't wear makeup and without the hairpiece to slow me down I was in my jeans and had my jacket on in a few minutes. I poked my head through Brenda Bodwin's door.

"Knock knock," I said. "Love you, Mom."

She was putting on some ugly purple jumpsuit.

"Bobby! You're so great, sweetie!"

"Thanks, Brenda. You too."

"You have to dance with me tonight at the party!"

There was a party, of course. There was always a party.

"Okay," I said.

And she bastardized another line from the show in response: "Attention. Attention must be paid to this woman!"

I swung back into the hallway and Richard broke off from his admirers long enough to make eye contact. "You going to the party?" he asked.

"Wouldn't miss it," I replied, too loudly, as everyone who had crowded around Richard seemed to stop talking at once to listen to my answer. As if they cared, I thought. Oh well. I didn't need them.

"See you there," Richard said.

As I turned to leave, a smart-looking man in his forties stuck out his hand. "Enjoyed your work tonight," he said. "Charles Levitt, Cincinnati Rep." He handed me his card. "Why don't you keep in touch, let me know what you're doing."

Where was Cincinnati? I thought. Wasn't it the Cheese Capital of the World or something? Wasn't it smack in the middle of some God-awful farm belt, with statues of dairy maids and Flossie the cow? All those eastern cities were the same; Pittsburgh, Detroit, Cincinnati. They all had ugly names, subzero temperatures and bad coffee.

"Thanks," I said. "Thanks for coming." And I put his card in my wallet.

I chose to walk home before heading over to the party.

I had come to enjoy my walks home from the theatre, and I always chose a route that took me by interesting houses. The houses themselves weren't interesting, just one boring 6C's-built ranch-style after another, but they qualified as being of interest if there was discernible life going on inside. At eleven o'clock, most good, hard working families were either in bed or laying it down for the day. One house always had its front drapes open, and often I would see a middle-aged woman moving around inside. Sometimes when I passed a nice house I wished I could see more of the inside. Some I wanted to live in. I wished I could be some ghost and inhabit the house, inhabit the people who lived there, know what it was like to live their lives, even for just a few seconds.

I walked briskly, and I found myself talking out loud. I wasn't just talking to myself, because I was describing details of my life and where I lived. "Down there is the Inn, that's where we hang out sometimes. You should see Rita Tasner dance on the tables. She really gets going. You'd like her, she's a kick." I was responding as the other person in my head and then verbally responding as myself.

"It's great here in the wintertime. There'll only be eight of us on the teaching staff. Noah Manning said he likes my work." And I was showing this imaginary person – the person I was having a conversation with – where I lived. "Tomorrow I've got the morning off, so I thought we could have breakfast at Connie's. Then I can show you around the theatre." And some stuff didn't make any sense. I'd change topics in mid-sentence. "Have you heard *The Wall?* There's a place here that makes pizza even better than Josephina's. And it has a salad bar." And once, when I got close to the apartment, I stopped and closed my eyes, and I imagined Santa Maria in the fall, and I smelled the fallen leaves of the ash trees, and I saw myself living in a pristine apartment with white walls, making spaghetti sauce in the kitchen. It was gray and raining out-side, and it was almost dark. The big picture window in my living room was reflecting my image, and steam was rising from the stove. I was starting a new book. I had real wooden bookshelves. And there was a woman on the couch, reading. She put down her book.

"I have to leave now, Bobby," she said.

"Was it so bad, Gina?" I asked. "Was it really so bad?"

Willie Loman had nothing on me.

AUGUST

12

"Take your pound of flesh," I said. I was aware of saying it even though I hadn't meant to.

"What?" Ripley asked.

"Nothing," I said. "Drifted off. Sorry."

We were on a bus again, Ripley and I. This time we were headed up the coast to San Luis Obispo.

"What's your favorite McCartney tune?" he asked.

"I've told you all that. There's a ton of them. He's just flat out a better songwriter than Lennon."

"How can you say that? Lennon was the catalyst! He was and will always be the soul of the Beatles. McCartney is a hack by comparison."

"Okay. What about 'Yesterday'? It's one of the greatest songs ever written."

"You can't compare that to 'You've got to hide your love away.' Same subject, less schmaltz."

And we went on like this all over again, as if the bus had triggered an auto-response in us both to discuss the Beatles. Ripley had the edge on me because he was so impassioned about the subject matter. I just wanted to use the two hour bus ride to catch up on some missed sleep.

Since Ripley had hooked up with Wanda Dare I saw him much less than I had when we started the season. But after the show Sunday night, Wanda drove off to meet her husband for a romantic tryst in Ojai, and Ripley and I had arranged to catch a bus on a Monday morning to visit a friend we both knew from grad school. I would have loved to have gone to San Louie with Angie, but it was rare to find Ripley without Wanda Dare, and it was a good time to do some big male bonding. Neither of us had to be back in town until our call for *Once in a Lifetime* on Wednesday afternoon. It was a company rule that if you went out of town overnight you had to leave phone numbers and addresses of contacts with the stage manager, tell at least five other company members where you were going, arrive back in Santa Maria hours ahead of your call (double the travel time) and check in with the admin office on arrival. Not many company members bothered going anywhere, partly because of the hassle, partly because nobody had any money. San Louie was pretty easy to get to by bus, making it NO BIG DEAL as far as our pocketbooks or the admin office was concerned, and we had two nights to crash with Paul Butler. He was an MFA director in our grad school who directed a *Macbeth* for his thesis project. Ripley played Macduff and I was Big Mac. *Macbeth* was pretty much how Ripley and I had gotten to know each other our first year in the program. Direction-less after grad school, Paul Butler drew the short stick and wound up at a non-equity (read *community theatre*) Shakespeare festival in San Louie. He said the shows stunk but he was getting laid a lot and he had a great place to live. What had he been invited to direct?

"*Macbeth*," Paul Butler had told me over the phone. "But this time it's going to be a lot better!"

I wasn't sure how to take that remark.

"And they wanted me to play Prospero in *The Tempest*."

"You? Prospero? I didn't know you could act," I said.

"I can't. But I'm the oldest person in the company."

I would put Paul Butler's age at just over 30. I told Ripley that at the first available opportunity, we had to get on a bus. This was something we couldn't miss.

Things had been only a bit calmer since we got the season open. The manhunt for Fred Norton was ongoing, and the police had had no breaks in the case since Fred's brief appearance onstage that day. Apparently he had vanished into thin air. Ephrem and Richard and Brenda Bodwin and I had all been called down to the police station and questioned separately. The police showed me some mug shots and asked me to identify the man I saw. The one I picked turned out to be Fred. Everyone else identified him too, of course. The police told us that besides the real estate fraud he was wanted for interstate transportation of stolen goods. It seems Fred had had some involvement in the robbery of a Portland area department store.

Bronson and Lloyd had been leaving me alone, but it was easy to tell they were up to something. I never saw them around during the day and they seemed to be having business meetings even when they showed up at the Inn after shows. Brenda Bodwin had a fling with Bronson. I found a prurient interest in this, and pressed her for details backstage one night before *Salesman*.

"Mom?" I said. "Have you been getting laid?"

She closed her dressing room door and gleefully told me she had run into Bronson at the store a couple times. Bronson was always buying huge bags of groceries. The second time she saw him there, she broke the ice.

"I know you're a big boy," she told him, "But can you really eat that much?"

"This is nothin'," Bronson joked. "I eat more when I have sex a lot. But things have been pretty slow this summer."

Brenda wound up giving him a ride on her Harley back to his place and staying longer than she should have. They only did it a couple times, now and then, she said, before the novelty wore off. So she thanked Bronson for the attention and roared off into the sunset.

"He's a strange one," she told me.

"How strange?" I said.

"Well, he's very secretive about some things. Very private. There's no phone service in that house. And like, his garage? I asked him if I could use his garage to do some work on my bike? He got all huffy and anxious. I mean, he and Lloyd have the only garage I know of. I offered to pay him for using it but he wouldn't have it. Said something about the landlord having stuff in there."

"So you went to bed with him so you could use his garage?"

She gave me a look that said "C'est la vie."

"Did you get a peek at it?"

"I tried. It's locked. Not a padlock, a real doorknob lock. And it looked like it used to have two windows but they've been walled over. He said he didn't have the key."

I nodded my head. "Lots of groceries, huh?"

"*Lots* of groceries."

And then the plot had thickened. It was a Wednesday, and a warm haze was lingering in the air as I walked down to the college for a matinee of *Once in a Lifetime*. It was seven minutes past call when Stage Manager Lou burst into the dressing room in a panic.

"Who owes me a favor?" She asked.

We all froze in various states of undress.

"Bob! you owe me for that hairpiece and jacket episode!"

I wished Lou hadn't brought up the hairpiece thing so I winced but quickly said "Sure. What's up?"

She signaled me into the hallway and closed the door behind us. "Bronson and Lloyd aren't here yet. It's not like either of them to be late and they don't have a phone at their house. I need you to run over there and see if you can find them. Do you have a car? Take mine. Hurry!"

She tossed me the keys as I ran towards the parking lot.

"You know where they live?" she asked.

I did. It was a dilapidated white stucco crackerbox with a weed garden in front. As I pulled up I saw the single car garage in back, facing the alley. It was fourteen minutes to showtime, so my blood was pumping pretty fast. I honked the horn, and called out their names as I ran toward their front door. I felt like Dick Tracy.

I banged on the door. Tried it. It was open. I took in the room quickly: sofa. Newspapers. TV. Velvet painting of John Wayne. Stained green shag. Open boxes. Food wrappers. Called again, louder. "Wake up!" I screamed. I was moving fast. Tried the kitchen. It was a shithole. Tried the hallway. Nothing. Bathroom. Nothing. One bedroom: mattress on floor. Dirty clothes. Poster of Farrah Fawcett. Next bedroom: cement block bookshelves. Milk crates full of junk. Mattress on floor. Nothing. Out the back door. Checked the yard: transistor radio playing "Free Bird." Towel, sunglasses on beat up chaise lounge. Playboy magazine folded open on ground. Lemonade glass, ice was melted. Sprinkler on weed bed. "Bronson?" I screamed. Heard muffled cry! Thought it came from inside the house. Ran back in. I yelled hello and waited, breathless. Nothing. Ran through house to kitchen. Looked on table: roach clip. Ashtray. Car Craft magazine. Note scrawled on yellow tab: "Bronson: Tell Lloyd I'm gone for a few days. Clean garage for extra $20 -" Garage! I ran back out the door. Heard yelling from garage. Knocked on door. Yelling from inside. Two voices. "Bronson?" I yelled back. "Ed Marie!" is what I heard. "What?!" I yelled back. "GET THE KEY!" They yelled. "Where?" "TABLE!" Raced back into the kitchen. Grabbed key from under yellow pad. Raced back to garage. Key in Lock. Free! Bronson and Lloyd. "Let's go!" "Lock the garage! Give me the key!" Bronson locks garage. Run to car. Pile in. Doors slam. Roar off. Everybody okay. Out of breath.

I wheeled Lou's Dodge Dart around like a maniac. Bronson and Lloyd were pretty shaken up, but we hit the dressing room at 1:57, and Lou would hold the curtain for the customary five minutes anyway, so we had plenty of time. Lou came in the dressing room and when the guys told her they accidentally locked themselves in the garage she wasn't angry as much as concerned about them.

"Don't you have a way to get out from inside? Couldn't you open the garage door?"

"Been welded shut," Lloyd said.

Bronson jumped in. "It was a stupid mistake. Tell you about it after the show."

It was clear to me that Bronson didn't want to talk about their garage. But I felt entitled to some answers. In the second act, he and I found ourselves offstage together. He gave me some story about how Lloyd found a garage key the landlord had hidden and they both went in the garage for the first time. Then the door shut and locked behind them.

"But the key was on the table," I said.

"There were two. On a ring. Lloyd took one and tried the lock."

"What's with that garage? It's like a fortress." My next thought was like a tagline from a horror movie. Was it meant to keep something out? Or keep something in?

Bronson was too clever. He would never confirm or deny any of my suspicions.

I hadn't heard from Gina in about three weeks, for which I was thankful. In our last conversation she had accused me of not facing up to my responsibilities.

"What are you doing there? Sooner or later you have to dive back into your life," she said, in her Gina way.

"This IS my life," I said, giving myself points for originality. Even though I knew it was temporary, I just didn't seem to possess the energy to do all the stuff Gina thought I should be doing. Like getting my resume photo taken and sending it out to all the casting directors in L.A. She always thought of junk like that.

"Noah Manning made noises like he was going to hire me," I said.

"So you're going to spend the winter there?" she said.

"It's a livin'," I said. I lifted that line from one of my favorite scenes in *Rocky*, where Rocky gets fed up with his trainer Mick (Burgess Meredith). Old Mick gets on Rocky's ass for hanging out at the gym like a two-bit palooka, and not seizing on his own talent to rise above the riffraff. And Rocky's been working for some sleazebag gangster as, in

Mick's vernacular, a "leg-breaker." Rocky has to defend himself.

"It's a livin'," he says.

And Mickey rips back: "It's a waste'a life."

But there I was, playwriting again. It's *never* that moving, that logical, in actual conversation. I said "It's a livin'" to Gina and she says "What are you doing about US?" Like I'm supposed to be doing something? Jesus! Like that reply even made sense? Was I supposed to be "doing something" about our divorce or our marriage? What about you, Gina? What are you doing about US? I hung up on her. True, I hadn't actually filed papers like I threatened to, months back, but there was some confusion about which state to file in and all like that. And no, I hadn't worn my wedding ring since the night I dropped it in Lou's Chock-Full-o'-Nuts can. I was working on my suntan, and that ring had left this unbecoming white streak around my finger. I had too much to do during the day to "work on my marriage."

Days in August went like this: I got up around 11:00. This is not too decadent when you think about it. I did work at night, after all. Breakfast was simple and I'd make it at home, usually a bowl of cereal that I'd eat on the front stairs in my bare feet. Even though the weather was idyllic most days I rarely wore short pants. I was a jeans type, and felt like I was walking around in my pajamas if I wore anything else. Sweat pants, never. Any guy that wore sweat pants in the summertime probably had a small penis and was trying to hide it. I rotated between four t-shirts: Three that I had brought along with me and a Lynyrd Skynyrd shirt I got for free at a local record store promotion, which I was very proud of.

Most days Angie and I would put on our backpacks and wander over to the Allan Hancock campus to take advantage of the facilities. I frequented the piano lab in their music department, and the swimming pool. Angie went to the library because her MA candidacy required that she complete her thesis on Goldoni and some detailed aspect of the Comedia del Arte. She had opted for the more study-intensive MA degree over the performance-heavy but sweat-free MFA like Ripley and I had. She was now regretting her choice.

Sometimes Angie and I would hook up with Ronni and head over to the mall to see a matinee at the movie theatre. If Angie wasn't available I'd often go play guitar with Hanover. He had an extra guitar he let me use, a Fender Mustang that I plugged into the second input on his amp. He had been able to bring a lot of stuff with him because he owned what I called a Child Molester Van, one of those white bricks on wheels with no windows in the back. A lot of guys cherried them out and carpeted them, put a bed in them, put huge walnut-cabineted speakers in them. Not Hanover. He just used it to carry his stuff, which I was grateful he had hauled with him to Santa Maria. We liked to write heavy metal songs and improvise. We called ourselves The Turds. If The Turds weren't re-hearsing I'd go to the record store and look through the record bins for hours. I liked to study the cover art and memorize the song order and producers' names for groups I liked. I never bought anything, but if you wanted to know the song order and length for Ian Hunter's *You're Never Alone With a Schizophrenic,* I could tell you.

There's something about the theatre that keeps you on edge. On any day that you have to perform there's a mild tension that permeates the day. You're never completely at rest, more than likely because, however experienced you are or however much some cynic like me tends to downplay it, appearing before a large audience of people on any given night is a stressful endeavor. On THE DAY OF you find yourself looking at your watch a lot, and if for whatever reason (poverty perhaps) you don't wear one, you annoy a lot of people by constantly asking "What time is it?" It was a mandate in theatre that you be where you were sup-posed to be on time.

Because you were aware of the clock ticking, a day's activities in Santa Maria was usually a safe endeavor, requiring a minimum of travel and never very far away, just in case. Sometimes company members would organize day trips, mainly to the river to go tubing, or to Los Alamos to go wine tasting or antique shopping. I would usually pass on the more fruity excursions unless Angie was going, and only then if she was going without Willie, which was most of the time. Even though Willie's schedule had slowed down, he still never seemed to be around very much. He had been interviewing in L.A., and Angie said he might take a job at Universal Studios as a scenic carpenter.

Of course, after the shows at night, we didn't have to watch the clock anymore. And that's when everything happened. There was the Inn. There were the parties. There were the recently discovered hot tubs near Los Alamos. Lou had brought news of the hot tubs back with her after she had been treated to a "Spa Day" by Noah Manning as a thank-you present for all her hard work. The tubs had quickly become notorious. They were natural hot springs run by hippies, and bathing suits were optional, meaning nobody wore them. It was basically a large outdoor sex pavilion frequented by exhibitionists and thrill seekers. Groups from the theatre had gone there after shows, gotten naked together and all piled into the largest tub, chattering drunkenly while doing Lord-knows-what to each other beneath the black water. I had never been there, but Angie and Willie had gone with a group the first week they arrived. They didn't go back. I had been curious about the tubs, and when Kathy Bishop and I became lovers I suggested that we give them a whirl. But neither of us had a car, and she saw the tubs as too obvious a place to have sex anyway, and said she wasn't interested.

Kathy and I were having sex about once a week, though technically she was still going with Rob Banister. Not that it was a major item of conversation, but all the women in the company knew that Kathy and I were doing it and none of the guys had a clue. Conversely, all the guys thought Angie and I were lovers, a rumor which I did not work hard at dispelling. The women knew the truth. Angie and I shared a deep friendship, observed the rules and closed our separate doors at night.

Kathy and I would vary our itinerary: Sometimes we'd hook up after a show but she really loved to do it outside, usually in the middle of the day. One Tuesday we went to a deserted Guadalupe beach to have a "picnic" and made it on her towel in the sand. Another morning she called me and woke me up and asked me to come over to her place. Rob's mother was visiting (from Riverdale, I guess. Lived next to Betty and Veronica) and they had gone to Santa Barbara or some nonsense. So I wolfed down a banana and hoofed it over there. It was a long walk. It was almost noon by the time I got there and I was burnt to a crisp. I had to take off my shirt and wrap it around my head so I looked like Lawrence of Arabia when I turned into her long dirt driveway. She was sitting on her tilted little porch in a sundress, and I could tell by the way it hung on her that she had nothing on underneath. She watched me approach, looking at me through lidded eyes. As I got closer she stood up, peeled off the dress and stepped off the porch into the sun. She stood in front of me naked, the noontime sun accentuating her body with deep shadows, making her breasts appear as if they were floating out in front of her. She stepped up to me and led me over to the "picnic" towel she had spread out on a little patch of mowed, dry grass. Tall cornstalks surrounded us and rustled in the warm breeze. I could hear trucks far away on the main road. Sun baked our bodies and made us slick with sweat. We didn't really talk very much, before or after.

"I see paint," I said.

I was suddenly aware of the silence and looked at Ripley. His brow was furrowed.

"What did you say?" he said.

"I don't know. What did I say?"

"You said 'I see paint.'"

"I must have been dreaming again."

"You've been staying up too late."

I didn't tell Ripley that in my dream I was painting the walls of an empty apartment with white paint. Somehow, Rocky Balboa was there and was eating Cheerios on the floor.

The San Louie bus depot looked like a California mission with lots of potted palms and Pac Man machines that I know didn't exist when father Junipero Serra was walking around in brown robes. Paul Butler was supposed to meet us in the boarding area that smelled like ammonia and diesel. There was no sign of him.

"Maybe he got held up," I said. "You got his number?"

"No. Do you?"

"No. I thought You'd bring it."

"He was supposed to meet us in the lobby," Ripley said.

"I know."

"So where is he?"

This was the sort of thing that freaked Ripley out. Things not going as planned, stuff like that. He got that little creak in his voice that told me he was agitated.

"Maybe something came up," I said.

"What a fucking bastard. I knew this was a bad idea. I never liked him anyway. He was always stuck up. You remember that play he wrote? What a bunch of self-centered garbage."

I liked Ripley better when he was smooching up Wanda Dare. She calmed him down.

"Let's just wait here," I said. "You want a hamburger?"

"No. Can you call Angie and get the number?"

It was a nice day. In good time, I thought. I was having fun watching Ripley squirm a bit. "He'll show up. Besides, she's at the library."

We eventually wandered outside and halfway down the street, keeping our eye on the parking lot and the front entrance of the bus station. It was another nice day. Ripley parked on a city bench, smoked and kept watch while I checked out some comics in the drug store, especially a new *Swamp Thing* I had been waiting to see. We had been in town an hour already. I didn't want to carry the *Swamp Thing* with me, but I bought an Abba Zabba bar, pulled it apart and gave half of it to Ripley.

"Straighten up, boy. You're slumping," I said.

"We might as well go home."

"I've never been here. Looks like a great town. All this brick and stuff. Look at that old movie theatre. This place is a lot cooler than Santa Maria."

I was about to say that maybe I should live in San Louie in the fall and commute, but I kept quiet. I hadn't told anyone except Gina about my little talk with Noah Manning. Ripley ground out his cigarette on the sidewalk. He was chewing the taffy and peanut butter loudly, with a horrible smacking of his lips. He had a tendency to smack his lips, even when he was humming some song. He used lip smacks as percussion. He would smack his lips the way somebody might tap their foot. Even with the Abba Zabba in his mouth he started to hum and smack his way through the bass riff of "Watching the Detectives." Then he said:

"We should have gone to L.A. (smack) Could have stayed with (smack) Margaret Boscovitz (smack)."

"Peg Bosco," I said.

"What?"

"Peg Bosco. She changed her name. You knew that."

"No I didn't. Peg Bosco? (smack) What a phony. Are you kidding? (smack) That's no better than her real name. She should have thought of something more glamorous than that (smack)."

"*Cher* was already taken," I said.

Finally he made an effort to swallow. "I don't think she had much talent."

"Gina says she's working in a restaurant."

"We could have stayed with her in L.A. though. She's a fox." He went back to humming Elvis Costello. Hum hum hum smack. Hum hum hum hum hum hum smack.

"I'll try to call Angie," I said. I walked down to the pay phone at the other end of the block. Willie was in L.A. and I was betting that Angie had not yet left for the library. I was right. She was still at the apartment.

"The guy stood us up," I said. "Why don't you take the day off and come up here to San Louie? This is a great town."

"Some guy called for you. Paul? He said he couldn't leave the line in the unemployment office and that you guys should walk over to his place. He gave me the address."

"Okay. But why don't you come up? They've got those hot springs up here. Maybe we could get a group together."

"Great. Me in a hot tub with three guys. Aren't you with Ripley?" She didn't like Ripley all that much.

"He can crash at Paul Butler's. You and I can see a movie or something or have dinner and drive back in the middle of the night if we want to. Bring your d-o-p-e."

She was a pushover. She said she'd leave in a few minutes.

13

Ripley and I walked over to the address Angie had given me. Paul Butler had an apartment in one of those cool brick buildings above a pizza place and a copy joint. We ate some pizza slices at an outside table and Paul Butler showed up around 2:30. He was a tall, generally loutish guy who wore Hawaiian shirts when it was inappropriate and should have exercised a bit more often in his lifetime. He was closer, friend-wise, to Ripley than to me, primarily because I had never really forgiven him for botching our *Macbeth*. I'm sure that if Ripley and I had not been stationed close in proximity to him neither of us would have seen nor heard from him again. He was wearing khaki shorts and a loud green silk shirt.

Geez, sorry I'm late, blah blah blah. Only day I had to file for unemployment and blah blah blah. He led us upstairs and opened the door to his place, number three. I was jealous immediately. It was a one room studio, with a nook for a kitchen, a bathroom and a closet. The place had atmosphere; wood floors, an exposed brick wall, a wrought iron balcony that faced the street. He even had one of those potted trees that look so good with brick walls and wood floors a ficus something-or-other, but it had lost most of its leaves.They formed a brown pile around the tree.

"Tree cost me fourteen dollars," Paul Butler said, "And it up and dies on me."

"You've got it in the fucking shade," I said. "Those things like light." Gina and I had one, and it had died too.

"Is that it? I've been watering the hell out of it, but the leaves just get brown and fall off."

"They look great in the plant store," I said.

Paul Butler had hung a Harvey Edwards dance poster in the middle of the brick wall. His bed was on the floor, unmade. His clothes were stacked against the wall. That was it.

"No wonder you've been getting laid a lot. This place is a real pad," I said. I was halfway serious. Ripley had sunk into a pizza stupor and wanted to lie down on the floor.

"Help yourself," Paul Butler said to Ripley. "You guys want something to drink?" He opened the refrigerator. There was nothing in it but a beer and a lemon. "I've got lemons. We can make margaritas."

I volunteered to go to the supermarket and bring back a six pack of those margaritas in a can. I had my hand on the doorknob when Paul Butler said "Hey, sorry about not getting word to you earlier. I've got *Macbeth* rehearsal tonight."

"Rehearsal? On a Monday?" Ripley said. Monday was the universal day off in professional theatre.

"Who said anything about this being professional theatre?" Paul Butler said.

"Jesus Christ, man," I said. "Haven't you opened that show yet?"

"Hell no. We had to wait for this out-of-town actor to become available."

"Ah! You brought in a ringer!" Ripley said.

"He's the only real pro they hired. Except me, of course. They wanted him because he had played Macbeth three times before. Turns out he had played the role in the opera *Macbeth*. He was a tenor. He didn't know a thing about Shakespeare. So we fired him and got somebody else. This guy's better. He's from out of town, too."

Ripley said "L.A. or New York?"

"Atascadero," Paul Butler said. "You guys feel free to come and go. You can come to rehearsal tonight if you want. It's a tech-dress. Might be interesting."

"Wouldn't miss it for the world," Ripley and I said, almost in unison.

Paul Butler's phone rang – a choppy, European-type ring, signaling that someone was at the street door.

"That's Angie," I said.

I raced down the stairs and out the lobby door. Angie was in cutoffs and a light blue halter top. It was good to see her.

"This is the place," I said. And before she could head upstairs I swung her around and led her down the sidewalk. "We're going to the store. You ever had those margaritas in a can?" I asked.

"Yeah. They taste like shit. Wine coolers are better."

"That's not saying much, is it?"

She rolled her eyes at me.

"Okay. We'll get wine coolers then," I said. "Hell, we could bring back bilge water and those guys wouldn't know the difference."

Angie was distant and morose.

"You okay?" I asked.

"Naw. I'm fucked up today."

"This okay for you? Being here? I thought it would be fun, get you out of the house."

"Bob! You know I've got shit to do! I'm trying to get this thesis written and it just gets deeper and deeper, you know? Like I uncover one thing and then I have to write a fucking novel just to explain myself. And Willie is gone again. I just... I can't wait to get out of this hole."

"You mean Santa Maria?"

"I mean Santa Maria and I mean this hole, this HOLE! Why do you have to be so goddamn literal all the time?"

"I'm sorry," I said.

"You're so... patronizing! You're so accommodating!" Then a second later she said "Oh jeez – I'm sorry. Just ignore me, okay? Pretend I'm not here today. I'm having an off day. And don't ask me if I'm on my period, okay? Because I'm not."

"I wasn't going to."

"Guys do that, you know. You have a bad day and they just assume it's your period. GOD I hate that! They're so stupid!"

I made a gesture as if to say "Yes, I'm a shithead."

"This marriage... this fucking Willie. Can you believe he's gone again? I'm happy one day and then the next I just can't stand myself."

"You mean... you can't stand to be alone?"

"I mean I'm sick of myself. It's always 'be a grownup. Learn to be self sufficient. Don't be lonely. Stand up for yourself.' It's like a tape in my head I can't turn off."

Whatever trip Angie was on, it was making me uncomfortable. I didn't say anything. I just let her talk. And after awhile she started thanking me for being there for her, for listening to her. But it seemed almost forced. I had listened to her much more intently at other times and my attentiveness went unappreciated. Fortunately our errand allowed lots of interruptions; finding the store, scoping out the booze, paying for it. By the time we walked back I was able to successfully change the subject to the studied gracelessness of Ripley and Paul Butler, and was even able to get Angie to crack a legitimate smile. "Paul Butler thinks God wears a Hawaiian shirt," I said.

We ducked into Angie's VW to fire one up before heading upstairs. Angie took a huge puff and went off on another rag about some other aspect of her failed life. Finally I felt like I had to do something.

"Angie, you remember that exercise in acting school?"

"Which one?"

"The blindfold test. You know, where you're blindfolded, and you make yourself stiff and fall backward, and people catch you and pass you around the circle?"

"What about it?"

"It won't work if you're uptight and scared."

"How do you know how I am?"

"I don't. But... I know you need to get out of your head for awhile. I mean, I do it all the time, get caught up in my head too much."

"That's why I smoke dope, Bob."

"But this is better. If things are so important, you just make them less important."

"How do I do that?"

"You know how, when you're acting, if you think of things too hard you get this huge mental block? And you know if you can just relax, it's so much easier. The lines come out different, more true, because you're more receptive to what other actors are saying. You can't listen if you've got all this shit in your head all the time. In fact, it's the only legitimate way to truly respond to stress. You have to make things not mean so much."

"Not mean so much? That's ridiculous. If nothing has any importance in your life then what is there to keep you going? Why not just say 'fuck it' and kill yourself?"

"Because none of our problems mean anything in the big picture."

She looked at me for several seconds. "This is not helping. I don't want to get into some debate about libations and what's not important. That is far too woo-woo."

I was getting nowhere, so I tried another approach. "Then you should get a dog," I said.

That did it. I could tell. Angie rolled her eyes and looked at me incredulously. "Great, Bob. Who's going to take care of it? In four and a half weeks Willie and I load up and head for Who-The-Fuck-Knows-Where and you think I should get a *dog?* What planet are you on?"

"I'm just trying to help," I said.

I expected her to turn away, but she looked deeply into me and her eyes filled with tears. I held her to me and let her cry. It was hot in the car and Angie smelled like dope. I felt her tears hit the back of my neck. "I would like a dog," she sobbed. "I really would."

"And a nice big house where it could play, with a big rolling, green lawn."

"And a spreading chestnut tree." She gasped, a laugh, and held me tighter.

"What would you call it?"

"Stan," she said.

"What if it was a girl?"

"It would have lots of little Stan puppies." She laughed. I did too.

She stayed clasped to me for a long time, and we rocked gently, holding each other. When she pulled back, I wiped the tears from her cheeks. We stayed, forehead to forehead, her arms around my shoulders, until I had to move.

"My leg is falling asleep," I said.

"Sorry." She jerked back abruptly.

"No, no. It's fine. You all right?"

"I'm good. Sorry."

"Angie! Come on. You okay? I've just got to get out of the car."

"Yeah. Time to go. They'll think we drank this shit ourselves." She had grabbed the wine coolers and was out of the car and up the steps ahead of me. I reached out to grab her and she took my hand, leading me up the steps.

14

Whenever the three of us, Paul Butler, Ripley and I, had gotten together in the past at parties and stuff, we had to dredge up our brilliant production of *Macbeth*. Unfortunately, that Monday was no exception. I was worried that Angie would get bored immediately, but she seemed interested. "Hey! I played Lady Macbeth in college," she said.

"Far out," Paul Butler said.

"Could Angie have matched the standard set by Deena Hamill?" Ripley said.

"Who's Deena Hamill?" Angie said.

Paul Butler struck a familiar Deena Hamill hamlike pose, his eyes wide, his hands flapping and his feet stamping. Ripley and I cracked up. "Deena Hamill was what was wrong with my show," he said.

"ONE of the things," Ripley said under his breath.

Paul Butler heard but went on anyway. "Fucking Al Robarts didn't recommend me for graduation because of her. He said her bad acting was my fault. Like I didn't try!"

"Deena Hamill was someone who acted AT stuff instead of just acting," I explained to Angie. She knew what I meant.

"First of all, she was too old for the part," Paul Butler said. "She was married and lived in the community. It was fucking Robarts who let her into the program! And then he blames me because she sucks so bad?"

"Robarts can eat me," Ripley said on an exhale through a cloud of cigarette smoke.

"*This* guy did some amazing work," Paul Butler said, waving in my direction. Then he looked at me. "I tried to cut her out of every scene I could for you, guy. I really did."

"Thanks," I said. Unfortunately, his cuts weren't enough to save my ass.

"I knew I had to do it when she wanted to hike her skirt up during the 'unsex me here' speech."

"Oh no," Angie groaned.

"No, really!" Paul Butler said. "Remember that, you guys? She was the biggest exhibitionist I've ever seen."

"But that speech isn't about sex at all," Angie said. "It's misinterpreted by stupid actresses like it's some sort of masturbation ritual or something."

"Right on," Paul Butler said.

"What she's really asking for in the speech is for her sex to be ignored. She wants all of her womanly virtues to go away so she can summon the courage to help her husband kill the king."

"You've got the part," Paul Butler said.

"Wish you could have been in our show," Ripley said.

"What did she do during the mad scene?" Angie asked.

Paul Butler looked at me, then burst out laughing.

"He cut it!" I said.

"You cut it? Oh my God," Angie said. "You cut the Lady Macbeth mad scene?"

"Two nights before opening!" Ripley said.

"Oh my GOD!"

All I could do was look up at the ceiling.

"She sucked so bad, I just had her wander through the castle holding a candle so no one could see her face," Paul Butler said.

"No 'out damned spot'?" Angie said.

"All I let her say was... what was it, Bob? Something about Duncan's blood..."

"'Yet who would have thought the old man had so much blood in him.'" It was Angie who answered.

"Right on!" Paul Butler said. "You still know it?"

She ignored the question. "Did that work?"

"No," Ripley said.

I told Paul Butler to tell Angie about the technical fiasco that ensued during dress rehearsal, but he said "You want to see a technical fiasco? Come with me. It's time to go."

Angie, her interest peaked, was the first one to the door.

The four of us walked down one of San Louie's spacious sidewalks to the middle of town, where the SLO Shakespeare Festival was in residence. It was a beautiful evening, still hot, and I could smell Angie's familiar perfume, some musk cream she bought at the Renaissance Fair, fresh from the small ceramic pot she kept on her dresser. It blended well with the smell of weed which hung around Angie, and gave her an exotic, Eastern European scent. I felt good, glad to be free of clock watching for two whole days. Paul Butler, however, was very much on the hook, and he walked much faster than the three of us. He disappeared into the theatre while Angie and I waited for Ripley to finish talking to an old guy in a sailor hat and bermuda shorts.

"You want a cigarette?" Ripley was saying, and the old guy took three or four from Ripley's pack.

"You didn't tell me you played Macbeth," Angie said to me over her shoulder.

"What difference does it make? It was a couple years ago. It's just air."

"Is that what you think? That it's all just air?"

"That's what it is."

She looked at me. "You remember that great speech? What Macbeth says at the end of the play. After Lady Macbeth dies?"

It came back to me without warning.

"Out, out, brief candle,

Life's but a walking shadow, a poor player

That struts and frets his hour upon the stage

And then is heard no more. It is a tale

Told by an idiot, full of sound and fury

Signifying nothing."

"Very nice. You believe it?"

"What do you mean?"

"About life. Is it that empty, do you think?"

It was a multileveled question, worth a better answer. "No," I said.

"You know why that passage is so famous?"

"Why?"

"Because it's everybody's worst fear, you know? The fear that there's nothing out there. No puffy cloud where all your loved ones sit, waiting for you to join them."

True, but our perspectives could not be compared. Macbeth was a murderer in a freezing castle in the 10th century. He had run out of spiritual options. I was talking to a winsome blonde from Kansas City on a sunny street in August. Our society had progressed quite a ways past broadswords and gruel.

"What do *you* believe?" I said.

She shifted her weight impatiently. "That's so like you. Answering my question with a question. I'm atheist, by the way. I thought you knew that."

"We never discussed it."

"That's why I'm asking you. Most people are too afraid to say they don't believe in God, because they think there's always some chance the Bible could be right and they'll burn in Hell. And saying 'I'm agnostic' is such a fucking cop out. You either believe in a deity or you don't."

So then Angie and I had this impromptu CliffsNotes discussion about faith right there on Broad Street in San Louie. I wound up telling her that I believed in the soul, and the perpetuation of the soul after death, i.e. reincarnation, but not in the existence of heaven or hell, and therefore not in God per se. And because of this spiritual bent I could not completely call myself atheist, though I could not necessarily apply a label to my belief system. She somewhat accepted this, though she questioned to what degree I was being sincere, and accused me of being noncommittal, even though I did the best I could to articulate my beliefs.

And Angie was standing so close to me while we were having this conversation that I couldn't help but ask "Why are you wearing that musky stuff?"

"Do you like it?"

She moved closer to me, belligerently pressing herself against me. She was really starting to annoy me.

"Cut it out," I said.

Finally the old dude in the sailor hat sauntered away, and Ripley walked toward us, counting the rest of his cigarettes.

"Guy is a thief," he said.

Angie looked away from me pointedly. "Give me one of those, will you Ripley? Noncommittal Bob doesn't like the scent I'm wearing."

This pissed me off. "That's not fair," I said. "I was honest with you. You may not agree with me, but don't insult me."

Ripley looked like someone had eaten all his cookies as Angie fished in his pack. Then he looked at me, wondering what the hell "Noncommittal Bob" was all about. My look back told him I couldn't figure Angie out, and I turned and walked toward the theatre to get away from her. Ripley lit her cigarette.

Paul Butler was having a heated conversation in the doorway with a short, balding fellow who was animatedly illustrating something with his hands. Paul Butler was doing his best to console him. Finally the short guy turned and stalked off. I grabbed the door from Paul Butler as he scowled at the floor and walked inside.

"That your stage manager?" I asked.

"No," Paul Butler said. "That's my Macbeth."

Paul Butler was one of these guys who had read too much science fiction when he was a kid. I knew the type well, because I was one my-self. A skinny, freckled geek in coke bottle glasses, kneeling on the floor, elbows on the plaid bedspread, trying to finish Arthur C. Clarke's *Childhood's End* before bedtime, racing through Ray Bradbury's *Something Wicked This Way Comes* only to turn around and start reading it again. Then, when puberty landed on us like a whale in a backyard swimming pool, we started lurking at the newsstand, sneaking peeks at the covers of *Creepy* and *Eerie* magazines, with images of near naked barbarian princesses, dark-haired and exotic, and grotesquely muscled warriors painted in an old masterly style by a clever illustrator named Frank Frazetta. Then it was Conan the Barbarian that kept us awake at night, with the imagery of Frazetta's covers occupying our daydreams and fantasies. I had jacked off more than once to that silky Cimmerian princess with the snake slithering up her leg. I had imagined myself swinging that broadaxe at the snow giants, riding that bucking, armored horse amid hordes of shadowy demons. It was powerful stuff, perfect pornography for us socially inept, pimple-faced punks. So no wonder Paul Butler held on to those images well into adulthood. No wonder he stood up in his graduate thesis meeting and announced to his advisory board "I want to direct *Macbeth*, the definitive production, the way it should be done," and then reveal, to the horror and disdain of the assembled faculty hardasses, the Frazetta painting of Conan chained to the floor with a monstrous serpent rising up from between his spread legs. "Here is the way Macbeth should look," Paul Butler said confidently, "Stripped of all aspects of civilization, naked, fighting his dark impulses in a murky world of witches, murder and lawlessness."

It was 1978. We were in the liberal arts. Al Robarts, the faculty spokesman, told Paul Butler he could do it. "But you better be prepared to defend your concept with Shakespeare's text," Robarts said, "Or you're setting yourself up to fail. And I'll be the first to let you know it doesn't work."

Smugly, Paul Butler went ahead with his production. I was cast, apparently possessing the right kingly manner and build for the enthusiastic director's image of Macbeth. And Ripley had the innocence and smoldering ferocity needed to embody Macduff, the warrior hero. We sat around Paul Butler's apartment for our first reading of the play. Ripley and I were skeptical of Deena Hamill from the start, but there she was, making small talk and sipping Diet Coke. Paul Butler burned incense and talked animatedly the whole evening, explaining his concept, giving us his numerous text edits, playing the music he would use in the production, all sturm und drang stuff, Wagner's *Gotterdammerung,* Led Zeppelin's "When the Levee Breaks," Penderecki's *The Devils*. He raided his comic collection to show us images that he was using as inspiration for the costume designer. The world Paul Butler envisioned was a tribal world. All references to Scotland were expunged from Shakespeare's text. It was a timeless story, he said, and it was to be born out of a maelstrom of blood and sorcery, myth and legend. The cast was to be dressed head to toe in red robes, like inhuman members of some bloody witches' cult assembled on the heath, and dance around a black cauldron. Macbeth was to be born out of the incantations of the robed figures, and rise up out of the cauldron. All the characters, when they made their first appearance in the play, were to be "invested" ceremoniously by the ensemble. That is, they were to shed their anonymous robes and be announced as the character they were to portray. All were to be naked except for loincloths and leather trappings, wristbands and such, intended to make us all look like Conan the Barbarian. Ripley and I agreed that Paul Butler must have cast Deena Hamill for her body. We couldn't wait to see what she looked like in a leather bikini and gilded breastplates.

We all agreed it looked great on paper.

The reviewer in the *Sacramento Bee* couldn't get over the naked flesh. "An off-putting device," the review read, "Horribly distracting. Director Paul Butler obviously didn't trust the timelessness of Shakespeare's words to do his work for him... Butler's comic book imagery cheapens the complex moral dilemma of the characters..."

Some undergraduate told me later he thought we looked like we were at some bizarre S&M party. Sure, Conan could get away with wearing practically nothing. But in actuality the loincloths, when worn in context with our modern haircuts, wound up making us look like a strange cross between Fred Flintstone and the Marquis de Sade.

The reviewer went on: "Hampered as they are by lack of clothing, the cast of attractive actors does its best to make sense of Shakespeare's text." That was all she said about the acting.

But Paul Butler was undaunted. Despite the rousing chorus of "We Told You So" delivered by the faculty advisors with Al Robarts as the featured soloist, Paul Butler stood up and defended his production. He lauded the actors, Ripley and me in particular, and lambasted the Sac State technical support crews, who, he said, were unable to create his vision. "My mistake was that I overestimated the competency of the tech support. My vision was much more grand than the $300 budget I had for sets and costumes!" Al Robarts said it was indeed Paul Butler's fault for attempting so grandiose a concept on a $300 budget, and recommended that Paul Butler spend another year at State, a recommendation that the faculty upheld.

He spent the year below the radar, surfacing only to audit directing seminars and mount a better-received production of *Krapp's Last Tape* in the spring. He told me at *Krapp's* opening: "You know, I really believe my concept for *Macbeth* can work. I've been spending a lot of time writing different theatres, selling them on the idea. I need a theatre with money to spend. I need a theatre that's willing to take the same risk I am."

So there he was in San Louie, and there were Ripley and Angie and I sitting in the 188 seat house watching Paul Butler fit a cardboard crown on a short, bald guy with no shirt on. Yep, Paul Butler was at it again, and I feared for his very soul.

I whispered to Angie. "I can't watch this," I said.

"Don't be such a wimp," Angie said.

"The throne looks like a toilet," whispered Ripley.

This was a huge problem. The central scenic device resembled an oversize commode that gave birth to Macbeth, doubled as a cauldron for the witches, and generally thwarted every attempt the actors made at being taken seriously.

"Goes to show," Ripley said, "You can't shine a piece of poop."

The actors spoke surprisingly well. Still, it didn't matter. As each character was "invested," and revealed in their near-nakedness, I couldn't help sizing up their bodies: Macbeth was too short, Banquo was too skinny, this guy had love handles, this guy's chest was too hairy. It was, as the reviewer had said about our production, horribly distracting. Only a short time ago, that was me up there.

What was *with* Paul Butler, I thought. What was he thinking? Why did he hold onto this ridiculous device despite everyone's condemnation of it? I was overcome with a sense of futility. How could I believe that what I was doing in my chosen profession mattered to anybody but me? We were naive children of postwar idealists. Did we truly believe that theatre could change the world? Or were we just in it for ourselves, seeking approval from small, assembled groups of parental substitutes? What hope did we really have of making a difference? How noble was it to strut around onstage in a loincloth? All our training, our personal discoveries, the joy of finding a mode of expression for our anger and our passion was of consequence to no one. How did our indulgence fix any of our social ills? How did this folly strike a blow against worldly injustice? How many of us were actually performing in prisons like we vowed we would, bringing our message of understanding to the disenfranchised, the lost and the forgotten? If this *Macbeth* had been performed within three miles of a prison, it would have only incited a massive gang rape. It was all about *me*, wasn't it? Who will see *me*? Who will love *me*? Who will recognize *my* talent and give *me* praise?

I remembered voicing the same doubts in a conversation with Ripley two years prior. We were in the gym, working out to prepare for Paul Butler's *Macbeth*. "Yeah. I suppose it's a self-serving occupation," he said, between sets. "But where else can you have this much fun? I just want to do this as long as I possibly can. Who wouldn't?"

The obscene black toilet mocked the proceedings on stage.

"I've got to get out of here," I whispered.

I felt like I was going to throw up. I stood up abruptly and made a move to exit.

"You okay?" Ripley said. I stumbled over his feet, mumbling something about getting some air as I found my way toward the aisle. Angie watched me go.

The street was in full dusk and lights were beginning to make an impact as I broke outside through the lobby doors. It was cooling down; San Louie obviously benefitted from the same sea breezes as Santa Maria. I bent over, my hands on my knees, trying to stop the ringing in my ears. The sidewalk went blurry, sight and sound melded into a constant hum. I was aware that I sat down, harder than I wanted to, and as the hum and blur subsided I was aware of two hands around my shoulders, and a familiar, welcome scent of sweet lavender musk and weed.

"Bob? You okay?"

Angie had said more but I had been unable to make it out. That much I could hear, and I replied. "Yes," I said. very loudly.

"I don't believe you. Can you hear me?"

"Yes, I can hear you. Just catch my breath. I'm all right."

I was aware of people's feet as they walked by, too close.

"Just stay put for a second, okay?"

The ringing and humming had stopped. I was in the middle of the sidewalk.

"Jesus!" I felt vulnerable immediately and made a move to stand. Angie caught me and helped me to my feet.

"Holy shit, Bob. You're dead weight."

Those were the kindest words I had ever heard. Angie helped me to the curb, where, without warning, I vomited up everything I had eaten for an entire week. She stood clear while I spewed brackish slime into the gutter, painting the dividing line between asphalt and concrete. I could sense some pedestrians in back of me as they hesitated and mumbled their concern. "Sorry," I said, to no one in particular. The convulsions subsided. I felt Angie's hand encircle my brow.

"Sorry," I said.

"Never be sorry," she said. "Sorry is a terrible thing to be."

I was staring between my knees at the unrecognizable remnants of a sausage pizza.

"Bad food?" Angie asked.

I knew it wasn't the food that had made me sick.

15

Angie put her arms around me and walked me to a nearby restaurant/ pub, one of those slick, corporate-owned affairs with waiters that introduce themselves by name. Our waiter introduced himself as Ray. He led us to a seat on the patio. Angie had a salad and I had soda water. I looked at Angie and remembered that sometime during Paul Butler's rehearsal, she had gone back to the bug to change into her evening clothes. She now wore her familiar jeans and white blouse. I was still a bit weak, but was feeling better by the minute. Talking seemed like the best remedy. I went on vomiting words, spewing out bile about how ridiculous it was to put one's trust in people like Paul Butler and the wicked Darkly Effeminate Mario, and went on a tirade about how actors have no control.

Maybe she was reacting to my distress, but Angie took charge. She seemed to have recovered completely from her bitterness earlier in the day. She was very soothing and calm, and had at least a passable answer for all my rhetorical questions.

"It's all too weird, Angie. You know how we're trained as actors: Trust. Be vulnerable. Is there any worse training to prepare somebody for getting along in life? 'I'll just trust that a job will be there for me tomorrow.' 'I'll just be vulnerable and sweet to this gang on the corner so they'll respect me and won't beat me up.' I'm sick of it."

"Bob – let me say that you're a very decent actor..."

"Stop it. I'm not looking for a compliment."

"...And you handle yourself well in this world. Your training hasn't, you know, turned you into a sheep. The fact that you're aware of the pitfalls doesn't mean that you're going to fall prey to them."

"So a guy like Paul Butler comes along with this concept. We have to trust that he knows what he's doing? We have no control over the overall end result."

"It's the same with a job in any corporate environment. You have a boss, you have a job to do. We may not like it but we do it. You also have to trust that there are better directors out there than Paul Butler. There's a Noah Manning. There's a Steven Spielberg."

Either Angie was too smart for me or I was conceptually compromised in my weakened state. I didn't put up an argument. I even felt good enough to have a beer.

"Tell me about Gina," Angie said.

This, too, caught me off guard. "What's to tell?" I said. "Game over."

"No it's not. And you know it. You're still so wrapped up in her you can hardly breathe. Come on, Bob. Why don't you tell me what's *really* bothering you."

"She's this great person. You would love her, you really would. Everybody does. Me too, except it's more difficult for me because... she expects, maybe too much from me. Or I expect too much from her. So we let each other down all the time. You know how that feels?"

"Sure."

"She competes with me. Maybe it has something to do with us going through college in the same department or something. But she's... I don't know, I'm sure I was just as guilty. I'm sure I competed with her. Maybe I put her down and didn't realize it. She could never confront me directly. I mean she could tell just about anybody her most intimate thoughts. She's terrific that way, really. But when it came to me... It's like she needed to be strong and invulnerable. So she would... She just wasn't direct."

"She would lie?"

"I don't even know if she knew she was lying. I think I just expected too much from her, and she felt she couldn't live up. So she made her own rules."

She asked me again. "Did she lie to you?"

"Yes."

"Did you lie to her?"

"Yes."

"Not much of a marriage, is it?"

What the fuck do you know about it, Angie, I thought? Can you look me in the eye and tell me you've never been deceitful?

"Not that people don't lie," she said. "I do. But not to the people I value. Not to the people I love."

It was only because Angie had answered my unspoken question that I let her off the hook. Some electric mariachi band was playing "Wooly Bully" in a club across the street.

"Wanna go dancing?" she asked.

"Can't. No spinning."

"Wanna go back to the rehearsal?"

"I'd rather go home. Say I was sick. They'll understand. I'll call Paul Butler tomorrow."

Then out of the blue she said "Want to stop by the hot tubs?"

All day, I was sensing a change in the careful chemical balance Angie and I had created between us to keep our feelings for each other in check. Perhaps I should have asked for clarification, asked if she was advocating a revision to the rules. But before I found my voice she leaned toward me and asked:

"Can you handle this?"

I made it easy for her. "Sure," I said.

We loaded in the V Dub and hit the road. It was dark by then. We headed south and got off the freeway at the proper exit, but there were a lot of unfamiliar backroads to contend with and we got turned around a few times. Angie hadn't driven on her first excursion to the tubs. There was a lot of "Do I turn here?" and "Was that it?" and other confused exclamations from us both. But eventually we rolled down a long, dirt driveway and parked in a lot with five other cars in it. The smell of sulfur and burbling noises told us we were in the right place. There was a small reception cabin with a yellow porch light where we paid a long haired, skinny hippie girl for our towels and sandals. She showed us the shower cabin and told us we could change there. Our tub was number six. She indicated the path to our tub and left us alone.

Angie and I went in separate stalls to change out of our clothes. For some reason, possibly because I was still a bit wobbly from puking my guts out, possibly because Angie and I had made many efforts to dissect and dispel the sexual energy between us, I wrapped my waist in a towel without having to think of asparagus to calm a raging erection. I figured, hell, It's only Angie. It'll be like seeing my kid sister naked. It was getting chilly outside, and I decided to wear my jacket with my towel and sandals. I wadded up my pants and shirt and shoes in a ball under my arm and put my hand on the knob to leave.

Angie had already emerged from her stall, and I heard her say "Heeeyyy!" in greeting to someone she obviously recognized. "How are you guys?"

I stopped moving, straining to hear the reply.

"Hi Angie!" said a voice. It was Ephrem.

"How you doing?" said another voice. It was Richard Siebert.

Then Angie started talking. No other voices chimed greetings. That meant Ephrem and Richard were not in a larger party. They were there together.

Angie and Ephrem and Richard were exchanging familiar theatre talk, commenting on the beautifully clear evening, making idle chatter. I was waiting for Angie to say something like "Look who else is here!" by way of revealing me, Noncommittal Bob, her date, but she gave no indication she was there with anybody else. I stood in the stall, my hand on the knob, waiting, but not waiting. I was hiding. That's when I knew that things had changed with Angie and me.

Ephrem said "You here with Willie?"

"No," Angie said, without hesitation. "He's in L.A. interviewing for a job. I'm writing my thesis. This is my reward for writing today. It's so fucking boring." No mention of me. I waited. Shortly, the three voices wished each other well and said they would see each other very soon. They were all chuckling.

"Bye," Ephrem said.

"See you," Richard said.

"Bye bye," Angie said.

And then I heard three sets of sandals move away along the gravel path. Angie had walked along the path toward tub number six, continuing the charade. I waited in the stall until the skritch-skritch of the gravel subsided. Then I pushed open the cedar plank door. I stood in the path until Angie walked back. She approached me slowly and stood in front of me in her puffy blue parka and institutional white towel. Her clothes were bundled under one arm. She brushed the errant lock of blonde hair from her eye, tossing her head in her familiar way.

"You coming?" she asked.

I was aware of our breathing. She wasn't smiling. I didn't need to say anything and she didn't either. She looked at me without expression. Finally, she held out her hand.

I took it, moving my thumb slightly to caress hers. Her hand felt warm, almost hot.

She turned and led me along the path.

For the next couple of hours, Angie and I made love in hot tub number six.

16

After we had gathered our clothes and showered the moon finally decided to come out, lighting the gravel in the parking lot as we made our way back to the car. Angie felt softer than she had before. She had little or no body fat, and it was a curious feeling pressing her against me, because I had known her as wiry and quick, loaded as tight as a catspring. With my arm around her, holding her close, it seemed her whole body had relaxed. It was as if her bones had melted. I wasn't fooling myself: I knew she had a skeleton in there someplace, working organs pumping blood, producing waste. I knew Angie too well to delude my-self into thinking she was something fragile or unworldly. For instance – that young woman I had that huge crush on? She was so beautiful it was hard for me to imagine that she had anything but sweet smelling herbs stuffed inside her. I couldn't imagine her taking a dump, for instance. That's why it never would have worked. Having sex with her would have spoiled the fantasy. Angie was a real person. We had farting contests, she and I, sitting in the library together. She usually won because of her fixa-tion on cafeteria bean salad, which she said reminded her of picnics in some park she went to as a kid. I knew Angie well. Maybe not better than Willie, but if you asked Willie where she bought her new sandals (Casual Corner) or what kind of tea she had recently discovered a liking for (dar-jeeling), or even how she held a bat when she stepped up to the plate, he wouldn't have been able to tell you. If he did, I could beat him in elo-quence, hands down.

Where was Gina in all this? In this postcoital mental landscape I was painting for myself? She was right there, present in my thoughts like a cloying, sentimental song to which you can't forget the melody. Sex with Kathy Bishop hadn't conjured any memory of Gina. None at all. Sex with Kathy Bishop was as innocuous as eating a spoonful of marshmal-low fluff. Satisfied the sweet tooth. And the guilt factor was proportional: Enough to make me wince when I remembered I ate it, but it tasted great, so what the hell? What was one little bite of marshmallow fluff? Angie was the equivalent of three pizzas sitting in my gut. I couldn't forget it.

So I had this feeling that I was going to cry. I had a lump in my throat about the same in intensity as in the days after Gina left. I didn't let Angie know, though I'm sure she was feeling about as raw as I was. She had cried when we were making love. She made her face wet with hot tub water to hide it from me, but I could tell. I wanted to cry with her, but my lust for her was overwhelming. Now, though I felt I should be seeing nothing but pink daisies and rainbows in front of my eyes, I saw the dark trees, smelled the sulfur, felt the hard gravel beneath my feet.

We didn't say a word until we were almost home, and then we only talked pleasantries. Let's cut this out, I thought. Let's get our relationship back. The house was going to feel different, too. At least we had the rest of the night to set things straight. At least we could talk about it over cups of tea, stay up until dawn and comfort each other, try to figure out our feelings for each other and how they were going to affect our lives.

It was about midnight when she turned into the alley that ran behind our apartment. She pulled the bug into her parking stall and we walked, single file, up the steps to the front door.

"Guess I left the light on," Angie said as she tried her key. But the door pulled open in front of her.

"Hey Ange. Hey Bob." It was Willie. I could feel Angie freeze. I would have bolted, but it was too late to head back down the steps and get out of there.

"Hey baby," Angie said. "I didn't expect you home tonight. Great! How'd it go?"

"Aw, just terrific," Willie said. "Randy and I were just so *up* from the whole interview we couldn't settle down. So we drove back home tonight. Save a hotel bill. I can't wait to tell you about it."

"Sure! Sure. How exciting. We were just over at the Inn. Let me put my stuff down." She kissed Willie and went into the bedroom with her coat and handbag and shot me a look of absolute horror over her shoulder.

"How you doing, Bob?" Willie and I stood, hands in our pockets, in the middle of our living room. I still had my jacket on, and realized it would look better if I took it off as I normally did when I came in.

"Good," I said, as calmly as I could. "Glad it went well for you down there."

Willie was tall and slender. He was about four inches taller than I was, which gave him an unspoken edge over me in conversational situations. It had always been slightly intimidating to talk to Willie because I had to look up at him. At that moment, his presence was indomitable, and it seemed like he had swelled to fill the room. Where before I had seen him as clueless, it suddenly seemed he possessed an inscrutable clarity that could look right through me and dissect my soul.

"Oh man, it was so perfect. It was like the job description was written for Randy and me. The guy did everything but roll out the red carpet for us."

"So... great. So... did you get the job, or...?"

"Aw, it's so perfect. I just gotta wait for – hey Ange? Come on out! I gotta tell you what happened!"

Angie fluffed her hair as she rounded the hall corner and went into the kitchen. She did it to hide her face. "Go ahead. I'm just going to put on some tea."

For the next half hour Willie told us how he and Randy fared at the job interview. I heard none of it. I could only search for opportunities to read Angie's eyes. Mostly they told me how sorry she was, how helpless she felt, and how much she wished it was just the two of us there. I tried to generate enthusiasm for what Willie was saying, hoping that I wasn't overreacting. I stayed in the kitchen only long enough to be polite and made moves to exit as soon as I felt it wouldn't appear unusual. I put my cup in the sink and raised my hand to signal I was going to bed, looking right at Angie.

"Hey, can I get that address from you?" Angie said.

I hesitated an instant. "Sure. My book's in the glovebox. You want me to get it?"

"Let me pop down there with you. Hold on, baby. I'll be right back." Angie got up and beat me to the door. "Put the water on again, okay?"

We ran down to Angie's car. She turned to me, and even in the darkness I could see her face was hard and impenetrable. "I don't know what I'm going to tell him. What do you think I should do?"

"Tell him how you feel."

"Don't do this to me, Bob. Don't give me one of your sitting-on-the-fence answers."

"How is that a sitting-on-the-fence answer? I can't be any more direct than that."

"I've got a husband up there that I love, and he and I have problems, and my idea of solving it is going to the hot tubs with you and fucking my brains out. You've got a wife, too. And even if you don't love each other anymore you've at least got a life in front of you. Do you see me in that life? Do you love me now, more than a little bit?"

"Yes, Angie. I love you now, more than a little bit." I let a beat go by. "Did we do it just so you could confess to Willie and make him pay more attention to you?"

She had been rigid, and she deflated and collapsed against the side of the bug. "I don't know. I don't know if I did it to get attention. It's all fucked up."

"I'm asking whether you were using me or not."

"How dare you ask me that! I am not using you. Bob." She grabbed me by the shoulders. "I feel closer to you than I've ever felt to anyone. What do you think I should do?"

And then I said it. "I don't think you should do anything tonight. Let Willie talk. Keep this to yourself. Let some time pass. Let's you and I sort it out. We've got some time."

She looked like I had shot her through the heart. "You want me to lie," she said.

She was right. That's what I had said. "It's not really –"

"That's how you would solve this problem. You would lie."

My throat dried up.

"You don't think I should tell him," she said.

"Angie, don't. Please. It's too early. Just let this sit. Give it a little air." And then I tried to rationalize. "You've already lied. You lied when you walked in the door. You lied to Ephrem and Richard at the hot tubs."

"Oh God. You're right. I did."

"It's not lying if you pick a time to tell him that's more conducive to..."

"But I'd be lying to *him*."

"Angie –"

"I can't let this sit. I'm not like that."

"Well for Christ's sake, Angie. Did you know all along you were going to tell him the truth when you and I were doing it?"

"I wasn't thinking about that. It just happened."

"Bullshit. You'd been thinking about it all day. What am I supposed to do when we're naked and grabbing each other? Now you tell me it was all a mistake? I feel set up."

"I warned you about this. I asked if you could handle this."

"That's unfair and you know it. The stakes got higher. Of course I'm in love with you now. How could I not be?"

"I'm sorry. I'm so sorry Bob."

"I'm sorry too. But it's too late now."

She had been hiding her head in her hands. Do you love *me*? I wanted to ask. I had never asked her. But I never asked Angie about anything she had to lie about.

"I've got to go." And she brushed by me. She stopped in the breezeway. "I won't tell him. Please come upstairs."

I didn't move.

"Do what you want," she said. And her voice broke.

Angie had always nailed me on my honesty, or lack of it. I was trying to figure out whether telling a lie in this situation would be a bad thing or not. Surely it was natural to me. I was an actor. And even my quest for finding "honesty in the work," and "truth in the moment," as acting teachers liked to call it, was in service to the success of the performance. And a performance was, by the very nature of the word, artifice.

I stayed outside but went upstairs after a few minutes, mostly out of a desire to control the situation, as if my presence in the house would exert some influence on Angie. If something happened I didn't want to miss it. If I had to confront Willie I wanted to do it square. If I could comfort Angie somehow, I wanted to be there for her.

She and Willie were sitting on the couch. Angie had her knees drawn up close to her. She didn't look at me when I came in, but kept her eyes fixed on Willie. Willie was leaning into her, gesturing with his hands as he talked. He stopped me before I could retreat into my room.

"Hey Bob. You know – you and I should go have a beer sometime." He was up and towering over me. He was beaming with enthusiasm, which made him seem even taller than he was. He reminded me of a big puppy. "We've been rooming together for three months and I feel like I hardly know you."

"I know. It's been... hard to catch you around here."

"Part of it's this place, you know. It's got me running all the damn time. But I feel like I can relax a little when I get this new job. Enjoy life, you know?"

"Yeah."

"I'm talkin' with Ange. Looks like we'll be in L.A. in the fall."

"That's great. I'll miss you guys." I caught Angie's eye over Willie's shoulder. She betrayed nothing in her face.

"She says you're a great friend. I know she's really liked hanging out with you, so thanks for keeping her company. Only a few more weeks to go now!" He looked triumphantly at Angie. She smiled back over her tea. "So I plan to enjoy it here more. Because we won't be back in Santa Maria!"

I smiled and nodded my head. "That's great. Happy for you."

Willie stretched his legs out like a big gangly spider puppet, a marionette show. It was how he walked. It took him two steps to get back to the couch and put his arm around Angie. He kissed her cheek.

"Goodnight Bob," Angie said.

"Goodnight," I said.

I snapped a mental picture of Angie. It included Willie, by her side, his arm around her and grinning broadly. Angie's tea was in her lap and she was looking at me with that tight-lipped smile, the one that gave nothing away, the one that was halfway a grimace. There was a sadness in her eyes.

"I like this new tea you bought," Willie said.

"Darjeeling," said Angie.

Snap. It was the first time Willie had been in the picture all year.

17

I heard them through the walls later, as I lay in bed. They were having "the talk." I heard the low tones in Willie's voice. All I could hear in
Angie's voice was utter despair. No words. I heard her cry several times.
And I heard Willie comfort her. I caught some of his words, sometimes
whole sentences. I'd heard the lines a million times on TV shows. It was
like he was reading from a script.

"I know things haven't been great between us lately..."

And "This'll give us a chance to start all over..."

And "Aw baby, just give me some time to get this started. You'll love
L.A. You can have your career... I can probably even open some doors
for you at the studio... I'd be making enough for both of us to live on.
You wouldn't have to wait tables or anything if you didn't want to."

It made me nervous that I couldn't hear Angie. She would talk for
long periods sometimes, her voice a low mumble, and then she would
break down and sob. Was she playing her part like I had asked her to?
Was she sticking to the script they were acting out? If she was, she'd be
uttering familiar and vague half-truths, composed with only enough
courage to hint at her discontent and her subsequent infidelity. Lines I'm
sure I said, lines I'd heard from Gina, substanceless lines like:

"I feel like you and I have lost touch..."

And "I've done some things that I'm not proud of..."

And "If you think we could make it, I'm willing to give it another
try. But you have to understand, it can never be the same between us."
Hints. Niceties. Lies.

Or was she adlibbing? Was she confessing to Willie outright, and
giving him reasons why she didn't love him anymore? Was she telling

him the truth?

But the truth was, she did love him. She told me that. She made it clear.

Despite what I had told her, I hoped Angie had thrown the script away. I hoped she was speaking from her heart as candidly as she could, as I wished I could. As the long minutes wore on, the pattern in their speech became telling. Willie was dominant. His voice was energized. Angie was weaker, plaintive. Nothing that she told him seemed to phase him. After a couple hours they moved into the bedroom. I had to remind myself to breathe as I heard the telltale signs: zippers, the rustle of bedsheets, soft vocalizations. And I stayed, too enthralled, too depleted, too weak, too sick to move. After they lay quiet for awhile I heard Angie cry, sounds that went, for the first time all night, unanswered by Willie. And somewhere in a half dream I remembered touching the thin wall that separated us, and I imagined her on her side, touching it too.

18

I don't know how long the phone had been ringing when I answered it. The day was bright outside. Windows were propped open and the sounds of lawnmowers and garbage trucks filled the house. Angie and Willie's door was open and they were gone.

"Hello," I said.

"I was just about to hang up." It was Gina.

"No. I'm here. How are you?"

"Did you know my season closes before yours?"

Frankly, I hadn't been aware. "No," I said.

"It does. Have you thought about what you're doing when you leave there?"

"Well – I thought we discussed this. Noah Manning asked if I'd like to teach."

"Is that what he said?"

"I told you that's what he said."

"Did he give you a contract?"

"No but... I mean he asked me and everything. I mean, what else does he have to do?"

She let a long moment go by. "I'm going to L.A., Bob."

I let a long moment go by. "Okay."

"I mean, that's where I pretty much have to end up. Mom's going to give me the first and last on an apartment. But I've got to get a job right away so I can pay her back. I'm going to stay with Margaret until I find a place. Then I'll start auditioning."

"Peg Bosco?"

"What?"

"Margaret. Peg Bosco. You're going to stay with Peg Bosco?"

"Jesus. Is that what she changed her name to? That's horrible."

"Are you alone? I mean, are you going to live alone, after Margaret?"

She took another long moment before answering. "Why do you ask?"

"I just... I don't know what your situation is."

"Are you asking if I'm *with* anybody?"

"Basically, yeah. That's what I'm asking."

"I've been dating someone, but... at least at the moment... There are no plans, if that's what you're asking."

It sounded like the gardener had hefted his lawnmower up the stairs and was mowing the living room carpet. I shut the window.

"Bobby, I've grown up a little. It could be different between us now," she said.

I was afraid to go into this. "Okay," I said.

"You'll see. What about you?" She asked.

"Have I changed?"

"No. I mean... is there anyone else?"

"I've been kind of dating. But... you know..."

"What do I know?"

She was going to force me to say it. I looked at Angie and Willie's open door. "There's no one in particular," I said.

SEPTEMBER

19

I usually fell in love with my female scene partners.

It was a natural thing, really. All the big ones did it. Katherine Hepburn, Humphrey Bogart. They all wound up writing memoirs about each other. I didn't know what it was like on a movie set, but in theatre, we created these wonderful, romantic worlds, formed temporary families in a nurturing, caring environment. It affected me. For me, I always thought hopping into bed would spoil it. Like the infatuation with the young woman I told you about? How having sex would have ruined the romance by lending a carnal realism to it all? Reality could never be as idyllic as those precious moments on stage. Because on stage, you embodied someone else. There were no histories, no "hot buttons," no significant others to explain things to. So, I told myself, I should just accept the romance, soak it up, hold it close and relish the memories.

I know a few women fell in love with me too. If they had boyfriends or husbands, it didn't matter; the stage world was inviolate. On stage we were in love, even if it wasn't in the script. It was all about trust. It was our job: we had to open up to each other completely, allow each other to see deep inside, expose stuff that ordinary lovers may never have been able to reveal to one another. And there was the give and take of lines and intentions, the moment-to-moment work one acting teacher called "stringing together the beads." It felt like sex. Lovely, intimate sex. And as I've said, it was better.

It was getting back to reality that was the hard part. Those romantic worlds were presented for a price, and when it was over, the wrecking crew came along and took out the screws and everything went away.

Does anybody like to say goodbye, forever? Does anybody like to leave home, time after time? How do actors do it, I wondered. How could such sensitive, impressionable people be so callous as to make a career of leaving the ones they love?

I broke it off with Kathy Bishop the day after my hot tub escapade with Angie. I called Kathy up and said it wasn't working for me anymore, and she said it was a good idea because Rob Banister had asked her to marry him. His father owned a plastic drainpipe business in Illinois, and was pleading with Rob to come back and help him run the show. Rob promised Kathy a rich and varied marital arrangement, with plenty of theatre opportunities in Peoria, a hopping social calendar and a large house with a maid. She was planning to refuse Rob's proposal, but out of courtesy, she told me, it would be best if we weren't still fucking each other on the side. Instead of joining the drainpipe dynasty, Kathy was planning to move to Berkeley, work in a headshop and enroll in a school of modern dance.

That is: When it was all over.

That's all people were thinking about. October first. The end of the road.

There were people who had places to go. Brenda Bodwin would reclaim her throne as department head at Cal Poly. Richard Siebert, Wanda

Dare, Verden Price and all the ACTers would head back to San Francisco and put in a busy season there. Ephrem had decided to travel north with Richard Siebert and become his live-in roommate. Ripley, at least at this point, was planning to ride with Wanda Dare up that pink champagne highway, glide into the City By The Bay, put on an apron and dust her three story Victorian walkup while she was off rehearsing *Hedda Gabler* at the Geary.

Ben Heller and Rick Kaiser were going to bicycle the length of Baja and winter in Cabo. Cal Munson was going to study at a Lutheran seminary and enter the ministry. Jean Martire was taking her marvelous looks and great set of pipes to New York, where everyone thought, and so did I, that she might even make it. Ron Odekirk, one of the spear carriers in *Hank V,* was going to start a theatre company in Corvallis, Oregon, and had convinced Trish Coleman and Laura Finn to go with him. Mark and Candice would pack up their bicycles, their stereo and their Oscar Meyer Wiener slip covers and dump them in yet another empty apartment in Seattle, where they had been offered a season at the Seattle Rep. At least Mark had. Candice had been promised a role in their Christmas show as an enchanted pumpkin. She planned to work in retail on the side.

Some people were postponing the inevitable by enrolling in grad school or finishing a degree somewhere. In this category were Ronni, who had somehow convinced her dad that lots of rich, eligible men hung out in graduate acting programs; the morose and asocial Peter Ross, who planned to write a thesis entitled "Theatre of Death and Dismemberment;" and Nathan Trask, who was continuing his education primarily to sleep with as many women as possible. By the way, one day I asked him why the dog in his song was named Embo.

"It's Bongo," I said. "Or Bingo. Bingo was his name. The dog."

"Yeah, but *this* dog's name is Embo."

"Okay... it's your song."

"Yeah. It's my dog, too. His name stands for Eat My Butt Out."

I wished him well in graduate school.

L.A. was, of course, the destination of many, including Angie and Willie (and Gina), but many had no idea what they were going to do once they got there. Rita Tasner could stay with a close relative in Van Nuys while she got on her feet. Hanover had a brother who owned a tire outlet store down south somewhere near one of the Orange County beaches. He could work there while he set himself up "as close to auditions as possible." Stories like this were plentiful. People couldn't wait to start banging their heads against the gates of Hollywood.

The desire did not burn in me nearly as brightly. In fact, I felt very little desire for anything. The flame of my spirit had been turned down to a little blue glow since that night with Angie. Since then, I had hardly seen her. Willie, to atone for his three-month vanishing act, now spent every waking moment with Angie. I was pretty disgusted with myself for allowing our friendship to evaporate. I was disgusted with myself for not cornering Noah Manning and pressing him for a contract. I was disgusted with myself for not having some sort of plan if he didn't wind up hiring me. Ever since Gina's phone call I had been plagued by a gnawing realization that my conversation with Noah did not in fact result in a solid job offer, but was only some vague hint at one, and that perhaps I had only imagined that he was interested in me at all. The fact that Noah had decided to go on vacation before starting fall semester did not help.

And I was disgusted with myself for saying yes to Gina when she asked me if she could visit.

It was as if somebody else had climbed in my body and was moving my lips for me. Some goblin ventriloquist had perched in my chest cavity and was reaching up through my trachea, working my mouth, making me form words I didn't want to say. I had been weak, my internal surveillance was compromised, and the invader took over my body when I couldn't defend myself.

"I think we should meet," Gina said on the phone that night. "Once and for all. If you think it would be worthwhile."

"Okay," the hobgoblin made me say. If it had been up to me, I would have said "Hell no. Why should we even open this door again? You and I are split. Let's leave it that way." But the thing inside me wouldn't let me say it. Instead, it made me agree to hosting Gina for a few days on her way to L.A.

Her visit could not come at a worse time. It would coincide with the last few days of the season. But I didn't call her back and say she couldn't come. Truth: I even found myself looking forward to seeing her.

"Who is driving this clown car?" I said to my brain.

"Burn in hell, white boy!" the hobgoblin at the controls answered back. He was out of control, and was steering me toward my doom.

I was definitely not myself. I was floating through the last days of September without savoring them in any way. Days were slipping through my grasp. I snatched at them as if in a dream, I collected nothing, no trace of their magnitude. And as the days passed, the afternoon shadows lengthened, the light before the evening shows took on a silvery glint, and a hazy chill settled after dusk, earlier and earlier each day. You could smell the damper, smokier scents of autumn in the air. PCPA was already a ghost world compared with those electric days in June and July. Ranks had dwindled precipitously since then. The directors were gone. The designers were gone. The tech ranks had been pared down to skeletal running crews. Noah Manning was gone. All the actors were still around, but everyone had their minds on other places, LIFE AFTER, and were already packing sparse belongings in preparation for the inevitable exodus.

Nothing, however, seemed to phase Bronson and Lloyd, who had faced the end of the season long before and looked beyond that bleak horizon to financial success.

"How's your business plan coming?" I asked Bronson one evening before *Once in a Lifetime*.

"Outstanding."

"Where will you go after the season ends?"

"Undecided. I have a few financial obligations concernin' our silent partner that'll keep me in Santa Maria for a while into the fall."

"Lloyd too?"

"He's part of the arrangement as well, yes."

"What kind of obligations?"

"Financial ones. Management stuff primarily. Keeping an eye on things for the guy until he gets some issues resolved."

I told Bronson I admired him for putting his financial affairs first.

"My goal is to become financially self-sufficient by workin' the entrepreneurial angle. An actor has to learn to be otherwise self-sufficient," he told me. "If the system does not allow for a comfortable existence, it's up to the actor to bend the system and make it work for him."

I agreed with him up to a point. And what he preached sounded pretty good. Real estate, a car, employees with health plans, and oh yes, watch the business for me while I'm in Boston doing *The Cherry Orchard,* will you? But it was a cake-and-eat-it-too scenario. The unspoken reality? It's one world or the other. The more time you spend figuring out how to make it in the real world, the less interest you have in the sacrifices inherent in the theatre world. The attrition percentage is high; casualties are many. There are far fewer older actors than young ones, because the frustrations of poverty and rejection wear on one eventually. Maybe you haven't had an acting job in six months, and the unemployment is due to run out. So you say "Well, I'll get a job as a night porter in a hotel for a few months. That way I can leave my days open for auditions." It works that way for awhile, white-knuckling it on the 405 freeway with the radio blaring and all the windows open to stay awake on the way to the audition, nodding off in the reception room, staring blearily into the camera. Then you go a few more months without an acting gig, and along the way you find a relationship to take the edge off. The relationship gives you comfort, so you invest more into it. After awhile you say to yourself, "I'm tired of being too broke to take my date out to dinner. I need a better job." But you find that in order to make good money you have to get a day job. "After all," you say, "The hours are better." So you get one, and then another one, and then another one, and though you tell yourself you can take off any time your agent calls, it becomes an effort, the calls come less often. Then there are promotions, job changes, the engagement, the pregnancy, the home in the burbs, and finally the mailed notice informing you that you've been dropped from the agent's roster. It arrives in the box on a day you're in Salt Lake City for a client meeting, and you hardly pay it any attention.

They call this growing up.

Evenings at the Santa Maria Inn were more subdued and much less well attended. I went there only occasionally, and though I put on a good face while I was there I never stayed long. I would walk to Lyon's Restaurant near the mall, because it stayed open all night, and I could find a corner, nurse a root beer and read. It was either all-night Steinbeck or the triple X theatre at the edge of the city on the way to Guadalupe. I admit I walked down there a couple times, but I never had the nerve to go in. I couldn't imagine what people did in there, and it made me hurl to think of the poor guy who had to clean the floors when the place closed. I wound up walking most of the night. Admittedly, this was strange behavior. I told myself it was because I enjoyed the exercise and looking at people's houses, and I did, but I also knew it was about not being at the apartment when Angie got home. I also think my interest in pornography was due to a dangerous but hopefully temporary hatred of women. I wanted to see them get fucked. All of them.

And maybe metaphorically I was walking to assure myself I was still alive. I often found myself walking beyond the triple X, almost as far as the dunes. I would walk until all signs of life around me had been subdued by those darkest hours. Not until I could hear only the sound of my own steps and perhaps the barking of a lone dog would I feel more alive than the rest of the sleeping people. Not until my aloneness was affirmed could I return home. But I did come back. My route was never a straight line. It was always a circle.

I wrote Angie and Willie a note and left it on the coffee table. I said Gina was coming to visit for a few days and that I hoped it wasn't an inconvenience, that she would take my room and I would sleep on the couch. When I got up I saw the note had been turned over and in Willie's hand was written:

"Hi Bob! No problem! Help yourself to cookies on frig."

Dear Mom,

Well, you were right.

It was the letter I hoped I'd never have to write.

Things aren't going so well. You were right about Gina and I getting married too early. We should have waited until – I don't know – maybe until after we had a kid. Like Aunt Susan and Marty. And then what'd I do? Went and fell for another girl who lied to me.

I saw myself going home on a bus, broke and disheartened, giving mom the sob story at the kitchen table over her meatloaf surprise and strawberry pie.

And you were right about that acting class you warned me not to take. Here I am, out of money and nowhere to go. And after following my hearts desire, I take a dive right into the unforgiving cesspool of life. And what do I have to show for it?

I'd sleep downstairs in the corner by the tv (my room having long ago been converted to a sewing room), and save my money from my job at the Quickie-Mart, attend night classes for an AA degree. Maybe I would tool around on a Vespa, and I would start wearing shirts with collars.

Theatre is the devil's spawn, Mom. It's wrecked my life. It's time I grew up and enrolled in business accounting classes like you said I should. You know that money I borrowed for graduate school? I'll pay you back, I swear.

At least I wouldn't be getting hurt all the time. At least I wouldn't have to have scenes like the one with Angie when she cornered me after I got out of the shower. "Will you talk to me?" she said.

I made my usual evasive moves, said my usual passive-aggressive things like "What's to talk about?" and "Are you sure we've got time before Willie gets back?" which usually just succeeded in pissing Angie off and reassuring her that her decision to stick with Willie was the right one, until she turned away and left the house in disgust.

But that morning my confrontation-destroying tactics were not having any effect. I even toweled off in front of her without making any attempt to hide my penis, hoping that some sense of propriety would drive her from the room. But it didn't work.

"I'm not going to let you go another minute without talking," she said.

So we talked. And all the talking didn't solve anything between us. Take any two enlightened, otherwise-encumbered people, put them in a close, humid environment, let them have sex, and then watch as they try to pick up the pieces afterwards. It's going to be messy. I think it would have helped if we could have had sex again, right there, just blown it out in one savage cataclysm, but that line would not, could not be crossed again. So instead of sex we had tea, in a miserable attempt at being civil and restrained, and we were everything that we didn't want to become for each other. If it weren't so near the end of the season I would have moved out right then.

Dear Mom,

Why couldn't I have had a sister so I could have realized that women are dangerous and not to be trusted? Especially actresses.

Can't wait to taste that strawberry pie.

Love, Your Son, Bob

I took all 27 pages of the letter and hid them under my sock pile.

20

It was the last Thursday in September. We were entering the final weekend; all but three nights separated us from Actors' Oblivion. *Death of a Salesman* was closing, and because there were no matinees on Friday, it was also the night of the end of the season party, a must-do event for anyone even remotely connected with PCPA.

The party was to be hosted by Ronni, who had spent a few weeks getting to know a guy, a former actor, who worked the box office and lived in a gypsy wagon. The wagon was parked out near Los Olivos, in an olive grove owned by some rich member of the theatre's board of directors. Apparently the rich guy found it on one of his travels to Europe, rotting in a field. So he shipped it over from Belgium, restored it, had it painted its original colors, and now it sat, rotting in *his* field. He offered it up to the theatre every summer to see if one of the bohos wanted to live there, and the box office boho nabbed it before anybody else even knew about it. (I was never able to remember the box office guy's name. I just called him Gypsy. I was always resentful of Gypsy for several reasons. One – he got to live in the fucking gypsy wagon. Two – he was nailing Ronni, while I, though I had been given my chance as you know, hadn't been able to raise my hammer. Hence, I'm sure, my psychic block regarding his proper name.) The wagon had electricity but no toilet or running water, but a stream was nearby. Plus, there were all the olives you could possibly eat. Ronni spent lazy September days with Gypsy getting in touch with her inner self, winding wild baby's breath into her lover's flowing dark hair (Reason Three – Hair! Bastard!), cavorting naked in the stream and eating psilocybin mushrooms.

So Ronni told everybody: "[Gypsy] and I are building a dance floor, outside, under the stars."

But in fact they knew nothing about carpentry and tried to build the dance floor out of fallen olive branches and woven grasses. It didn't work. Willie was going out to the gypsy wagon later in the day to put his finishing touches on the new improved dance floor, Angie said, because Ronni had announced:

"[Gypsy] and I want to host the final season party! It will be an all-night event, starting after the shows and ending whenever!"

I wanted to store up sleep for the long night ahead but I couldn't relax. I was jittery about seeing Gina, and I was trying not to think of anything, but I wound up thinking of *everything*. It seemed like everybody's emotions were all screwed up. Brenda Bodwin had called me earlier that day in a panic and lamented over the closing of *Salesman*.

"There's something so special about our show, Bobby. I don't want it to end. It's such a depressing story but it's so wonderful to do the work, to exist in that world with you and Richard and Ephrem. What am I going to do?"

And Ephrem had called too. He had been morose for a week and a half, and I knew it was because the world we created and existed in as brothers was coming to an end.

"Just wanted to say it's been great working with you and this has been..." his voice broke a little.

"I know, Eph," I said. I made it easy on him. "Me too."

After I hung up Ripley called.

"She's going back to her husband," he said.

"You're kidding. I'm sorry for you, pal."

"It's such bad timing. She doesn't even want to talk to me. We had plans. I was going to live in San Francisco. And she doesn't even love him. Now what am I going to do? We have one more *Henry* and two *Major Barbaras* to do together."

"Really sorry..."

"I'm not going to let her get the better of me. I'm not hiding. I'll show her what she's missing. I'm going to be the life of the party tonight. But stick close by. I may need your support."

I told Ripley about Gina's proclamation. "She says she's *changed*," I said.

"Let me sniff her out," Ripley said, a hint of lechery in his voice. "I can tell if she's faking it."

So Gina had picked one hell of a day to arrive.

It was a sunny day. I walked over to dink on the piano in the music lab and kill some time. It was clear the season was coming to an end; the place would have been swarming in the middle of July, but looking around, I only saw two joggers doing the perimeter on the north side. I stopped by the call board at the theatre. Alongside the usual hand-scrawled notes advertising bicycles for sale or roommates wanted was a very un-hand-scrawled poster placed there, apparently, by the FBI. It showed two photos of Fred Norton side by side. One looked very much like the fellow who wrestled Officer Wadleigh on the *Death of a Salesman* set. The other one was Fred in a beard looking very much like a camel trader in Casablanca. Above the photos in large block letters was one printed word: "WANTED." Below the photos I read the phrase "$20,000 reward for information leading to arrest and conviction."

I looked around for someone to whom I could raise my eyebrows and make woo woo noises, but the building was all but deserted. So I walked over to the admin office to find an audience. Lou was the only one there. She was at her desk, her cane propped against the wall.

"Hey Lou, you see that wanted poster for Fred Norton?"

"What poster?" she deadpanned.

"The one on the call board."

I could tell I succeeded in getting a rise out of her. "Well, some woman from the police department came by and got permission to post something. But I didn't know it was a wanted poster." She widened her eyes and stubbed out her cigarette. "You serious?"

"And there's a $20,000 reward for his capture. Check it out."

Lou wouldn't let you walk any slower than you normally did when you walked with her. In fact I had to hurry to keep up. She lit another cigarette and she reminded me of a steam train as she catapulted herself across the grass. "How's it goin'?" she drawled.

"Okay. When does Noah get back from vacation?"

"He should be in tomorrow. Why?"

"I have to ask him about something."

"He's going to be hard to get ahold of if I have anything to say about it. We need answers from him on about 15,000 questions." Then she stopped her locomotive gait, swung around and asked me straight out. "You want to know about your winter contract?"

"Yes!"

She sucked on her cigarette. "It'd be nice to have you around," she said, without a trace of emotion. "I know he likes you. Have you seen the season?"

She meant the winter season lineup. I had. Gracing the main stage would be *Sherlock Holmes, The Sound of Music, Arms and the Man* and *Kiss Me Kate*. In the smaller studio theatre: *Wait Until Dark,* some horrid thing called *Apple Pan-Dowdy* and *Bleacher Bums,* just in time for baseball season. Not a trace of Ionesco or Sam Shepard. Just safe, controversy-free audience-pleasers.

"Sure," I replied, trying to sound enthusiastic.

"Seems like there's a lot of roles you could do," Lou said.

Yeah. Maybe I could play a burnt cake in *Apple Pan-Dowdy*, I thought. "Seems like," I said. "But it would be nice to know for sure what was going on. Summer's over in a few days."

Lou looked at me like she was Ann Landers and I had just tried to pick up my salad fork with my butt cheeks. Apparently, any inference of impatience with Noah's administrative decisions was a serious breach of etiquette.

"I mean... you know?" I said meekly.

She looked around, as if there were loads of people within earshot. Around the quad, sprinklers rhythmically ticked off long shoots of water.

"Noah said he'd come back with the list of who's going to be asked to stay. So I'd expect to know tomorrow sometime."

"Sure. But, I mean, it's a little late for some of us to make plans, Lou. I mean, why is Noah leaving town for two weeks without letting anybody know if they're going to be here or not?"

Lou stared at me as if in warning that I was treading on soft ground. "It's his vacation," she said.

"Well, okay. But... it seems... somewhat badly timed."

She took another long drag and studied me carefully. "Look, Bob. I like you. I really do. And I hope Noah wants to keep you around for the winter. But – do you really think this is all about you? Do you have any idea how many decisions have to be made over the course of a given day?"

"I'm sure... but –"

"I defend to the death Noah's right to take his vacation. Do you have any inkling about how hard he works? I tell him not to, but he even works while he's in Mexico. This place is in his blood. I say bless him for it. We all owe him a tremendous debt of gratitude for keeping this place going the way he does. You too."

I looked away, smacked my lips, looked back at Lou. "I gotcha. I hear you. You're right," I said. She was.

"But I appreciate the talk, and you have a valid point. You're just ill-informed. You're a good man, Bob."

And the train huffed off, smoke billowing. She beat me to the door by ten paces and was in the hallway before I knew it.

"Where's the poster?" she asked.

"Right next to the call sheet."

But as I approached the board I could see why she sounded perplexed. It was gone.

"Where'd it go?" I said.

"You sure it was here?"

"Sure. Not ten minutes ago."

Then she gave me a stare that said either "You've been smoking too much dope" or "I guess Noah was wrong about you" depending on how paranoid I happened to be at that given moment. But I was too dumfounded to be paranoid.

"I swear," I said.

She humored me. "Nobody should be taking anything down without permission." Then she turned and said "Let me know if you find one somewhere else." And she disappeared into the ladies' room. I stood there studying the tack marks in the board and muttering incredulities to myself.

I went outside and headed toward the neighboring music lab. Only one bicycle was parked in the rack. The door opened and out stepped Bronson, rolling up a sheet of paper and stuffing it in his backpack.

"Hey!" I shouted. "What *is* that?"

"What's what?" he said.

"That paper. What are you doing?"

"Just some sheet music." He was already on his bike, and was making no motion to linger behind and talk to me. By the time I got to the rack he was gathering speed.

"Did you see that wanted poster?" I called after him.

"What wanted poster?" But it was clear he didn't want an answer as he disappeared around the corner. I trotted out to the parking lot and caught sight of him outside the cafeteria. He stopped his bike at the message center by the empty picnic tables. I saw him reach up, take something off the board, and stuff it in his backpack. Then he rode off. I knew if Bronson had his way, Lou was never going to believe that there was a reward being offered for Fred Norton.

Angie and Willie were sitting around reading when I got back.

"You nervous, Bob?" asked Willie.

"A little," I said.

"What's that about?" Angie said.

"You know. The expectation. Seeing her again."

"You afraid of getting your feelings all messed up?" Willie said.

"Oh, I'm pretty solid on my feelings about Gina."

Angie dropped her book to her lap, suddenly interested. "So what are those feelings? You still love her, don't you?"

"Sure I love her, you know, but... we have so much history. I mean, she's Gina. But she's... well, you'll meet her. She's a tough one sometimes."

"You mean she's difficult? Or is it your relationship that's difficult?"

"Both, I guess."

It was me and Angie talking now. You could wring the subtext from every word.

"But I mean... is she a difficult person? Is that what you're saying? She seems really nice on the phone."

"Sure, but you haven't lived with her."

"Well, I'm just curious whether you mean it's difficult because relationships are difficult or whether you think she's *wired* wrong or something. I mean, Are you saying *she* was the problem because *she's* difficult?"

Willie put a hand on her shoulder and patted it concernedly, cocked his head, tried to make eye contact with his wife. Angie had her eyes glued to mine, awaiting an answer.

"You'll meet her," I said. "You'll get a chance to judge for yourself."

Angie went back to her book. I could tell she was disgusted with the reply she got from Noncommittal Bob. "Oh, I'm looking forward to it," she said. "It's so easy to rag on people when they're not around, isn't it?"

Willie thought Angie was out of line and he said something like "Hey, Ange..."

"Sorry," she said. But I knew she didn't mean it.

Gina arrived about four o'clock. She had the car, the yellow Toyota, the one I had driven all over Sacramento, and Bellingham before that, since our freshman year. We had gone on dates in the car, driven to the laundromat, the supermarket, the Thin Lizzie concert, visited Gina's brother in Elko, Nevada. And now she stepped out of it like it was hers all along. Actually, it *was* hers all along. She had brought it into the relationship.

I met her in the theatre parking lot because it was close off the freeway and easy for her to find. She drove into a space, waved, and popped out of the car before I could get to her. "Hey kiddo," she said.

I'm sure it was the way the light hit her. But it was not yet Golden Hour, the time of day cinematographers love, when the sun, sinking low on the horizon, rims everything with a golden highlight. Regardless, golden light played across her shoulder length auburn hair, which seemed to bounce far too much for someone who had been in a car for three days. She was taller, thinner, prettier than the image of her I held in my memory. This was the woman I had married. This was the woman who had cried in my arms when I told her how much I loved her.

"Hi Gee," I said.

We embraced easily, tightly, for long minutes. Then we looked at each other and smiled. I noticed a hitch in her breath when she sighed. She meant to say my name but nothing came out. Then she cleared her throat. "What am I going to do without you?" she said.

21

I showed Gina around. We walked along the curvy sidewalk, past the vacant cafeteria, science building, math hall. She told me about her roommates, her big role in *The Rainmaker*, and picnics on the banks of the Mississippi. Gina insisted we take the bus to Solvang instead of driving down separately. "I want to experience it just like you do," she said. "We'll have plenty of time to talk about things later, just the two of us." So I showed her the theatre and took her down to the stage, which was all set up for *The Country Wife*. Then we sat in the lobby and made more small talk while we waited for the rest of the cast to show up. And when they did, one by one, I introduced them to Gina, and as I expected, instead of saying merely "Hi, nice to meet you" and turning to me to commiserate on the closing of our beloved show, each of them stayed talking to Gina long after the introduction had been made. Gina had a knack for making people feel comfortable, making them believe they must have known her from somewhere in their past. She truly did enjoy people and take interest in who they were. People sensed this in her and warmed to her immediately.

Like Brenda Bodwin: "Are you staying until Tuesday? We must have lunch!"

And Ephrem: "You and Bob should go swimming with us on Sunday!"

And Richard Siebert: "Did you work with Colette Blake up in Minneapolis? She's a good friend of mine."

By the time we got on the bus Gina had packed her social calendar so full I wondered if we'd actually have time to say anything to one another.

Gina wore a new blouse and familiar khaki shorts that had been a standard uniform for her throughout our graduate school years. We sat on the bus together in a seat toward the front. She held my hand tightly, and I wondered if this was the way a divorcing couple should be behaving. It felt good, laughing at Ephrem making chihuahua George "dance" to "Another One Bites the Dust" on the bus radio, watching Brenda show us what it was like to wear a dress while riding her Harley. Gina fit in seamlessly. I'm sure everybody on the bus wondered how on earth I could be breaking up with such a wonderful person.

Gina and I had time to go out for coffee before the show. We sat by ourselves in a corner. She told me about watching funnel clouds, the humidity, and mosquitoes the size of June bugs.

"It's why they have screens on everything back there. And bug zappers. And everybody plays baseball. In the evenings people sit on their screened-in porches and sip lemonade and listen to baseball games. It's very America."

I listened for awhile. Then I said "Gina, you know you're welcome here and all, and it's great to see you and everything, but why are you here, really? Do you think this is a good idea?"

"Why would it be a bad idea?"

"Well... I mean, we split four months ago. You showing up here now doesn't fix what's already been done."

"I know that. But we spent seven years together. I think we owe each other the courtesy of a meeting without all that anger, you know? I mean, we're worth more than that. I still have feelings for you, Bobby."

I started to say *well of course – I have feelings for you too* and blah de blah, but all of a sudden I became self-conscious. So I said "Well, what are you saying, Gina? Do you want to try to get back together?" And that changed the tone a bit.

"No. That's not what I'm saying. Do you?"

"Unfair question."

"It's just not easy, is it?"

"Then what? You want to be friends, then?"

"Sure. Don't you?"

"Not sure."

"Really?"

"Yeah. It's confusing enough without seeing you again. It's not like I've had an easy time of it."

"Neither have I."

"It might be a little early for me to forgive and forget. I guess you can, though, huh?"

She leaned in and looked at me. "Hey. This is hard for me. Give me some credit."

"Fine," I said. "Credit given."

"So you're just going to close me off. Your mind has been made up."

"Yours hasn't? That's a new one." My anger was rising. "I'm not the one who spent three weeks on the floor of Margaret's apartment. You couldn't stand living with me anymore. You left me, remember?"

"Does it really matter to you who left who? I couldn't stay at our house. Somebody had to go. And I was the guilty one, remember? I cheated on you."

"I was about the last to know, wasn't I? Here I thought you just 'needed some space,' and went off to live with Margaret. And all the time you were…" She knew I was going to say *cheating on me with Mark Sanders*. But I didn't. I said "How could you do that? How could you do that to me?"

"Go ahead and blame me, Bob. But it's more complicated than that. You see the affair as the cause and I see it as the effect."

Who put that convenient label on it? "The effect of what?"

"I couldn't live in the house with somebody who hated me."

All of a sudden I couldn't say anything. Dead stop. Nothing. I looked at the counter. A beefy blonde girl in a Heidi outfit had been eyeing us, and she looked away when I caught her.

"We should go," I said. "Sorry I got angry."

Gina stared at the tabletop. "I shouldn't have come. I was wrong to have come." She blinked once and a tear fell on the table, and she fished in her bag for some Kleenex.

"No. I wanted to see you. I'm glad you're here." And there was more of this talk, this smoothing over, an abrupt about-face, to try to erase what we said and what we felt, to salve over the hurt and dispose of the wreckage of our anger. We walked to the theatre.

Why did she think I hated her? How could she have thought that? But somewhere, way down, down in the primal stew of my gut, I knew what she meant. Down there, bile and acid and testosterone and genetic shards of a savage ancestry churned and fumed and spiked thoughts and impulses and desires untamed by manners and education and learned behavior. Down there, a black pit bull paced in a cyclone pen, waiting to lock jaws on the hand that left the food. Hate her? I couldn't admit it, couldn't begin to vocalize why that statement had hit home.

22

It was the last time we would say those lines. The words of *Death of a Salesman* went into the cool night air and disappeared, over the lights, over the fake turrets, gone. Those moments onstage would never be lived again, as if we never lived them. The tech crew barely let the audience leave the auditorium before they attacked the set and brought it down. I couldn't watch. Gina found her way backstage, hugged me and we shared in the customary post-mortem with the rest of the cast.

"Did the hair thing bother you?" I asked her.

"What hair thing?"

"You know – the fact that I was playing a fourteen-year-old with a bald spot?"

"You don't have a bald spot. Do you? Maybe you do. Let's see." She tried to turn me around.

"Never mind," I said.

We all gathered around Richard Siebert because Ephrem had opened a bottle of champagne and poured it over Richard's head. Everybody in the cast was toasting each other for all our hard work.

"And wonderful times," said Ephrem, tears streaming.

"Here's to Noah Manning!" said Bill Morris, and a big cheer went up.

"I'll miss all of you," Richard said.

"Oh Gina," Brenda said, reaching out her big arm and drawing my estranged wife into the circle, "We all love each other so much!" And then she started to cry again.

Gina just smiled and folded into the group.

The bus let us off in the parking lot and Gina and I headed for the Toyota. I instinctively went to the driver's side door, but stopped myself in time.

"Whoops," I said, "I don't have the keys anymore."

"I'll drive," Gina said casually. "Hope you can fit."

The car was packed to the roof with boxes, and the passenger seat was forced up to the dashboard, but I managed to squeeze myself in.

"So," I said, "When you meet Angie... like I told you, she's pretty direct."

She smiled. "You know, I appreciate that trait these days. It's very refreshing."

"Yeah, but sometimes it comes off as rude."

She looked at me. Streetlights flashed across her face as she drove. "You have a crush on her, don't you? Are you in love with her?"

This was not the Gina I knew. In all fairness, I told myself, and I don't think I was imagining this, the old Gina would have pouted for days and thrown tantrums no matter how I answered that question. Even if I answered *no*, she would have known I was lying and thrown even worse tantrums. The new Gina, if a bit more detached, seemed self-aware and eminently more accepting.

Or maybe she just didn't care anymore.

She smiled and turned away. "You don't have to answer if you don't want to. It's none of my business anyway."

She turned into the empty parking stall beside Angie's VW. Lights were on upstairs, and I steadied myself for the introduction.

"Angie, this is Gina," I said.

Angie was dressing for the party. She had left her door ajar, as she usually did, and was putting on shiny, fake leather pants. "Hi!" she said, and came out to greet us, no attitude whatsoever. "I feel like I know you," she said, and other, patently cordial things that were intended to make Gina feel at home. But I could tell Angie had her guard up. Before our big fallout she would have been riveted by every blink of Gina's eye. Now, she was formal and efficient. But her distaste for me didn't put the brakes on her candor. She didn't let two minutes go by before she said "So Gina – I've heard it from Bob's side. How about you? What's the word on you two? Are you trying to patch it up together? Or is this like the summit meeting to decide who gets what."

Gina looked at me. *What did I tell you?* my eyes said.

Then she waded right in: "Well, the problem is, We could leave it here and part as friends. At least I could. I don't know about Bob. He still has to forgive me for cheating on him. But, and I think I'm right in saying this... we still love each other quite a bit. So if we decide that we want to stay married... and I don't know if it's even a real option – for both of us – we'd have to work really hard to get over the guilt, and the hurt, and to learn to forgive each other. And frankly, it may just not be worth it, you know? I mean, I'm sure you know – it's hard living with someone else. And neither of us are especially easy people. It would be easy to be friends with Bob, for me, anyway. But my mind was made up a few months ago – to end it. And I know Bob's was too. The trick is not to let all the emotions involved with seeing each other again get in the way of figuring out what's right for the both of us. What's right for me may not be what's right for Bob. You know what I mean? So..."

Any trace of skepticism on Angie's face vanished and was replaced by awed respect.

"So that's why I'm here," Gina said. "No easy answers."

Angie stared blankly at Gina. "How about some tea?" she said.

I watched Gina's spell swirl around Angie in a cloud of pink fairy dust. With all of the good feelings that Gina spread, like rose petals strewn from a gilded basket, I was beginning to feel more and more like the ass end of a donkey. The two women sat at the kitchen table and conversed like best friends, while I lurked around gulping tea, cringing at the frankness of the conversation. Mostly they compared marriages, talked about their challenges and needs in ways that two guys, even if they had known each other all their lives, would never have been able to vocalize. Eventually I had to do something, so I brought some of Gina's boxes upstairs.

"Bob!" Gina beamed as I passed by, "Let's all go to the party together!"

If it had been just Angie and me in the house, having all the lights on would have done nothing to dispel the cold gloom that would lay, wraith-like, in the corners. But Gina's presence made the place glow again. It was as if Gina was allowing Angie and I to see each other in a different light, one, I hoped, that would make us more accepting and ease the tensions between us.

I was wrong. Angie plopped herself in the back seat of the Toyota after I had cleared a space for a second passenger. I had claimed my familiar place at the wheel, a decisive move on my part, and we waited in the car while Gina finished changing.

"So Bob. Gina seems NICE," Angie said sarcastically. "Understatement!"

"Nice is not the word. She's great. Everybody loves Gina."

"Funny, you know. Somehow I had a much different picture of her. Here you've been talking about her for so long. And to answer my own question, I don't think she's difficult at all. In fact, I wondered why you hadn't been calling her Saint Gina."

"Thanks for your opinion Angie."

"Makes me curious about how you see me. If Gina is this certifiable basket case, I must be some overwhelmingly cruel, bitchy whore. Vampirella. You know what your problem is? You're the same age, but you're way too young for her."

"Girls mature faster than guys," I said.

"Fuckin' A," said Angie.

She only quieted down when Gina appeared, radiant in a polka dot dress, red scarf and a bomber jacket. How did she know exactly what to wear? "You look PERfect!" Angie said, delighted, as Gina sat down. I drove, they talked. I didn't say a word.

We drove northeast until the city lights dimmed behind us and stars became visible. It was a gorgeous, clear night, with a moon that was almost full. It was warm, and it seemed to be getting warmer the further we got from the ocean. We turned off the county road and fell in line with three other cars that I recognized from the theatre, and followed the herd through a column of large olive trees.

"Must be getting close," Angie said. "I better toke up. Anybody?"

Gina and I both passed.

"This's my last one this summer," Angie said, inhaling.

The olive trees gave way to pastureland dotted with the occasional scrub oak, and we rolled over a cattle guard and parked with a bunch of other theatre cars in a makeshift dirt lot. Our headlights revealed what looked to be a mockery of a formal ball, where, instead of exiting from grand limousines chauffeured up to sparkling terraces, people tumbled out of packed VWs and Ramblers and stepped in cow shit. Nobody had announced a theme, but everybody had the same idea about what they wanted to wear. There was Rita Tasner in a sequined dress with her feather boa and hiking boots. Laura Finn wore a strapless evening gown over camouflage pants. Hanover wore a tuxedo coat over his tights from *Henry V.* Angie wore a combo of black leather and taffeta, and looked like some cycle harlot crossed with a fairy from *A Midsummer Night's Dream.* Even I had combed the thrift sores and found a horrible green and orange plaid sportcoat, which I wore with cowboy boots and my customary jeans. People stood in the dirt lot and seemed in no hurry to go anywhere. Women touched up their makeup in vanity mirrors. People passed bottles around in groups. We came upon Curt Harnick and Barbara Ledbetter, who were already so drunk or high they could barely walk. I figured it was useless introducing Gina. But the five of us, now a loose group, began following others along a beaten path through a thicket of deerbrush marked by a string of miniature lights and felt penned signs. "LOVely ParTY!" "CeleBRaTe!" "FuN FuN!" Barbara read each one of them aloud and laughed. A stream burbled somewhere nearby, and music, a bootleg Grateful Dead tape, got louder as we walked toward it. Soon we emerged in another clearing, a cow pasture actually, and there was the gypsy wagon, strung top to bottom with white Christmas lights. Strands of lights looped to the dance floor, which jutted from a gentle slope and extended a few feet over the stream. Willie had done a nice job building it. The platform was being used as the buffet and bar at the moment, and it was easy to see why. It was the only level surface in the area, as the rest of the grounds sloped up, covered in dry grass grazed to lawn height, to the main house (a wood, glass and white stucco mansion), which you could see perched grandly atop the hill overlooking the olive grove a few hundred yards away. The owner must have been gone, as the house was completely dark. Music blared from speakers hung from the occasional oak tree. The whole scene smelled of patchouli, cow manure and beer.

"Fucking paradise," said Barbara Ledbetter, who tripped, fell to her knees and laughed helplessly while Curt tried to get her to her feet. I was glad to leave them behind.

I was wondering why Angie continued to hang around in the vicinity of Noncommittal Bob one instant longer than she had to, but she did, long enough for Ronni to notice and hurry over to us. She was dressed in a spectacular white, flowy linen dress that dragged on the ground behind her and had other fabrics, leaves, wildflowers and bits of lichen sewn to it. In her dark hair she wore a garland of baby's breath. "I'm a bride of the forest, queen of the gypsies," Ronni said proudly, rapturously, to the oohs and ahhs of Angie and Gina. I wanted to puke. Angie was quick to introduce my wife, and Ronni clasped her hands together and swelled like a balloon, her Linda Rondstadt eyes now quite dilated, and engulfed Gina in a welcoming embrace.

Ripley was lurking a few feet off and he pulled me away while Gina was busy.

"What are they," Ripley said in my ear, "New best friends?" He had raided the costume shop and was dressed like Lil' Abner Yokum.

"It's been a wild day," I said. "Gina has been on her absolute best behavior."

"What's with her, anyway? Nobody changes *that* much."

I had forgotten I was supposed to be Ripley's support, not vice versa. So I quickly asked him how he was and if he had seen *her* (Wanda) yet.

"Not yet," he said, glancing furtively about. "I'm trying to get really drunk so I can make a huge scene. Has Angie got some weed?" And he stumbled past me into the fray. "Hi Gina!" he called to my wife, who saw him and embraced her old classmate somewhat hesitantly. But it was Angie that Ripley really wanted to see, and at his first chance he pulled the leather fairy aside and hit her up.

"Bob, do you have a show tomorrow?"

It was Nathan Trask. He was standing too close to me, his huge Cheshire Cat grin spread like butter across his face.

I shook my head. "No," I said.

"You want one of these?"

From behind his back he drew a crackly sheet of clear styrene plastic backed with tinfoil. Little round domes in the plastic, evenly spaced across the sheet and separated by dotted perforations, held blue pills of some sort. Most of the domes were empty.

"What are they?"

"This," Nathan said proudly, "Is original Owsley acid."

"What kind of acid?"

"He was this chemist at UC Berkeley in the 60's who experimented with psychedelics? So he like, distilled the most pure form of it and wound up supplying Ken Kesey and Timothy Leary and all these famous heads. It's real, man. Go ahead – look at it. You want one?"

I held the sheet up to a string of lights. Stamped into the top of each diminutive blue tablet was an indentation of an owl head-like design. "Wow! Where'd you get this?"

"From Timothy Leary himself. I did this show in San Francisco last year about Timothy Leary and I played Timothy Leary and Timothy Leary himself came on opening night and came to our party and before he left he bestowed this on me."

"Quite an honor," I said. I was serious.

"You want one? Free. I can't take the stuff. I go epileptic."

I was far too much of a control freak to try LSD. "No thanks," I said.

Along the path and into the glade, Wanda Dare made her entrance on the supportive arm of Verden Price. Both were conservatively dressed, and both looked around the gypsy camp, smiling widely, as if it had all been done for them. I looked at Ripley. He was laughing much louder than he normally did, so I figured he had spotted her and was showing off how "okay" he was. Suddenly he seemed in no big hurry to leave the group of attractive women. Wanda and Verden found a clique of ACTers and quickly sealed themselves off from the rest of the spear carriers.

"Hey Nate," I said. "How come half that sheet is gone?"

He just smiled his mischievous grin and waved his hand grandly. "I got rid of some of it," he said. On the slope, in the moonlight, several partygoers wandered slowly, aimlessly up the hill.

"I'll take one," I said.

"Oh wow," Nathan said. He broke a tablet out of the aluminum backing and put it in my hand. "It's an unbelievably clean high. Take half a tab. Or a quarter. You'll come down quicker." Then he winked and said "Take it with someone you love."

I waited until he left and then popped the little blue pill into the pocket of my plaid sportcoat.

I decided to check out the gypsy wagon. It was Command Central for the long haired sound guy, who was monitoring the Grateful Dead with racks of stereo equipment under the glow of a single lamp. "Come on in," he said, waving a joint. But it was clear all the action was happening outside.

I waved to him. "Just wanted to get a look," I said. The wagon had lots of hardwood cupboards and shelves, a closet, and behind open curtains, one skinny, built-in bed which was strewn with pillows and colorful throws. This was how actors and vagabonds traveled a couple centuries ago, I thought. They never left home. They took it with them. I turned to leave but Ronni had come up quickly behind me and I almost bumped into her.

"Hi Bob," she said. "I like Gina."

"Oh yeah, thanks," I said. "She's great." We had to yell to hear each other over "Uncle John's Band." "Where's..." And I couldn't summon myself to remember Gypsy's name. "...Where's your boyfriend?"

"He's tripping, I think. Hey Bob – Gina says Noah talked to you about filling an Artist-in-Residence slot during the winter. Have you heard yet?"

"No. He's not back from his vacation yet, I guess."

We stood by the door of the gypsy wagon. Ronni made no moves to leave. "Guess what?" she said.

"What?"

"He called me today and hired me. I'm going to be here this winter." And she squealed happily.

The icy hand of dread stuck out its first two digits and walked them, mockingly, up my spine. I was happy for Ronni. But the affirmation of her employment created an odd jumble of emotions inside me. I have to say I was surprised. Not that Ronni was asked to stay, necessarily, but surprised at the suddenness and finality of it all. This is how it would be decided. In one moment, my nagging uncertainty would be resolved. Noah would answer my question with one phone call. Or perhaps, If he had decided *not* to hire me, his answer would be silence, which might lead me to approach him, respectfully, while he was in his office, to ask for a minute of his time. I would have to stand there and inquire if he had thought about "what we talked about a couple months ago." And perhaps he might respond "What did you and I talk about?" and I would have to say "You know, the Artist-in-Residence position." And then, he might diplomatically apologize for inferring that our conversation was even close to being concrete, that there were obviously plenty of variables that he had to consider during the summer and that it just, well, wouldn't be a good "match" for me this year, but that he appreciated my interest, and that I should audition for him again next summer.

Then again, he might have tried to call. And he might have been apologetic for stringing me out and making me wait so long before he set his roster. He might have even been surprised that I had any doubt in my mind whatsoever, as he intended from our conversation to hire me all along, but that he was so busy planning the season and running the theatre he neglected to check back in. "At least I knew I had you as a starting point," he might say. "It was the others I had to think about. Welcome aboard."

My heart was beating far too fast. I hated to have had to think about my future, not with Gina there and people tripping in the olive groves. I hated to want something so badly. I hated that I had made it so important. I hated that Noah's decision was so far out of my control. I hugged Ronni and told her how pleased I was, and was able, for a few moments, to hide my face.

"I'm surprised you haven't heard," she said.

"You know Noah. He's got lots of things on his plate. When did he tell you?"

"Late this afternoon. Were you out? He probably tried to call. Do you have a message thing on your phone?"

"Yes. I mean, yes, I was out. Who else is staying, do you know?"

"The only other one I know of is Bobbi North. She heard right before the show and she was so excited…"

"So no grad school for you, then, eh? You got a nice place to live, anyway." I patted the side of the gypsy wagon.

"It's okay, but now that I'll be making some real money, I'm gonna get a new place in town, one of those modern townhouses out on Willow. Oooh… I hope you get hired! We can hang out!" And then she hugged me again. She grimaced in glee, and she was off, her long sackcloth gown gathering straw from the ground as she walked away.

Then I just walked up to Wanda Dare like we were best friends.

"Can I talk to you a minute?" I said. She tried not to look surprised. She smiled, somewhat embarrassed, and excused herself from Verden and the other ACTers. We found a quieter place to talk. I knew I was risking Actress Armageddon but I figured I had an even chance to exploit her sense of guilt rather than peak her wrath.

I gave Wanda the whole "good friend" story, how I had never known

Ripley, "Jake," to be so *into* a relationship, and that it was really difficult to see him get hurt, and how I felt that she hadn't played fair with him because he certainly hadn't been aware of the "ground rules" as she called them, and that maybe she had it all worked out in her head, the "boundaries" and all, and I had no idea if the husband was aware or anything like that, but she had led Ripley down the proverbial path. "I felt like we *bonded* that evening we talked. And I know you to be honest and up front with what you feel. All I'm asking you to do is honor your own feelings for Rip... I mean, Jake." She was actually very receptive and admitted that she felt horrible, and that she had entered the affair despite her own reservations, but that she couldn't help herself, and that her first allegiance was to her husband, and that she owed it to him and their marriage to this and that and blah blah blah. I looked over at Ripley. He had moved away from Angie and Gina and closer to Wanda and me, and I gave him the evil eye and waved him away. He got my signal and stood clear.

Wanda was standing there empty-handed. "Can I get you a beer?" I said.

"Thank you. I'm very thirsty. I guess I could use one," she said.

Why Wanda, I thought, how absolutely audacious of you. "You know," I said, "When I move away from you Ripley is going to glom on to me and he's going to want to know what's going on and so I thought, rather than me coming back here with your beer, it's really him you should be talking to anyway, and I was wondering if it would be all right if we just skipped a few steps and I sent him back here with your beer. What do you think?"

"Oh! Well... I hadn't wanted to –"

"I really think you owe him one last conversation, you know, and this is a good place. He really needs just to have... some tender words. And some finality. What do you say?"

Wanda pursed her lips and looked over at Ripley thoughtfully.

"You still feel something for him, don't you?" I asked.

She looked at the ground and sniffled. "Very well," she said. Then she turned away. "One last rendezvous. I guess I owe him that much."

She wiped her eyes.

I put my hand on her shoulder and patted it consolingly. "Stay here a minute," I said, and headed over to the bar. Ripley didn't let two seconds pass before he was in my face.

"What are you doing? What'd she say? Were you talking about me?"

"Everything's fine. Let me handle this," I said.

"How are you going to handle it? How can you handle it? What do you mean handle it?"

"Wanda's too much in charge of this thing right now. You need to get this relationship back on your turf. You *need* her too much. So... we just have to level out the playing field. I think she's ready to talk. I think you'll see a change in her." I was filling a plastic cup from the keg. "Give me your cup."

Ripley handed it to me and looked over at Wanda. She was alone, her arms crossed, looking in the stream contemplatively.

"She hates me, doesn't she. Do you think she still loves me?"

"Do you have a pocketknife? Oh wait... never mind."

"She's just a little girl, really. You know? I don't blame her. These things are hard to sort through..."

Ripley wouldn't have noticed what I was doing if he was looking at me dead on. But he wasn't. He was looking at Wanda. And while he talked I took the little blue tablet from my coat pocket, set it on the edge of the picnic table and crushed it with a wine bottle. Then I gathered pieces and sprinkled them evenly in the two cups of beer. I swizzled both cups a little in my hands, and then presented them to Ripley.

"She wants you to take this to her." He took the cups of beer. I squeezed his arm. "Be gentle. Don't let her out of your sight. And for God's sake, straighten up, boy. You're slumping."

He nodded, turned, and headed down to the stream. I watched him approach Wanda tentatively. Both of them kept glancing about at various places on the ground, looking everywhere but at each other. Finally Ripley said something and they made eye contact, and Wanda seemed to melt somewhat, moving slightly, instinctively nearer to him. He gave her the beer, and motioned that they move even further away from the crowd, and they crossed the small stream to sit on the opposite bank. They sat on a large, flat rock, Wanda perching a bit awkwardly, and they talked and sipped their beer.

It must have been around three o'clock when the party truly began to swirl down the rabbit hole. I wouldn't have been surprised to see a hookah-smoking caterpillar in one of the oak trees. The music got louder and the stoned sound guy began playing a lot of Van Halen records at top volume. People started whirling and stomping on the dance floor, which caused one of the support struts that spanned the stream to crack and bow severely, enough that the kegs and picnic table full of booze toppled into the water. Several people, well out of their minds, kneeled downstream of the crash site and lapped up the wine, bourbon and creek water cocktail that burbled over the rocks. The fun new sponginess of the dance floor invited even more people to crowd onto it. People stood at the edges of the floor and clapped in unison. Something equivalent to a limbo line began to form, as dancers took turns launching themselves into the center, and, using the springy floor as a trampoline, bounced and flailed into the crowd. Some large tech guy stepped through the plywood and severely tore his leg up, but he was too far gone to care. Then the entire thing collapsed, taking several people with it. A water fight ensued.

Other revelers who sought a more serene experience wandered into the olive groves or strolled up to the front yard of the main house and lolled on abandoned lawn furniture.

Meanwhile, a lot of energy was being spent by Hanover and Rick Kaiser as they tried to capture a cow for the incredibly high Kathy Bishop. She had told Hanover that she would strip and do a bovine version of Lady Godiva if someone would find a cow for her to ride. The boys hadn't been able to get close to a cow, but spent hours trying, and had only been successful in scaring a couple into stampeding through the clearing. Kathy had long since lost interest in the cow hunt, and, as she had a thing for sex in the outdoors (as I knew well enough), reportedly led her old boyfriend Peter Ross into the olive grove and disappeared for awhile. This angered the recently dumped Rob Banister, who apparently still had it for Kathy in a major way. When Peter and Kathy returned to the clearing, Rob confronted them and engaged Peter in a shoving match. Hanover, back from the roundup, took off his pitted tuxedo coat and tried to join the fight, looking for any excuse to pummel the annoying Peter Ross, but I pulled Hanover away and held onto him.

"Fuck you!" Peter Ross shouted.

"Fuck you!" Rob Banister said.

"Everybody just STOP IT!" the incredibly high Kathy Bishop said.

I felt bad for Rob Banister. I wished he could just sink into the pages of the Archie comic he came from and disappear, pick up Veronica and Jughead and hang out at the malt shop. This woman has wronged you, I thought. You deserve better. You are better. Walk away from this.

But then Rob Banister spoke.

"Now Kate, I am a husband for your turn

For by this light, whereby I see thy beauty.

Thy beauty that doth make me like thee well,

Thou must be married to no man but me."

I could feel everybody assembled press their palms to their foreheads in unison. We all knew the verse was from *Taming of the Shrew*, and I could feel the crowd's sympathy for Rob take a dive. Shakespeare, now? Wrong place, wrong time. And his phrasing sucked.

Kathy Bishop stood with her mouth open. Peter Ross smirked and looked around, trying to kindle group laughter and direct ridicule toward Rob. But no one laughed. So Rob kept it up.

"Did ever Dian so become a grove

As Kate this pasture with her princely gait?

Thus in plain terms: you shall be my wife.

And will you, nill you, I will marry you."

Peter Ross laughed derisively, but a couple guys clamped their hands on his shoulders and shut him down.

"What do you say, Kathy?" said Rob Banister. "It's the last time I ask."

Kathy almost lost her balance as she shook her head defiantly. "I told you once already, it's not going to happen," she said.

At this, I felt the crowd turn in favor of Rob again, forgiving him his transgressions with the verse. It was all feeling very uncomfortable, and the vibe was bad, but then, out of nowhere, Verden Price stepped forward.

"Fie, fie," Verden said. "Unknit that threatening unkind brow,

And dart not scornful glances from those eyes,

To wound thy lord, thy king, thy governor."

He was as riveting as he was the first day of rehearsal for *Henry V*, before he started to second-guess himself. His voice was clear, his command of the language impeccable. We were all glued to him.

"What do you know about it?" Kathy Bishop said.

Verden looked Kathy right in the eye and moved toward her.

"A woman mov'd is like a fountain troubled,

Muddy, ill-seeming, thick, bereft of beauty.

I am asham'd that women are so simple

To offer war where they should kneel for peace."

Verden stood directly in front of Kathy. "You should be more accepting of those who love you," he said. "Love is a precious thing in this world, and you should never take it for granted."

It appeared as if Kathy was going to say something, but she hesitated for a long moment. Then she turned, swayed a bit, caught herself, and walked out of the grove with as much dignity as she could salvage.

Verden put a hand on Rob Banister's shoulder. "Good for you, sir. But don't give her a second thought. You deserve better."

Rob watched Kathy disappear into the trees. Then he turned back, gave us all a stalwart smile, thanked Verden, bowed graciously and left the grove. We gave him a big hand. Peter Ross shook his arms free and slunk away, muttering. The crowd went back to doing whatever they had been doing.

Oddly, no one milled around Verden Price, a sure sign the season was over and there were no more social points to be gained by association. So I went up to him and shook his hand.

"Nice work with the verse, Verden," I said.

"Thanks, Al," he said, and walked off.

Yes, he called me Al.

23

As the night progressed and the temperature dropped, people packed into the Gypsy wagon like it was a frathouse phonebooth. I peeked inside once and it was shoulder to shoulder, loud and smoky, and people were passing panties over their heads and tossing them out the open door. Eventually the music stopped. The equipment had either been crushed or cleared to make room for more bodies. Then the wagon cleared out and most of the party migrated to the parking lot, where people continued packing themselves into different cars, running the heaters and playing stereos, gradually winding down. I kept tabs on Ripley and Wanda Dare for awhile. They stayed on the rock near the stream most of the night. Once I observed them staring into each other's eyes, hopelessly lost in one another, slowly touching each other's faces.

Gina dropped in on different scenes from the party like she was a foreign correspondent at the Russian Revolution. She checked in with me often, giving me energetic accounts. The guy in the football helmet lit a tablecloth on fire, the overly loud woman passed out, stuff like that. Fatigue caught up with me so I told Gina I was going to sit it out for awhile. I crossed the cow fence and wandered up the hill, and sat at the base of an oak tree where I could look down on the gypsy wagon, the wrecked dance floor and the stream. The moon was so bright I could see remarkably well. I was about fifty yards from the sprinkler line at which the sparse brown grass turned into the lush green lawn of the main house, which jutted, dark and empty, from the hillside above. After awhile Gina followed me. I watched her climb the hill slowly, almost seductively, a ghost in the grey moonlight. The breeze picked up her skirt and made it billow softly about her. She stood in front of me, her hands in the pockets of her bomber jacket.

"Hi," she said.

"Hi."

She made some half-hearted attempts to climb the tree.

"Help me. Boost me up."

I stayed put. "Too tired," I said.

She slumped against the tree and pounded it with the flat of her fist. "I met Willie," she said.

"Oh. Is he here?"

"You don't like him, or what?"

"No, he's fine. He's a nice guy. So I guess Angie is hanging out with him now?"

"I guess. I think they're in the parking lot." She swung from a large branch overhead.

"You bored?" I said.

"No. I'm cold. You want to hold me?"

Where was I when another woman tried this tactic with me before? Outdoor parties seem to bring out this primal mating urge in women. I stood up, almost obligingly, and enfolded Gina in the plaid jacket. Her hair smelled like the herbal shampoo we both used until she got fancy and started buying hair care products through her hairdresser. I wanted to ask her "Did you go back to using that herbal stuff?" but I figured it wasn't the right time. Gina's eyes were closed as I lifted her face up to mine and kissed her open lips.

"Everybody's fucking," Gina said. "Somebody's making love in the gypsy Wagon. You can hear them. It might be more than two. And then some other couple is getting pretty close to it down by the stream."

"Probably Ripley and Wanda Dare."

"She was taking his pants off." She reached up and bit my lower lip. "Does it make you think about it with me, honey? Did you miss me?" She took my hand and placed it under her skirt.

"Gina..."

"We could do it right here."

"This is so complicated now."

"What's complicated about it"

"I mean between us. It's complicated."

"I know," she giggled. "It's horrible. But we're still married. Don't you think about it?"

"Yeah, but..."

"But what?"

"Would it mean anything?"

A look of absolute dejection spread across Gina's face. "What do you mean 'would it *mean* anything?' What kind of... oh my God." She broke away from me.

"What I meant was, how could it be the same?" I said. "How can anything be the same between us?"

"Why does it have to be the *same*? It would be great if it *wasn't* the same, don't you think? Sex is one place you and I can meet, Bob. I don't care who you're with or who I'm with. I don't care about any of that. This is you and I, Bob. This is US. And we had this moment together, and now you've hurt my feelings..."

It felt wrong, but I said "I'm sorry, Gina."

"For God's sake. It isn't like I was a virgin when you met me. Is it because I've been with other people? Is that what's holding you back?"

Other *people*? I wanted to say no. But I couldn't.

"It is, isn't it? This is what's hanging you up? A two week affair with Mark Sanders?"

"It's not *what* happened. It's the *way* it happened."

Gina paused, speechless, and shook her head. She eased down the tree into a squat and pulled her dress over her knees. "All of your preaching about letting it all go. I thought 'This will be fun. We're married. Who really cares?' Now I just feel like shit."

"I can't turn my feelings off like that," I said. "Making love now. It just seems false."

"Who wants you to turn your feelings OFF? Hell! Feel me! Let me in. Let me affect you. Let's change it. Let's..." She sighed. "Never mind. Why don't you just talk about what's bothering you?"

"That's a big subject," I said.

"Well, like I've got something better to do? Talk to me."

I took a minute to gather myself. "Okay. What did you mean when you said I saw the affair as a cause and you saw it as an effect?"

"I can't explain it any other way."

"But how can you even begin to justify something like that?"

"I can't. I'm not trying to justify it."

"And you said that I hated you? Come on, Gina. How could I hate you?"

By example, she told me again how she had felt manipulated into starting Weight Watchers to please me, because I had shut down and given her the silent treatment for months as punishment for my perception that there was something wrong with her, she said. I didn't shut down, I said, I was busy and preoccupied with school. She said my silence, my withholding, was directed at her, and she said somebody who truly loved her would have accepted her at any weight she happened to be. Every time she had to drink one of those milkshakes in a can she resented me. She said I saw what I needed to see to justify my contempt for her. She told me how I hurt her self-esteem, and that her therapist helped her realize that she was being manipulated, that I was taking out my aggression on her physical image.

Inside, I had to begrudgingly accept what she was saying. I was not above being detached. And sometimes in those periods of detachment I truly wished Gina would disappear. Maybe with Weight Watchers she would starve herself into nonexistence. Or at the very least change how she appeared to me, because anything would be better than what I saw her as: A drag. An embarrassment. An encumbrance. Yes, I did feel that way sometimes. Did I hate her? I hated what she represented; a cage built of my own choosing.

But instead of telling her this, I was defensive. "You asked me! 'How do I look?' What am I supposed to say? You want me to lie about everything?"

"You mean you lied to me about other things?"

Yes. The affair with the young woman that I worked so hard to cate-

gorize as a non-affair was in actuality, an affair. There was no actual pen-
etration, but that didn't change it. And I was probably in love with her.
But instead of admitting this, I had to deflect the question:

"Jesus Christ," I said. "You asked me what I thought about everything! Every goddamn thing. You didn't make a move without consulting
me first. And what am I supposed to say when I know what I say means
so much to you. You hung on every word. You can't imagine the pressure, Gina, when I know whatever answer I give you you're going to re-
sent me for saying it. Like – do I think that girl is attractive? What am I
supposed to say? No? As if by any stretch of the imagination I could
convince you of that. Then you ask – do I think she's more attractive than
you? You put me in this place where I can't win, and I have to fight for
my life, and it's all about you, because somehow, somewhere you suspect
that I don't love you *enough,* so you're always trying to win my approval."

"It's because you're so withholding! You never demonstrate it. You
always make me feel like I'm nothing! I hate like hell to have to ask for
it all the time!"

And then the argument dissolved into the familiar pattern of insult
and recrimination that had infected our marriage like a cancer. And when
I felt thoroughly hopeless and disgusted with myself, and felt like endur-
ing any more would break my skull in two, this calm of the stalemate
settled around us. And miraculously, like a breath of air, Gina started
talking.

"I DO care what you think. It means more to me than anything."

I took off the ugly plaid jacket and spread it out on the grass. We sat
at a tentative distance from each other as the night slowly gave way to
dawn.

"I almost lost my mind in Minnesota," she said. "Those first few
weeks without you... I felt so lost. You were my best friend, Bobby. I
loved you so much. Forget Mark Sanders. That was nothing. That was
me trying to get you to notice me. So I left, and you were out of my life
for the first time in seven years. And I had to do something, because all
those habits I had with you were so IN me. Even though I know they

were bad habits. I based myself around you, lived my life for you, because I wanted to, but I didn't know how to live on my own. So I cried and cried in Minnesota, and after a few weeks I said 'what would Bobby do in my situation? How would he get over this terrible loneliness?' I admired you because you were so easy-going. I was the high-strung one. I held onto things. You just rolled with it. You weren't always that way. Do you remember when we first met? Do you remember the first thing I said to you?"

"You said 'Don't you ever smile?'"

"Yes. Because you were so serious. You had this most serious scowl on your face all the time."

"It was some sort of defensive posturing or –"

"You opened up to me Bobby. It was so wonderful. It's what endeared you to me. It's why I fell in love with you."

Being with Gina was easy for awhile. Truth: It was exhausting living life before her. It took a lot of energy to hold the world up. With her, I realized I didn't have to do that anymore.

"Then you became so confident, and I seemed to get more dependent. I was afraid of you, the power you had over me. And I began to hate you because I began to think that this calm you possessed meant you didn't care about me anymore. And that was the trouble I was having, Bobby. Because I cared so desperately for you, and I thought if I 'let go' like you did, I would make our marriage less important, and I would stop loving you. And, see, I can never do that.

"You remember when we were breaking up? Things were all screwed up because we saw each other in class everyday and I was living at Margaret's and we weren't even speaking? I was working and working on my audition pieces and auditioning all over the place, and I was so worried about it. And then I auditioned for Noah and didn't get called back. And I remember when I came to get my things, and we finally talked, and I had heard you had gotten this job and I thought 'How wonderful!' But I also thought 'How did he do it? He didn't work half as hard as I did.' And I was horribly jealous, to top it all off. And I asked you how you did it and you told me about how you just let it all go."

"My Freefall Theory."

"I remember you told me, and I think the line might be from a movie but I don't remember if it is or not. One time you said to me 'Gina,' you said, 'Sometimes you just have to say to hell with it all.' Remember? Was that from a movie?"

"I don't remember. Probably."

"It didn't help at the time you said it because it sounded like a lecture. So I never thought about it. But the only way I could get to sleep at night in Minnesota was if I imagined myself falling. Just falling into space. And all the time, like a mantra or something, I'm saying to myself 'Just put it in freefall.' And I never landed. It calmed me down. Then when I started to have anxiety about – whatever – I would just... go there... I said to myself 'He's gone, anyway. He doesn't want me anymore.' And I thought 'I can do this.' And I stopped lying to myself. It's like I wanted things to be so right, and when they weren't I told myself 'Yes they *are!*' And it was forced, and it was no good when I forced it, because it was a lie. And I started to see how easy it was for me to get all caught up in the way I thought things should be and not see the way things really are. I needed to see where I fit in the world before I could tell if I liked where I was.

"And then I met a man. I hope this isn't hard for you to hear, Bobby. A wonderful man. He was older, and it was easy being with him, and he helped me get centered about things. And I learned that things don't have to be so black and white all the time. I don't have to be good all the time, and hate myself when I think I've been horrible."

What did she say?

Wait. Back up, I thought. Don't tell me this.

"It's not what you think, Bobby. It's about healing. It's not about anything else. I don't know how long it will last or how long I want it to last. But for right now..."

Wonderful... older... man. They were truly the only words I distinctly heard. Of course she would find others. Another. I should have known – did know. Expected it, truthfully. I had moved on. I had found others. That was the point of it all, to get beyond where we were. We had been stuck, for years. Now Gina was moving on. Why was this surprising?

"...was hard to give you details over the phone... I know you asked, and... I *did* tell you... but I had to get things clear..."

She was telling me the truth. She was being honest.

I left *her*. Somewhere in it all, I let her go. I turned my back. I could have stayed with it, tried to understand. There were chances. I had chances all along. I could have asked her what was bothering her. Instead I ignored her. Because she wasn't *strong*. Too needy: *Get over it, Gina*.

"So, I guess... if you were truly going to be out of my life..."

Now she had fallen in love with someone else. And everything else diminished in light of this new flame. Even me.

"...just *happened*..."

Who was this strange creature before me? How could she have wanted to make love just now, under this tree, and then go off to live with someone else? Who was this person? How did things get so out of hand? So complicated? So messy? Where was the familiar Gina, the girl I grew up with? How could she be so independent, so unpredictable, so free? Why didn't she *need me anymore?*

"...showed me how to get beyond it..."

We had lost each other, sure. I could admit that. I could have held her hand in the movies. I could have tried to understand about the credit card. I could have waited for her on the hike. But this. This was cruel, this visit, this flaunting of my failure, our failure. Why did we need to wear it like a shirt? Just cover it up. Dig a hole. Make it go away. Pull off the road, it's late. Let's not go on from here. Jesus Christ, Gina. Find a fucking motel. This is too dangerous.

"...not saying it'll be better or even different..."

The lump, once so familiar to me in the weeks and months after the breakup, rose back into my throat, bigger than ever, bigger and dryer than Arizona, and a flood of anger and sadness gathered behind my eyes. Sure we had problems. Sure there were lots of bad times, but there had been just as many glorious ones, and regardless of the level of comfort I was feeling at any given time in our marriage, life with Gina was *home*. Who cares if I wasn't happy? With Gina, I *meant* something. What would life be like without her, truly, without her, after the power I held over her was gone? When I wasn't there in her life like a searchlight, guiding her. Step here. Step there. Watch me? See? Do it this way. Walk with me, it's cold out here. I felt like screaming, like holding her to me and begging that she never let me go, begging her to make it the way it used to be. Remember the conversations in the dark? The song about the cat? The nights of Hamburger Helper, Saturday Night Live, the trip to Sea World, the funky green apartment, the night Elvis died, the waterbed, the walks down M Street, the Raggedy Ann doll. Remember? I was *her Bobby,* the first, the most important. There were so many memories, so much history, so much life that we shared, I could wait out any temporary, incidental love she might come across.

I COULD FIX IT.

"...not sure how serious this is, or if he continues to be serious about me..."

She's leaving the door open. She wants me to save her, to make it the way it was between us. Fight for her! I thought. Have I ever truly fought for anything? Did I ever truly risk it all to win something? Was my whole life just an exercise in giving up? Did I stop worrying about things because I truly didn't care anymore?

I found myself winding tighter and tighter until I thought I'd explode, but somewhere in my maelstrom of anger and hurt I realized the horrible narcissistic truth. I was only thinking of myself. Wanting Gina back was the pinnacle of selfishness. We had grown up, grown past each other, grown apart. There was Mark Sanders. There was the young woman. There was Weight Watchers. There was Angie. There was this new guy. Wanting Gina back was my attempt to take control, to salve my feelings, to ease my loneliness. I wasn't thinking of Gina, what was best for her, what would help her heal. I knew we couldn't work, but in our marriage I had failed to accept it, in much the same way she did. And worse, I was playwriting. Trying to make it *the way it should be.* But I couldn't erase what we had written. There were words in the script that I couldn't cross out.

It was April.

I was in acting class. It was a sunny morning, with dew on the grass and the smell of jasmine floating over all of us in our tank tops and sweatshirts. Ripley was there, and Sue Westerberg, and Gina, always Gina, and that skinny fornicator Mark Sanders, and we all dropped our bags in the corner and stretched and went "Ahhhhh" and let it all shake out, yoga-like, like we did in those days. We gathered in a circle, and our instructor asked us to clear our heads, let all our worries drain from us, and gave us lots of hudu-guru homilies like 'find your center' and crap that I had never really paid attention to, had felt *better than*. But I had not really seen the light until that day, until it was my turn.

We were playing that acting game, the blindfold test, the trust exercise. I stepped up into the center of the circle, and someone, I think it was Ripley, tied the blindfold around my eyes. This would be easy. I could do Richard III. I was Macbeth. This was a kid's game. All I had to do was fall. The group spun me around, lots of hands touching my shoulders. I was spinning, disoriented. "Let go," someone said. "I am," I said, defensively. "Relax," someone said. Was this hard for me? Why was this hard for me? It *was* hard for me. I tried to fall freely but resisted, and I put out a hand to stop myself. I almost gave Sue Westerberg a black eye. The circle fell apart. "Sorry. sorry." Shake it out. Try it again. How could something so simple be so hard, I thought. I was a fucking actor, for God's sake. I could do anything. "Let go, Bob" somebody said. I was struggling, struggling, not falling right. Were there rules to this exercise? How do you fall right? "Let go, Bob." I think it was Gina. There was Gina. We were in the pasture, and morning was coming. My eyes were closed, and hands were all over me, supporting me, keeping me aloft. Why did I struggle? Gina was there, her hands on me, and I realized that struggling was futile. "Let go, Bob." Resistance would cause too much pain, too much damage. "Let go, Bob." Fighting was not helping. Fighting was destructive. I could float there, freely, forever, peacefully. I could. "Let go." And instead of fighting for control I could relinquish it. I could. I let go. My defenses fell. I fell. I was At Mercy, falling backwards into Gina's arms, trusting that she'd be there. And she was. Everything fell out of me, all my truths fell out. I confessed everything to her, and she listened without judgment. Gina was there, and it was wonderful, beautiful, pure. And in an instant, I was able to let her go. In that instant I found true love for Gina, truer and purer than anything I'd known. Ego was gone, my need to control her was gone, and what was left was clean, like sifted snow, and I saw her simply for the first time, even as she held me while I cried and she cried and said she was sorry and I said she didn't need to be, and I told her that I was happy for her, and I meant it.

"It's scary out here without you, Bobby. But I think I can do it. I think maybe I'll be better off in the long run."

"No old habits."

"No old habits. It doesn't mean I..."

I put a finger to her lips. "I know, Gee." I wanted to say it first. "I love you too."

24

It was still early, probably around seven a.m., when Gina and I pulled into the parking lot at the admin building. She was driving, I stayed in the passenger seat while the Toyota's engine idled.

"You sure you want to do this?" she asked.

"I'm sure." I looked into my lap at the note I had written.

Noah,

Please take me out of the running for an Artist-in-Residence position this year. I have made other arrangements. Thank you for considering me.

Best Regards, Bob

"I don't understand," Gina said. "I thought you wanted to stay."

"I think there's a difference between wanting to stay and not wanting to leave."

"What's the difference?"

"I don't want to stay because I have nowhere else to go. I don't want to stay because I'm afraid of change. I can't be an actor right now, Gina. At least not here. Maybe somewhere else, sometime."

"Why can't you be an actor?"

"Lots of reasons. I'm too sensitive. I'm too fucked up. I've got to feel like I have some control over what I do. I want it to be my choice, not theirs."

She smiled and nodded. "Mr. Freefall wants some control," she said.

I smiled back at her.

"All right, Bobby."

I got out of the car and walked over to the admin door, slipped the note under it, then got back in the car and Gina drove us back to the apartment. We slept until about four, together, on my bed, like spoons, me holding Gina from behind, as was our custom.

Noah didn't call that day. The phone didn't ring. At least I didn't hear it if it did.

She said she slept well and felt rested enough to drive. We had agreed she should leave earlier than she had planned, that there was nothing more to talk about, really, except the papers and filing and that sort of stuff, which we could do by phone. It would be a simple divorce; neither of us owned anything except the car, and it was clearly hers.

"Whenever we get around to it," she said. "Filing the papers, I mean."

"Whenever we get around to it," I said.

Then I helped Gina pack up, we kissed each other goodbye, and she drove off about 6:00.

25

On Monday I slept late and spent the rest of the day playing guitar with Hanover one last time, before we hefted his amp up into his van. We swore we'd send Turds songs back and forth to each other over the winter. I got back to the apartment about 6:30. I had tried to delay my return as long as I could, hoping to give Willie and Angie enough time to clear out before I got back. Willie had said they hoped to be gone by 3:00. But as I walked up the alley, the doors and hood of the bug were wide open. Willie saw me before I had a chance to duck out of sight.

"Hey Bob," he said. "Glad you caught us before we left."

Angie had been leaning over the passenger seat stuffing the last box in the last space available. She looked at me and looked away, closed the car door and went upstairs.

Willie and I stood in the carport. He talked animatedly, but I didn't really hear a word he said, something about how the place in L.A. was near the studio or something. I nodded and probably kept glancing toward the stairs, waiting, but not hoping for Angie's return. Finally she did come back, smiled, brushed by me, opened the passenger door and announced "All clear upstairs."

"Well, I guess this is it, Bob," Willie said, and he came awkwardly around the car, practically leaping over it, and crushed me in a neanderthal embrace. "We'll miss you, guy. Won't we, Ange?"

Angie smiled, her tight-lipped non-smile. It was her turn. She stepped up to me and hugged me absently.

"Goodbye, Bob," she said. "Keep in touch."

"Goodbye," I said.

And then she sat down and closed the door.

"Ah hell. My keys! Wouldn't you know it!" Willie bounded out of the car and up the steps to the apartment.

Angie sat in the passenger seat. She looked at me once, then turned and fixed her gaze out the windshield. I crossed my arms. Angie cleared her throat. The last glint of sunlight disappeared from the tops of the buildings. I was aware of the sound of the freeway, many blocks away.

Finally, I said "There's just one thing I want to know, Angie."

She dropped her head, gathering herself. She sighed once and looked at me defensively. "What's that," she asked.

"You know that night at the hot tubs?"

"Yes..."

"When you saw Richard and Ephrem outside the changing room?"

"Yes..."

"Do you think Ephrem had his chihuahua in our tub?"

She sighed, relieved. "Wouldn't surprise me."

"George was there, wasn't he? Do you think he peed in it?"

She tried not to laugh. "Wouldn't surprise me," she said. Then she looked at me, differently this time, the way the old Angie used to look at me.

"There you are," I said.

"I owe you a huge apology," she said.

"You don't owe me anything."

"I do. Because I think I had a lot of judgment about you, and it wasn't fair. I think I was holding you to a standard that I couldn't live up to myself."

This was sounding a lot like what I had said to Gina in the olive grove. "Nah. Listen," I said. "I brought it on myself. You warned me."

"All I've been is mean to you. But it's just because I'm mad at myself. I'm sorry."

"Never be sorry," I said. "Sorry is a terrible thing to be."

Her smile was her old smile, the way I knew her.

"So there's just one thing I want to know, Bob."

"What's that, Angie?"

"Are you still in love with me a little bit?"

And I'd never seen her smile quite so brightly.

I heard the jingle of Willie's keys. "You've got my Mom's address," I said. "Send me a postcard with your address and phone number when you get settled. If you feel like it."

"I will," she said.

Willie hopped back down the stairs and stuffed his gangly frame in the driver's seat. "You know where they were? On the floor against the toilet. I dropped 'em there while I was takin' a poop."

Angie laughed freely, the first time I'd heard her laugh that way in a month. Willie started the car. I banged on the roof. "Good luck," I said.

The bug putted down the alley, tilting in the ruts. Willie reached his hand out the window and waved. The car stopped at the curb and the brake lights came on, visible now in the dusk, then the turn signal flashed, Willie gunned the engine and turned onto College Boulevard and the car disappeared.

I went upstairs and stood in the middle of the empty apartment, now still and hauntingly quiet. Earlier in the day, the power had been turned off. A gloom had gathered inside, and the pastel light of the darkening sky glared in stark contrast through each window. My two big army duffel bags were packed and waiting against the wall. My bus left the next morning, so I had twelve hours to kill. I figured I'd see a movie, read at Lyons, then come back and catch a few hours' sleep on my bare mattress.

I turned around and sat down on the stairs outside. A fog bank was rolling in from the west. I smelled barbecue and heard Mexican music from down the street, and heard the landlady's tv through the open windows of the main house in front, a commercial about vitamins. Her orange tabby cat walked along the top of the cedar fence, then stopped, its tail switching as it stared at something in the neighboring yard. This was no longer my home, I thought.

So I grabbed my duffel bags, locked the door behind me, dropped the key in the landlady's mailbox, and walked toward Main Street. I got a locker at the bus depot, stashed my bags, and headed west into the fog. After I had finished walking, hours later, past the Triple X and all the way to the enchilada place on the outskirts of Guadalupe, I came back to the bus depot and parked myself in one of the blue fiberglass seats in a row against the back wall, and under the greenish glow and vacant hum of the tube lights, as the Pac Man machines sang their theme song, I nodded, arms folded on my chest, until morning.

OCTOBER

26

I found out a few days after the end of the season that Fred Norton had been apprehended, and more interestingly, that Bronson and Lloyd had been responsible for his capture. I got the details by calling Bronson myself, and even though he was swamped at the time with local media attention, he seemed happy to talk to me.

"We set a trap for him. Lloyd hears this bangin' one night out there during the summer. We go out in the morning and it looks like someone broke in to the garage. So I set out to reinforce the place a little so it won't happen again. A few days later looks like whoever it was had come back. So then it becomes this war. I seal up the windows, weld the door shut, board up the place. Still, every so often we'd notice somebody tampered with the lock and got inside. So we decided to set a trap for him. I made sure the place was sealed up tighter'n' a drum, and we set this lock to lock from the outside, so when someone goes in, they stay in until we let 'em out. So nothin' happens for awhile, and then a couple nights after the season closes we hear all this commotion out there and call the police. And guess who we caught?"

Bronson's story held up despite intense scrutiny from the local police, and despite a strikingly different account of the proceedings by Fred Norton. Norton claimed that he paid Bronson and Lloyd to let him live in their fortified garage, that they had, in effect, acted as accomplices by providing him with shelter and by running errands for him, bringing him groceries and keeping quiet about the whole thing. Norton claimed he had paid Bronson and Lloyd over twenty-two hundred dollars in cash as rent, over and above grocery money. Norton had free access to the garage with his key, and would come and go as he wished, often staying in the garage for days at a time. On the night of his capture, Norton said, he had returned from a trip and found his sparse belongings cleaned out, and was pushed from behind and locked in the garage until the police arrived. There was no evidence that Norton was telling the truth, no evidence of the cash transactions, and no evidence that Norton had stayed for any duration in the garage as he claimed, due, Norton said, to the fact that Bronson and Lloyd had burned all evidence of his extended stay while he was away trying to set up another real estate swindle in San Bernardino.

As to what Norton was doing that day Officer Wadleigh spotted him at *Salesman* rehearsal?

"I think he wanted to see the show, so he decided to sneak into a run-through," Bronson said. "He said he liked Arthur Miller."

So the boys were left with a sizable reward. I asked what Bronson had in mind for the $20,000.

"Right now we're still in negotiations to lease some real estate, and if it goes through you'll be the first to hear from me. We haven't forgotten what you did for us, with those button designs and all, so we'd like to make sure you're involved in some way, if you're comfortable with that prospect."

I said I would be, as I was still in the area, and my plans were still formulating as well. We agreed to meet sometime and talk business.

"In the meantime, let's see a movie or somethin'," Bronson said.

"Sure," I said. "If you guys want to come up here. I'd have to take the bus down there. There's better movies in San Louie."

I had moved into Paul Butler's apartment in San Louis Obispo after the season ended. I had called him up and asked him what he was going to do with it when he left.

"Nothing," Paul Butler said. "I leave September 30. You want it?"

"Yes," I said. "I think it's a great place."

So I took the bus up, and with Paul Butler vouching for me, talked the landlord out of having to pay a flat sum for the first and last month's rent, which I didn't have. "I can give you the first month plus fifty dollars," I said. "And I'll give you fifty dollars extra every month until that last month's rent is in your pocket."

I also told the landlord that I would clean the apartment myself, after Paul left, and the landlord was an older guy and liked my enthusiasm, so he agreed to my terms. I dropped my duffel bags in the middle of the floor, took Paul's dead ficus tree and threw it in the trash, and then walked down the street and got a job at Skippers fish and chips.

NOVEMBER

27

The weather had turned wonderfully dour, and wet storms blew in off the Pacific twice a week. But I was dry and comfortable in my second story brick with high ceilings and wood floors and utility kitchen. After I got my second paycheck I bought a used tv and a new ficus tree, and I made sure to put it in the lightest spot in the apartment. After all, you can't live in a place with exposed brick walls and wood floors and not have one of those trees. I bought food and cooked in every night, and even learned to like asparagus.

Ripley ended up following Wanda Dare to San Francisco, though I couldn't guess as to what extent their relationship was still in flower. I got a postcard from him, one of those tourist-type airbrushed sunsets with "San Francisco – the City by the Bay" written in gaudy script over the Golden Gate. All he said was "Got cast at Eureka Theatre doing midnight show. Selling tuxedos on Pope Street during day. May try Chicago in the spring."

I sent him back a postcard. It said: "Straighten your shoulders for God's sake."

Gina called once, twice actually, when she had gotten especially lonely, and we talked for much too long. Luckily it was after 11:00 and she was paying the bill. Seems her new guy had postponed his trip to L.A. for awhile and she was wondering whether or not he was going to keep his word about coming west.

"Is he an actor?" I said.

"Why do you ask?"

"You can't answer a question with a question."

"Yeah, but what relevance does that have to anything?" Gina knew damn well what relevance it had. But I just smiled let her go on: "He could be a stockbroker for all that matter," she said. "You're too quick to jump to conclusions."

"Gina, where are you going to meet a stockbroker? I suppose there were quite a few guys from Merrill Lynch hanging around the summer theatre, trying to get a piece of those massive investment portfolios."

"Oh! Speaking of money..." And then she launched into a long story about how Peg Bosco had lost $600 by falling for some dumb actor scheme. She took a "class" from a "professional director" to rehearse scenes from cancelled sitcoms and perform them for a group of casting directors, but it turned out that the "professional director" made porn films and the most high-powered person in the audience was a guy who filed scripts at Paramount.

"So are you referring to me as your ex-wife now?"

"Not yet."

"Then how do you think of me? What am I to you?"

I thought of the time Gina bought me a Van Halen record for my birthday. It was the wrong one. She bought me the second one, with "Dance the Night Away," whereas I had requested the first one, with "Runnin' With the Devil," produced by the one and only Ted Templeman, who truly had gotten the most thunderous and ominous sound out of the band, and David Lee Roth hadn't become such a clueless dork yet. But Gina had gotten confused. I didn't tear the cellophane, and she took it back and exchanged it. But I knew I hurt her feelings. I should have accepted the gift (even though I felt it would be a black mark in my collection, containing, as it did, the unredeemable "Beautiful Girls") and simply bought the first album myself. But times were tight. These things mattered. I told her thanks, and sorry I was so picky. She baked me a spice cake with raisins, my favorite.

"How is our divorce coming along?" I asked.

"I'm filing? I thought you were filing."

After we hung up I revised my monthly budget to allow for the occasional late-night phone call to Gina.

Bronson called me up the next day and offered me a job.

"We open Friday," he said. "Bronson and Lloyd's Used Car Mega-Store. On the old Occidental Highway South, down near the Pic-n-Save and the Fosters Freeze, across from the Ford dealership and on the way to everywhere, Gateway to the Golden Southland. Get behind the wheel of this better-than-new 1973 Buick or this sleek and sexy 1966 Plymouth Fury and feel those horses giddap."

"You offering me a job or are you trying to sell me a car?"

"Just practicin'. What do you think? Do you own a suit?"

"No."

"Hmmm. Maybe we could work somethin' out. You'd be a great salesman. Make a lotta money."

"Well, I appreciate the offer but I got another job."

"What, that fast fish place? C'mon, Bob! We're talkin' about some major commissions here. You'd make more in one hour than you can in a week."

"No, I mean a job job. The guy at the Cincinnati Rep gave me his business card after the opening of *Death of a Salesman*. I didn't think much about it at the time. But I called him at the end of the season and said I was available. And he called me back the other day and offered me two shows. The Gentleman Caller and Cassius in *Julius Caesar*, back to back."

Bronson was happy for me, even though he was sorry to lose his top salesman. I told him I started in two weeks, and they paid my way back and everything.

"Congratulations," he said.

"I need someone to sublet my place," I said. "You think Fred Norton is available?"

"Not for at least thirteen years."

I hung up the phone and pulled on my black polyester slacks and Skippers blue polyester shirt, and got ready to begin my shift. I wanted to get there a few minutes early so I could give notice. Just as I grabbed a banana the phone rang, that short, European-style ring that signaled someone was at my door. It shocked the hell out of me. It was the first time since I moved in that someone had rung my bell. So I went to the balcony and leaned over to see who was there, but it was raining, and whoever it was had taken cover in the entry alcove.

"Who *is* that?" I said.

I heard the rustle of a familiar blue parka. A woman stepped out into the sidewalk and looked up at me, squinting against the rain.

"Bob? It's me," Angie said. "I left him."

ABOUT THE AUTHOR

Kevin McKeon spent two years as an Artist-in-Residence at PCPA. He moved on to a career in advertising and graphic design, while staying involved in theatre on the side. He has adapted several literary works for the stage, including David Guterson's *Snow Falling on Cedars* and Tolstoy's *Anna Karenina*. He lives in Seattle.

www.ingramcontent.com/pod-product-compliance
Lightning Source LLC
Chambersburg PA
CBHW060926180626
46817CB00004B/1415